NIGHT MOVES

There was the faintest rasping of the tiny shells in the driveway.

In an instant Marcy had disentangled herself from the bed's cobwebby folds of mosquito netting and got to a window.

She went without a sound, she was sure. Yet nothing, nothing at all moved in what she could see of the courtyard.

Perhaps he had moved into the house. No; the house doors were bolted. She waited, almost afraid that the thudding of her heart would alarm the night prowler.

All at once, the ugly feeling of being under observation from somewhere — by someone — caught her again. She waited.

But time went on; the scent of flowers was sweet; nothing moved below — yes! Something did move out from the shadow and start across a starlit open space.

A dark, shapeless figure...

★　　　★　　　★

W9-CDP-192

MIGNON G. EBERHART

THE BAYOU ROAD

WARNER BOOKS

A Warner Communications Company

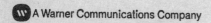

Remembering Mignon Marcy,
whose given name I am proud to bear,
and my Aunt Abbie Bryan,
two young women whose elegance and charm
captivated a very young child

ONE

The now-familiar sense of listening, waiting cautiously for something, struck Marcy Chastain again as she stood before the mantel, one hand beside the little clock. A gilt-bordered mirror, which went, French fashion, to the ceiling, reflected her still, intent face. Some little animal, hiding within an unprotected covert, might have felt the same instinctive sense of danger.

She didn't know, she couldn't identify, either the time when that sense of threat had first touched her or the reason for it. She knew only that it was recent, yet had become suddenly a part of her consciousness. Some inner voice seemed to tell her to beware, look out, to be on her guard at all times.

There was not a sound in the house, nothing to hear. Probably there were sounds in the kitchen or upstairs in the tiny library which M. Lemaire had taken over, the rustling of his newspaper, if he had contrived to get one, or even the squeak of the old armchair. But from where she stood in the salon, Marcy heard nothing at all.

As far as she knew, nobody was in the house who ought not to be there. No one was in the garden who ought not to be there. It was, of course, barely possible that someone, a prowler, could have stolen into the garden and the house at night. She was never absolutely sure that the door into the stable mews was barred. She had given strict orders about that; she was not convinced that her orders were obeyed. Yet she had never seen anyone actually approaching the house, certainly not entering it. Besides, there was little left inside that an intruder might want.

So her sense of being watched had to be completely mistaken. There had been no stealthy shadows moving about in the garden in the night, no stealthy footsteps along the galleries, no signs of a trespasser, nothing but her uneasy sense of some furtive surveillance.

She crossed the room, slid louvers apart and looked down into the garden. There were only flowers and vines and the white-shelled driveway, overgrown now with weeds.

She went back to consider the candelabra on the mantel.

The French clock beside her struck twelve in musical tinkles; it always struck quickly, as if impatient to get on about its chore of measuring the hours and eager to discover what lovely gifts time held for it. After a good thirty seconds, the great clock near the closed street door struck twelve also, but with a deep, ponderous *bong-bong-bong;* this clock had no frivolous delusions about time. The candelabra, one on each end of the mantel and flanking the French clock, glittered dimly in silver; an unbidden ray of sunlight from one of the louvered windows struck a glass prism into rainbow colors. The room was quiet and dusky in the lazy warmth of April noontime.

The French clock might bring in some money—not what it was worth, but something. It was small, delicately made, with its glass sides showing the fine mechanism it held; the frames of the glass, even the lovely pendulum, were minutely and beautifully ornamented with colored enamels. Yes, it might bring in some money.

The two great candelabra just might be worth something, too; greedy bargain-hunters bought almost anything that savored of age and beauty. However, they were beginning to bargain shrewdly; there was too great a supply for them to choose from.

The clock in the hall would be difficult to sell. It was too big, too solemn, too ponderous to be moved easily, although some particularly efficient officer had contrived to get the piano out of the house.

The Aubusson carpet still held jewel tones. It had always been protected from the sun; the long louvered windows were always closed during the daytime. But gleams of light danced here and there, picking out the gilt of an armchair, the glow of yellow or gray satin; one of them touched the huge portrait of Henri Chastain, solemn as the hall clock but handsome. Marcy, his daughter, knew only that he had been sent away from New Orleans. His determined chin, his firm mouth and dark, defiant eyes had landed him she did not know where.

There were other portraits hanging on the walls, framed in massive gilded wood. Some of them might be sold and passed off by the buyer as ancestors, even though a beholder might guess that they were indeed spurious relatives.

On the tables, in the gilded *étagère,* there were, by now, gaps. No one mentioned these empty spaces; everyone in the house knew why they were there. Some of them had been filled by family heirlooms, others by later purchases, as when Marcy's brother, Brule Chastain, had made the grand tour of Europe and bought extravagantly whatever he found attractive. It was good that he had had that long trip in France, Germany and England, good even that he had married, good, as a matter of fact, that he had a son, even though the son was not to be legally claimed and could never be an heir to the Chastain property—if, of course, there was any property left to inherit.

The point just now was to select something more to sell, something which might fetch a large enough sum to make it worth sacrificing. It seemed a pity to denude their home. Yet the whole house and all its contents might be confiscated any day.

Marcy wondered again, as she did during frequent worried, sleepless nights, where, if the house was taken over, she could send its occupants and how she could feed them.

There was only one place of possible refuge, and that was the plantation, Nine Oaks, up the river on the Bayou Road, if the Federals hadn't already taken over the property. If so, then there was no refuge at all. Their friends would be quite justified in refusing to take them in, lest such a welcome endanger their own safety. Safety. What a world had come upon them in which every moment, every hour of the night, every breath they drew, was influenced by that one word.

So it was in April of 1863, with the Federals still in control of New Orleans, with her father refusing to take the oath of allegiance to the United States of America (the Ironclad Oath, or the Eagle Oath, they called it) and sent away as punishment; with really no man in the house except M. Lemaire, that remote cousin of her mother's who had lived with them ever since Marcy could remember, coming and going idly, wandering around the city, apparently cadging a cigar, Marcy was sure, whenever he could, but never missing a meal, sitting in the library, doing nothing, yet good-natured, kind, friendly—and, Marcy thought crossly, slippery as an eel. Certainly he was no pillar of strength. Only Marcy and Liss, the cook, undertook the task of selling whatever could be sold.

Claudine, Marcy's sister-in-law, Brule's widow, merely raised delicate eyebrows when the subject of money was brought up—as if to say, How vulgar—and lifted a white hand to adjust the blond ringlets hanging over her pretty ears. But Liss knew how and where to sell what could be sold.

There was no use in even thinking about asking for Armand's help in selling anything. For one thing, he was still slowly recovering from the bullet which had all but shattered his right leg, and also, already he seemed to regard Marcy's property or any property she might ever conceivably inherit as his own.

The bell at the gate gave an easy, slow clang. Someone coming?

Her heart gave a leap as it always did at the sound of the gate bell ever since the men had taken her father away.

No one ever used the street door now; this opened directly upon the street, and its great iron knocker had disappeared during General Butler's reign over New Orleans; a conquered city, his soldiers thought, so why not loot? General Butler had set an example.

Again she went to the window overlooking the courtyard and the carriage gates. These, too, were iron, wrought iron in a lacy design, big and heavy enough to defy anyone to steal them. Within one of the great doors, however, was a smaller door, easier to open and close than the great gates, which had been designed for the passage of horses and carriages. No one even bothered to wonder what had happened to the Chastain horses and carriages; they were just gone one morning.

Marcy pushed open the tiny slit in the jalousies so that she had a narrow view of the courtyard. Jason was hobbling along to open the small door.

He looked frightened; he seemed to shrink inside his black jacket, but he held the door wide and bowed, and a tall figure in blue came into the courtyard. In blue! What did they want now?

She had not been asked to take the Ironclad Oath; yet she would be obliged to do so before the provost marshal could be persuaded to give her a pass out of the city someday, if ever. But this soldier—an officer, by his gold braid—might have come to confiscate the house. The Federal Confiscation Law was an effective handle for taking over any desirable property.

The sunlight fell warmly upon the flowers of the courtyard and upon the shining brown hair of the man in the blue uniform. A major, she thought, peering at his epaulets. He spoke to Jason, and the old man, ducking and bowing, replied with a gesture toward the house, toward the room where Marcy stood. So, he had asked for her. She thought back swiftly for anything she might have said or done recently which might be construed as showing disrespect for the conquerors. But Butler was gone; General Banks had taken his place, and everyone said, although still in whispers, that General Banks was a gentleman, more lenient, less cruel than "Beast" Butler. Her conscience was reasonably clear, and just then the man in blue, Major Whoever-he-was, looked up squarely at the window where she stood, and she took a quick breath of utter astonishment.

She moved a little away from the jalousies, as if afraid he might see her. Even now, after two years, her pulses began to pound. She could feel pink coming up into her cheeks. Then she whirled around instinctively to look at herself in the mirror over the hearth. She was not a little flushed; her black hair was not very neat. She patted and poked at it, smoothed the faded gingham dress she wore and jerked up the hoops.

Jason opened the door so quietly that she knew he was deathly afraid of the man who stood behind him; he was a soft plum color from fright.

"Major—" he began, his old voice trembling, his grizzled head almost shaking, too.

Major John Farrell came forward and put out his hand. "Miss . . . Chastain."

That one night he had called her Marcy and then Darling. Now it was Miss Chastain.

"I hope you remember me. I'm John Farrell. We met at Senator Davis's house."

She remembered far too much and too well. But had he come now to haul her off to Yankee headquarters where she might be accused of almost anything anybody chose to present as an excuse which would allow the Federals to appropriate the house and everything in it?

He said, "I hope you don't mind too much, but I have been billeted here."

She hadn't known that she was holding her breath until it came out in a gasp. "Billeted."

"During my stay in New Orleans. I'll try to be of no trouble. I'll not need meals, you know. Only a place to stay. And I may be out of the city often. I trust it is not asking too much."

"Too much," she repeated blankly. Directly it occurred to her that he might mean safety for all of them, safety for the house and everything in it. Safety.

He said, rather gently, "You have nothing at all to fear, Miss Chastain."

"Thank you."

His gray eyes were darker than she remembered and suddenly both very serious and very kind. "By the way, I'm empowered to pay you for my room. It would oblige me to stay here, if you are so kind."

So formal, so polite, as if those moments in the past had never been. She must have nodded. He tucked his gloves neatly into his sash, produced a purse from a pocket inside the hateful blue tunic, opened it, bit his lip for a moment, as if considering, and then put some gold pieces on the marble top of a small table near him. "They told me at headquarters to pay by the month. I hope this is satisfactory."

She was drawn, but absently, by the gold pieces. No need to sell the clock. No need just now to sell anything.

"I'm not sure that is enough," Major Farrell said unexpectedly. He added a few more coins to the little heap of gold. "I forgot that my hours may be a little—a little irregular. Coming and going—upsetting you and—well—irregular."

Pride told her to say that the gold was too much; her urgent need told her to take the money. "It is enough. When do you wish to come?"

"Well—if it is convenient, at once. My orderly has what clothes and belongings I have with me. He is waiting on the sidewalk. I believe you call it the banquette."

It didn't matter what anybody called it. Nothing really mattered but the man facing her. That and safety. It was clear now, preeminent in her mind. With him here, no one, no Yankee soldier, would dare loot; no Yankee officer with his position gone to his head would come around and tell her the house was to be appropriated.

He said briskly, "I'll be back this evening. I don't know what time. If the—the man who let me in could help bring in my gear?"

"Yes, certainly." There would be his room to prepare.

She didn't realize that he had put his hat down on a chair until he bent to pick it up; it was a black slouch hat, turned up on one side; his sash had a gold fringe which moved as he moved. "Thank you," he said courteously. There was

not the slightest hint that he remembered soft strains of
dance music from the house on a gentle spring night—or
anything else.

He opened the door and only then glanced around the
dimly lit room, dim but so charming, she thought, in its gilt
and pale yellow and pale gray. The carpet with all its lovely,
delicate colors and even the portraits seemed more dear to
her now that she need not consider their sale.

"I'll take you to the gate," she said.

He bowed again. She slid the gold pieces into the deep
pocket of her skirt; they walked out along the hall, between
more rows of painted ancestors, out the side door and into
the courtyard. The perfume from its flowers rose to meet
them.

The fragrance, the massed colors and the hazy sunlight
seemed to strike him with pleasure. He paused, holding his
black slouch hat in one hand, his other hand on the hilt of
his sword which she had not noticed until then. It was
almost as if he were posing for a picture, but obviously he
had no such intention; he was only looking around him, half
smiling.

Since it had been a late spring, the flowers had come out
almost at the same time, and now in the warmth of April
were full and rich, in red and white and pink and mauve and
purple, with the greens of wisteria and honeysuckle twisting
upward along the wrought-iron railing of the galleries and
providing a background for all that color.

The house itself, brick painted white, ran around two
sides of a rectangle; the great front gates made a third side.
The fourth side comprised the stable, another less elegant
carriage driveway leading to the mews door, the barnyard
and then to a street behind the stables; and near the house,
the kitchen and servants' quarters. It was, that day, like a
lovely box, glowing with color.

The driveway was made of tiny white shells which were
not now, as before, neatly raked. The vines needed pruning,
especially the wisteria, which seemed purposely to twist
around wherever and as stubbornly as it chose. The great
blue pots of roses, heliotrope, camellias, gardenias, had not
been tended either.

But all the same, there was an almost suffocating beauty of color and fragrance.

Major Farrell said, "Everything is so beautiful. I didn't notice when I came in."

"Nothing has been tended. We have no gardeners just now." She said it a bit too sharply, for it reminded him at once that he came as a conqueror.

He flushed a little, very slight red under tanned cheeks. "No, I suppose not. Well then, thank you very much, Miss Chastain. I shall be back this evening. Thank you." He bowed and strode away from her, the shells rattling softly under the steel heels of his boots; he swung open the small door and did not look at her again as he disappeared, walking briskly along the banquette and out of sight.

A soldier, obviously the orderly, came into view, saluted sharply and apparently on instructions from the major, brought some saddlebags and one large suitcase into the courtyard. She directed him to take the luggage into the house.

He did so, depositing all of it just within the door, then he gave her a kind of salute and trudged away and out through the small door, closing it behind him. She must tell Jason what to do with the luggage. It was a welcome thought that it looked substantial, as if Major Farrell might be expecting to make a long stay.

She stood for a few moments, clasping the gold. She suspected that the entire incident had been observed from behind the shuttered windows, and as she turned back into the house, Claudine came toward her.

Claudine looked shocked, angry, yet still elegant. Whatever happened, Claudine was almost always lovely with her shining blond curls, her gardenia-white skin, her air of aristocracy and pride. Probably, Marcy had thought, her beauty was one of the reasons for Brule's marriage to her—beauty, the Dupre name, the one-time Dupre money and the fact that it was considered an excellent marriage. Her father and Claudine's uncle, dead since then, had made the marriage pact. Also, Marcy was a little sadly sure that Brule had known in his heart that in marrying Claudine he need not give up Angele.

At least he hadn't given her up, and Claudine had kept her knowledge of the situation to herself, and in her cool and lofty Dupre manner had simply ignored it—until Marcy had brought Brule's little son home to care for. This had struck icy fire from Claudine's beautiful pale-blue eyes.

As always since Brule's death, she was dressed in black. Black set off her exquisitely delicate beauty, Marcy reflected sourly. She reminded herself that Claudine was her sister-in-law, her widowed sister-in-law, and had been Brule's legal wife, so they must all be very, very patient with her—especially since Bébé Brule had come to live with them.

Claudine was angry but quite coherent. "That was a Yankee! You were talking to him! You were showing him the garden!"

"He didn't come to arrest any of us! He came to live here."

"A Yankee officer."

"Look!" Marcy pulled the gold from her pocket and displayed it.

Claudine stared, her pretty mouth opened and shut. Behind them, Tante Julie said, "You girls must come in out of the sun. You'll ruin your complexions."

"I'll explain," Marcy said briefly, then walked inside the dim hall and told them. She did not make much of having seen Major Farrell before. The gold was enough. Every one of them had learned a practical lesson.

Each, however, had her own reaction. Claudine said coldly, "But he can't have a room with *us*. Put him in with the servants. He'll never know."

M. Lemaire appeared from the direction of the library. He said what Marcy had only thought to herself: "Now the Yankees won't come. Now they won't take the house. Not while there is a Yankee officer here. We must make him welcome."

The three women had turned to look at him. M. Lemaire straightened his shoulders beneath the black frock coat, adjusted his black silk stock, and with his gold-headed cane tapping the parquet floor, returned to the library and took his usual chair. The women could hear its familiar creak.

"Well!" Tante Julie said with a puff which came from the

depths of her thick, stoutly corseted little body. She shrugged and adjusted her hoops with a fat, still-ringed hand; the jewels glittered. "In that case, you must see that this major has a good room. Your father's, perhaps. It must be put in order."

Claudine had her gaze fastened hungrily upon the gold. Marcy wouldn't put it past her to snatch one of those beautiful, shining gold pieces and put it to her own use. "I'll see to it," Marcy said firmly and started for the stairs beside the dining room. She caught sight of Jason shrinking back, looking at the major's luggage as if it might explode. "Put it in my father's room," she told him. As she went up the stairs, she knew that Claudine and Tante Julie were watching her closely. She yielded a little and leaned over the bannister. "We can have some flour and spoon bread and chicken and maybe even coffee and—"

"Put it away, child," Tante Julie said, understanding.

Later that afternoon, Claudine went out, bonneted against the sun, her hands in lace mitts.

Marcy enlisted Liss, who, sour, ugly, but still loyal, had stayed with them in spite of the examples set by some of their slaves who had disappeared, headed for Yankee territory.

The two of them cleaned and dusted and straightened the room, which looked down upon the street and the courtyard. She removed only a few objects which reminded her too forcefully of her father, the silver-backed brushes, the small portrait of her mother framed in gold (she had never been able to bring herself to sell that), articles of clothing which still bore, heart-breakingly, the shape of her father's erect, tall figure. But all the time she worked in a kind of dual consciousness; she was thankful for the gold with the deep gratitude of one who has been far too near the edge of no resources at all. But deeper than that was the knowledge that he had come, John Farrell. Yet for months and months she had told herself that a few moments in the spring night in faraway Washington had meant nothing to him. She and Tante Julie had been invited all the way from New Orleans to visit the senator and his wife, who had given a ball. That seemed long ago, before the war actually began. Yet her heart had thudded like a drum when she saw John Farrell walking through the garden.

He acted, however, as if he had only a pleasant, perhaps, but faint memory of their earlier meeting. Indeed, if he thought of her at all, it was only as a dance partner and a momentary flirtation.

It was merely a coincidence that he had been sent to her home for billeting.

The money he brought was welcome; she would concentrate upon that and making the room comfortable and well aired. Whether or not he remembered what she remembered, he was welcome, and not only for the money and the safety. She would no longer feel any sense of being watched, more than half afraid of something she could not identify. Nobody would dare slide into the garden like a shadow, threatening them, when the major was living in the house.

It had been, of course, an idle, silly fancy on her part. All the same, that sense of listening could be forgotten now.

She was mistaken.

The sun was setting when they had finished. Major Farrell had not returned. But Marcy had barely washed and brushed her hair until it shone and got into a freshly ironed, if patched, blue poplin dress when Armand and Gene Dupre, Claudine's cousin, arrived.

Claudine came and told her. "They wish to speak to you." Her lovely chin was lifted in triumph.

"What about?" Marcy said abruptly.

"Why, this man. This major. This Yankee. What else?"

"But this has nothing to do with Armand!"

"You are to marry him. You have exchanged formal agreements. You are to be his wife. Anything you do is his concern."

Oh, dear, Marcy thought in dismay. Nothing that I do quite suits Armand. She said, "Thank you, Claudine."

She went slowly down the stairs.

Armand came, limping, to take her hand and kiss it. Gene Dupre merely took her hand.

"This man—" Armand began.

"This major," Gene Dupre said. "We must discuss him. May we be seated?"

"Certainly, sir. If you please." She sat in an armchair and tried to adjust her faded poplin gracefully around her.

"He's got to go," Armand said sharply.

"He's got to stay," Gene Dupre said as sharply.

TWO

Behind her someone slid quietly into the room and then closed the door. M. Lemaire so invariably made his entrances and exits in that manner that she did not even turn to look; she braced herself only for argument with Armand.

Armand, with his thin, pale face, his fiery black eyes, his high cheekbones and thick curly black hair, was both Spanish and French. His arrogant nose sometimes seemed to her all Spanish; it would be easy to suspect a certain Spanish strain of cruelty in him. His mother had been a charming, plump and determined lady of Creole blood, which meant French-born in Louisiana. His father, Juan Ortega, was descended from the early Spanish conquerors of New Orleans. There were many such blood strains in the city, which was not only bilingual—French and English—but in which also, among the older families, there lingered a strong feeling for the Spanish language and customs.

In Armand's view it was his responsibility to control Marcy's actions. He was her properly recognized and contracted fiancé and by custom had a right to object to any action of hers. Armand had always been rather like a loaded dueling pistol with a hair-trigger temper. He had been certain of himself, dashing, charming and naturally properly practical at the time they were formally engaged. It was an arranged but suitable betrothal; both families agreed, and in the usual procedure all her present (or later to be inherited) property was listed, item by item, in their marriage contract. That had been early in January, over two years ago. Everyone had known the war was coming. Armand and her father, too, had wished the arrangement settled before Armand would join the company of chasseurs, which his father and Marcy's father and many of their friends had helped to finance. A year and a half later, in the autumn, Armand had been wounded, so seriously wounded that he could no longer fight. Fortunately, he had returned, paroled, to New Orleans early that spring, after General Butler had gone and his successor was in command. General Banks was apparently determined to undo some of the harm General Butler had done and to make friends in the conquered city; thus he had permitted Armand to remain, out of uniform, in the city—not in his own home, for that had been confiscated, but in the St. Charles Hotel.

But Armand had come home a different man. She didn't then think of the differences, but she knew that in one way he had not changed: he still had that hair-trigger temper. It would be wiser and certainly more peaceful to try and speak softly.

She didn't. She said flatly, "He is paying us well. We need the money. He'll stay."

Armand's bright black eyes blazed; then tears came into them, and she felt desperately sorry for him.

"I can't give you anything." He sat down and put his curly head in his thin white hands. "I was rich. My father was rich. All his cash was put into Confederate bonds. He left everything else to me, but the Yankees have taken it. I've barely enough to live on. I can't give you money, Marcy. You must know I can't." He lifted his head; a rather calculating gleam came into his eyes. "I've thought of asking you to let me live here too."

She shook her head. "There's not enough room now, Armand. The major has taken the empty bedroom remaining—"

"You brought that child here."

"Brule's son."

"How do you know he's Brule's son? He could be anybody's son."

They had argued about this so many times before that she only said wearily, "Just look at him, Armand."

Gene Dupre decided to take a hand in the conversation. In some ways Armand and Gene could have been cut from the same pattern in the same cloth; yet the stitching had been different. Gene was very fair, with light, thick and wavy hair, a slim yet muscular body such as poor Armand had before receiving his wound, and the same daring will and charm which Armand had always had. When Gene, too, was paroled after what luckily had proved to be a minor wound, he had been permitted to take charge of his father's bank and business interests. The Yankees now in command were very hopeful of keeping up the city and the city's commerce, so Gene had been welcomed. He knew his dead father's affairs, and he had been very efficient in assuming command. He and Armand were not precisely like brothers, yet neither had resigned himself to the Yankees' occupation of the city. Neither had resigned himself to wartime conditions. Both were coiled like springs for any kind of action. Marcy believed that both were members of the clandestine group of hot-headed, paroled Confederate soldiers who were suspected—accurately, Marcy surmised—not only of perpetrating a series of kidnappings and small but troublesome riots, but even, on occasion, of assassinating one of the Yankees whose government had been thrust upon them.

But Gene had better control of himself and his words than Armand. He said now, "We all know Marcy's motive in bringing the little boy here. Somebody had to look after him. Besides, I understand that Brule paid quite a price for the boy's mother."

Armand poked at a rosy flower in the Aubusson carpet with his clean but shabby boot. Gene went on, "But this is not the problem. Armand wishes this Yankee major to leave. On the other hand, I understand why you allowed him to be billeted here."

"A Yankee," Armand said between tight lips. "A brute and a bully. No gentleman—"

"He is a gentleman!" Marcy said sharply. "And he will protect us. This house will be safe, and we'll be safe from any Yankee interference as long as he stays here."

"That's what I must talk to you about, Marcy," Gene Dupre began, but Armand cut in: "No gentleman! You can't trust him—"

"I think I can." Marcy was so tired that she became positive. "He *is* a gentleman."

Armand's head jerked back alertly. "Why do you say that? You've only seen him—"

"I met him in Washington. I was introduced to him at the ball given by the senator's wife." Armand's face was white with a sudden wave of anger, but she couldn't stop herself. She said wickedly, "I danced with him. He's a very graceful dancer." Better not mention anything else; better not even think of it.

Armand shot to his feet, yet leaned pathetically on the arm of his chair in order to spare his lame leg. Even his thin lips were white. "How could you!"

"He was invited there. So was I."

"I knew you shouldn't have accepted that invitation to go to Washington City! I tried to get your father to stop you. He said you ought to see a little of the world before the war began. My God, so you did. You met and danced with a major in the Yankee army."

"He wasn't a major then," Marcy said quietly, regretting she had aroused the swift Ortega temper.

"It doesn't matter. Now you have taken this man into your house. Why, you—you—" Armand's eyes sparkled with fury. "It was no coincidence, then, his coming here. He came because he knew you! And you knew he was coming! You invited him!"

"No! He just came. He said headquarters had sent him. He was to be billeted here. I didn't know he was coming. I certainly did not invite him." But she was touched with anger at herself for springing to defend herself so quickly. Armand's anger almost always struck a spark of anger from her. It really wasn't the basis for a happy marriage. But then marriage wasn't supposed to be particularly happy; it was an arrangement for mutual benefit of money and property. There was a time when she had attempted to refute that widely held credo, but since then she had had too much to do, too much to worry and fret about, to dwell on speculations about marriage. Gene said, "I must insist that you keep this young major here as long as you can. You see, I have found out that he is a liaison officer between headquarters here and General Grant's army." He paused. "Now do you understand?"

Armand's head jerked toward Gene Dupre. A flash of comprehension lighted his face. He gripped the back of his chair. "You didn't tell me! I won't have it!"

"It's perfectly safe," said Gene.

"No!" Armand's black eyes blazed at Marcy. "You're not to do it! You're not to keep him here at all. I'll not have him here!"

"Armand." Gene Dupre advanced and put his slender hand on Armand's bony wrist. "Armand, think of what she may be able to do for us."

Armand's eyes flickered. "But suppose—no!" he cried again. "That means she would be expected to be friendly with him, on confidential terms. No, I will not have it!"

Gene's face was very intent. "You *must* have it. Besides, Armand, surely you can put complete faith in Marcy. I know her. I couldn't possibly ask her to do anything unbecoming."

"But I don't see—" Marcy began, and M. Lemaire said, "Dear me! He wants you to act as a spy. He wants you to discover what you can about General Grant."

"Me!"

"In more specific terms," Gene said in a measured way, "we want you to find out just when, where and how Grant intends to attack Vicksburg."

"*No!*" Marcy said.

Armand sank back down into his chair, his hands in fists upon his knees.

Gene resumed in a quiet but persuasive way. "Grant has tried every possible way of approaching Vicksburg and has so far failed. But they say he is a man of great determination. He must have some other plan of attack. This man, your major, must know what that plan is.'' He came to Marcy and took her hands in his own. "And he can tell someone he likes what that plan is.''

Marcy sprang up. "No! You'll not use me like that!''

Armand sat like a deflated sack of black clothing, his eyes half closed.

Gene said, "Dear Marcy, I am not asking you to behave in any indecorous way. I think too well of you. But I know I can trust your judgment. Armand needn't object about this perfectly straightforward and simple request. We—I—want you only to show—oh, some friendliness, make the major feel welcome in your house. The slightest politeness will please him. These Yankees are so far from home, and they know themselves hated. Only a few merely friendly gestures might encourage him to talk of his work. Please, Marcy.''

There was a long silence in the dim room. Marcy could hear her own heart beating hard; she couldn't, she wouldn't, try to revive some wayward, silly impulse felt once in a moonlit Washington garden. "I won't do it.''

Gene sighed. "There are many women in our fair land who would be only too thankful to give their assistance—''

"Then get one of them,'' Marcy flashed. "Get Claudine!''

Armand said sullenly, speaking apparently to his boots, "Claudine wouldn't do it. She's beautiful but—she wouldn't!''

Gene sighed again. "I know. My cousin Claudine may be most delightfully lovely, but she would never undertake any possible risk to herself of—oh, anything.''

Armand was still angry. His dark eyes gave Gene a fiery glance. "You mean risk discovery and being reported as a spy. Yet you are asking Marcy—my fiancée.''

Gene gave a half laugh. "I'm only asking that she offer friendship, a welcome, so to speak, a meeting ground of—let's say cordiality. She is intelligent. She'll find a way to discover what we want to know.'' His voice hardened. "What we must know. All the Defenders—there, I ought not to have mentioned the name.''

"She knows,'' Armand said sulkily. "Everybody knows.''

"I know there is a group of returned soldiers—most of them paroled. I know that they call themselves *les Défenseurs*.''

"More than that she shouldn't know," M. Lemaire said.

No one so much as looked at him; they were all accustomed to his familiar and unimportant presence. Gene said, "Now, Marcy, I've come to a very disagreeable argument. I am loath to use it, I do assure you. I am obliged to. My—my associates insist."

"You—"

"The directors, men who own part of my bank and some others. They instructed me to remind you that the bank holds mortgages on this house and on your plantation up the river."

The little French clock ticked as merrily away as if nothing really ugly could ever happen.

Marcy's heart went down, it sank, almost literally, it seemed. She could feel the sickening sensation of that plunge.

He meant that he was instructed to threaten her, to say that the bank would foreclose the mortgages, take over the plantation, take over everything Marcy loved and the only shelter she had—the only shelter for the whole household.

She managed to lift her head and speak. Her impulse was to flash into fury, yet her voice emerged in pleading. "Gene, you can't do this to me. You've known me all my life. We've known the same people, the same—everything. You can't be serious." Another instant and she'd be sobbing.

Gene shook his head. "I told you I hate the idea. I could have cut my own throat before I suggested such a thing to you. But I cannot cut other people's throats. Not as the war stands. We must not lose. We can't lose. I was told to bring every pressure I could to induce you to see this—this really very small task in the right way. It is only a patriotic request, Marcy. Only that . . ."

The clock ticked on; she counted ten, twenty, thirty, seconds. Thirty pieces of silver, she thought fantastically: Major Farrell's gold. Get Major Farrell's confidence, worm any secret he held out of him, take any information she could gather about General Grant's intentions or plans to Gene. She was asked to betray John Farrell, enemy Major Farrell now; she must remember that.

Armand was sometimes extraordinarily sensitive. He was

this time, for he suddenly said, "You can't have any special feeling for this man!"

It was not even accusatory; it was merely a very perceptive comment. Armand's black eyes saw too much. She said too quickly, "I've met him before. I told you. That's all."

Armand's eyes were still bright and watchful.

Gene said, "Don't have any hesitation, Marcy. Naturally, I realize that this is a role no lady would wish to play. But I'm convinced that you can do it easily, beautifully, to help save our Southland."

That, of course, was not fair.

But Armand at last seemed conquered. He sighed. "Remember those mortgages, Marcy. You'll have to do it, Marcy. The house, the plantation—you'd have nothing left."

He means *we* would have nothing left, Marcy thought. Yet he was practical, he was right.

Gene took her acquiescence to logic for granted. "I knew you'd see it our way," he said and came to her again, lifted her hand and kissed it. Then he moved away. "Come, Armand. We can depend upon Marcy. She is a loyal Southern woman."

Both men, however, seemed subdued. In spite of his agreement Armand was still smoldering; he wouldn't look at her; he bowed jerkily. They went out, Armand limping heavily.

Marcy wouldn't cry; besides, her throat was dry—where would tears come from? M. Lemaire said briskly, "My dear child! It isn't so terrible. We need spies—"

"Don't use that word—"

"There, there. I mean all the information we can get. The South is fighting for her life."

He didn't understand, or did he understand too well? She believed Gene when he said he loathed bringing the potent financial argument forward; he himself must have given in to pressure. Armand, too, had been won over by sheer logic. She thought again, with a trace of cold cynicism, that he had thought of himself and her property. A Creole with a good dash of Spanish blood never forgot the solid, material facts of life.

"What's that?" M. Lemaire cried. She rose as he shot

across the room and flung back brocaded draperies and shutters. *"Nom de nom!"* He slid into French. *"Qu'est-ce qui se passe?"*

She ran to stand beside him.

In the courtyard below, Major Farrell stood, a solid blue figure. Gene and Armand stood too, facing him. But Armand was talking, almost screaming. The puzzled look on Major Farrell's face vanished; he stepped back swiftly just as Armand's hand struck at him. He must have struck the major's jaw, for the major put a gloved hand to his mouth. Gene's slender figure darted between them. He seized Armand by the wrist; he pushed Armand ahead of him, through the flowers, out the gate and onto the banquette, where they disappeared. Major Farrell had turned to watch them. Even his square shoulders seemed astounded. He simply stood there, like a rock, staring after Armand.

There was a low, pleased sigh behind Marcy; Claudine said lightly, "Now they'll have to duel, won't they?"

M. Lemaire turned abruptly. "Certainly not! Don't suggest such a thing. We must make Major Farrell welcome in this house. Armand was very foolish, very impulsive. Marcy, you will be obliged to explain, tell Major Farrell something, anything. Armand, of course, has been very seriously wounded, he is very nervous, very feeble."

Claudine laughed low, again. "Not so feeble that he couldn't slap a Yankee."

Major Farrell turned again, this time toward the garden and the side door of the house. They could see his face, still puzzled rather than angry, but there was a deep red mark across his jaw and he was frowning. The flowers around him were like a rainbow of color; their fragrance in the late-afternoon warmth must have caught his attention, for he paused, glanced around him and bent to look at a *rose de gloire* blooming near the shell driveway. As he bent, little Brule came running along the driveway, sending out a shower of tiny white shells. He stopped, too, and stared at the unfamiliar man, the unfamiliar blue uniform.

What a beautiful child he is, Marcy thought as she had many times before. He was a very pale color, not quite white, with lustrous dark eyes and a graceful way of moving, almost like a flower himself, bending and swaying on a stalk. The major looked down, smiled at him, and suddenly they were talking. Not a word could be heard, but the child was smiling too; as they watched, he slipped his hand into the tall major's hand, and they advanced toward the house together.

Claudine drew a sharp breath. "If you don't get rid of that child, I will."

From the first she had refused to call him Brule. Others of the family were naturally reluctant to use his name in Claudine's hearing. They had compromised with small names, le Petit, le Bébé, sometimes little Brule when Claudine was nowhere near. It was a reasonable objection on Claudine's part. No one could truly blame her, for little Brule was, without any doubt, Brule's son. He had something of his mother's coloring, that was true. But even his baby face was the image of Brule Chastain: square chin, square brow, firm cheekbones under the childish plumpness. He was Brule's son; there had never been any doubt in Marcy's mind since the drizzly, cold Christmas Eve when she had met Sister Mary Ernesta at the steps of the cathedral and had seen Brule, bundled against the chill, huddled against her black robes.

Major Farrell swung the child up to his shoulder. Brule gurgled happily, his wide eyes sparkling. Major Farrell, laughing, came toward them along the gallery. There was still a puzzled something in his face and certainly a blotchy red spot where Armand had struck at him. He put Brule gently down.

No, it was an impossible feat which had been demanded of her.

Tante Julie had materialized behind her. Tante Julie in the black she always wore, not for mourning but because she was a French lady over fifty. Her hair was only touched with gray; her eyes, her round, pink-cheeked face and her smile were all welcoming.

"We are hoping, sir, that you may have supper with us," she said. Her smile was gracious, her dimpled hand extended. "I was not here to welcome you earlier. We are indeed thankful that it is you who is to be our guest." The garnets at her plump white throat seemed to wink approvingly.

Major Farrell's gaze was puzzled but in a different way as he looked at Marcy, who gave a swift thought to the larder but could only add to Tante Julie's invitation. Besides, she thought tartly, he would see just how they were living.

"Thank you," Major Farrell said. "That is very kind."

Not kind, Marcy thought; she is trying to entrap you too.

Claudine said coldly, "How very odd, Major, that you were billeted here. A strange coincidence. Since you knew my sister-in-law before the war."

Major Farrell's eyes cleared; his gaze was now rather searching, his aplomb unshaken, however. "No coincidence, madam," he said cheerfully. "I remembered her and recognized the Chastain name. I asked to be billeted here. It's very kind of you," he said again.

So he remembered having met her. That was all he remembered. She was another girl he had danced with and walked in the garden with and had champagne with—too much champagne, Marcy told herself. Clearly it had meant nothing to him.

Yet in fact, there hadn't been much for him to remember. She had to admit that. She said sweetly, "How very kind of you to remember me."

She said it too sweetly. Claudine's feminine perception operated instantly; she shot Marcy a swift glance.

THREE

When Jason touched the supper gong, which hung outside in the lower gallery and could be heard all over the court-yard and the house, the major understood it and came promptly from his room, along the gallery and down wrought-iron steps to the ground floor gallery, as if he knew his way.

The galleries followed the lines of the house. It was a lovely house, designed and built with a graceful nod to the prevailing French architecture, but wider, more generous in its spaces. Marcy's maternal grandfather had built it, and he was what the Creole French called then and still call an American. By that they meant one of the vigorous, some-times wealthy tribe of North Americans who came to New Orleans after Louisiana was sold to the United States.

There was, indeed, a whole district in the city called the American District, and so beautiful that it was also called the Garden District. With the advent of the Americans, the city had lost some of its early Spanish flavor, though not its early Spanish buildings. The French, too, were not averse to taking advantage of the growing importance of New Orleans as a port, and some of their architecture remained.

It seemed remarkable, Marcy thought as Tante Julie ladled out a very thin gumbo from a beautiful Sèvres tureen (which could have been sold already but for its size), that in so short a time the war and the new conquering army of Yankees could have reduced her own family and many others not quite to starvation but frighteningly near it.

Supper was not plentiful. Marcy planned to take one of the major's gold pieces the next day, give it to Jason and tell him to go to the French Market, to take two baskets and fill them as best he could. Liss must go with him; Liss was muscular, big, bad-tempered and a magnificent cook. Somehow she had managed to feed them all during the period of something too close to famine, except for those times when she wouldn't cook at all but simply disappeared. No one knew where she went during those moods; she usually came back the following day and resumed her cross attitude but remarkably good cooking, even if there was very little to cook. Marcy knew that the other servants firmly believed that Liss was a party to strange affairs, voodoo, something occult. But Marcy was reasonably sure that Liss merely went to spend some time with her circle of friends, gathering gossip. She seemed to know everything that happened in New Orleans, especially any tale of slightly or more than slightly scandalous character. She often related to Marcy some of the news she had picked up. Although Liss had highly approved of giving little Brule a home and attached herself to him, Marcy had no doubt that her own action in taking him into the house had been the subject of much talk and discussion.

Marcy wondered if the major would ever inquire as to the reason for Armand's sudden attack. What could she tell him if he did? Oh, that was easy. She would tell him the truth: Armand had been in the Confederate army; he had suffered from battle wounds; it was only the sight of the uniform he hated, in the house where he was to be a part of the family, married to Marcy—yes, tell him that. It was enough.

Perhaps. She eyed the major as he replied to some smiling sally of Tante Julie's, and the thought occurred to her that it would be really very hard to deceive him.

Even if, in the end, she had to submit to Gene's argument.

They had coffee from tiny cups, which were one of the treasures of the house, made in France many years before, delicate and thin.

Candles had been lighted. Even the big candelabra on the mantel were alight. Using up candle wax, Marcy thought with a surge of indignation. Tallow was all they dared use so lavishly; it smoked and smelled but gave light.

Tante Julie poured the coffee; the huge silver coffeepot had not gone the way of some other more easily portable pieces of silver.

She wouldn't think of the phrase "pieces of silver" —pieces of silver, pieces of gold, deliberate spying, deliberate betrayal.

All the same, down deep in her consciousness were the facts Gene had so reluctantly outlined for her: Grant's approach to Vicksburg, its importance to the South, the mortgages the bank held on this house, on the plantation. Tante Julie carried on a light conversation with ease, telling the major of the beauties of New Orleans, something of its history, Spanish, French, then American. The major must see some of the beautiful buildings, the old buildings of the city. Had he visited the Cabildo, the Pontalba apartments, Jackson Square? Oh, of course. She'd forgotten Yankee headquarters. But there were other places; one of the girls— her bright black eyes singled out Marcy—would be delighted to show him around.

Claudine sat in lovely, icy silence. At some time M. Lemaire drifted into the room carrying a bottle of Marcy's father's cherished brandy and liqueur glasses on a tray. How he had secured the bottle and protected it, Marcy didn't know, but he was so long and thoroughly established a member of the family that no one questioned his right to do anything he chose to do.

Tante Julie might almost have been in league with Gene, for she sent Marcy to take her guest to his room and show him how to swathe the bed with the mosquito netting.

This small gesture would have astonished Marcy if the

major and his gold had not provided Tante Julie with a reason for so flagrant a breaking of the stern law of chaperonage, which had always existed for unmarried females in any decent and respectable family, particularly a family with French blood. No young woman was ever left alone with a man; marriage ended this chaperonage but nothing else. Tante Julie's flaunting of the custom would have amused Marcy in any other circumstances; even as it was she felt the corners of her mouth twitch. However, she rose obediently. Claudine was already blowing out the candles, and the smell of snuffed wicks drifted through the room. M. Lemaire picked up the brandy bottle and disappeared. Tante Julie, bright eyes sparkling as she smoothed her dress, said good night sweetly to Major Farrell.

He went with Marcy, climbing the stairs and along the upper galleries. The night fragrances of all the flowers were almost sickeningly sweet, yet so lovely, Marcy thought, so dearly loved.

He had already made himself at home in the big corner room, which had been her father's. Brushes lay on the marble bureau top. Uniforms hung in the great armoire; the door was open, so that she could glimpse the neatly tailored and pressed blue folds.

She swept the netting from its loops around the great four-poster bed. "This is important. Mosquitoes are already here. Their bite is vicious."

He eyed the thin netting doubtfully. "You mean I wrap myself in that stuff?"

"Oh, no. Shoo out any mosquitoes that have already found their way around the bed, then when you are in bed—" Dear me, she thought, how indelicate, speaking of beds and what not. She went on sternly: "—wrap it around. Tuck it under the mattress. Like this."

She showed him one corner of the netting, first shaking it hard. She listened for the whine of a mosquito, did not hear it and said, "That's all. If you need anything, Jason will bring it to you." She glanced swiftly at washstand, pillows, curtains, made sure all was in order and said, "Good night, Major."

She was not to escape questions so easily. "Miss Chastain."

She had to stop, her hand already on the silver doorknob. Her heart gave an unruly leap. Now—now he would speak of that long-ago dance. She was mistaken. He said, "I met someone in the garden as I came here this afternoon—"

"This evening. I mean, I forgot you Northerners call it afternoon. Yes, I saw—"

"Well, why on earth did he try to start an argument? Good God, I don't want to fight him. I don't even know him."

"He was—well, I suppose, still is a Confederate soldier. He was wounded and paroled. He is—" She had to swallow hard to get it out. She used the clear way of escape. "We are formally betrothed to marry."

Something changed in the major's eyes. She turned away, pretending to adjust a curtain.

"Oh," said Major Farrell at last. "I see. A long engagement, I suppose."

She fussed with the embroidered muslin curtain. "Yes." She made herself face him. "We became engaged just before I visited Washington."

After another long moment, he said, "And you are still engaged to marry him."

"Yes." She pulled at the curtain. There was no way in which she could explain to him the multitudinous reasons for continuing her formal betrothal to Armand. She almost cried out, "But I'm not going to marry him!" when he said coolly, "He is to be congratulated, I'm sure. Thank you. Don't tear that curtain to pieces, Miss Chastain."

She looked with surprise at the torn lace in her hands. The major must be thinking of those unbelievable moments in the moonlit garden. She felt a flame of color come into her face. A coquette, he was thinking. In his arms, willingly returning his own ardor fully, yet newly engaged to another man. But then, she had thought that of him too—a man accustomed to casual flirtations.

She moved toward the door. John Farrell said softly behind her, "Of course, I expect in your code his unusual conduct would call for a duel."

"No!"

"But I've been told—"

"No! That has been stopped. It's against the law." Was it? If so, no one paid any attention to a law forbidding a dueling: it was a custom.

Major Farrell said briefly, "I am not here to fight duels. Good night, Miss Chastain. Thank you for your kindness."

She went away, sweeping quickly along the narrow corridor, turning the bolt of the door of her room almost as if she had been pursued, as certainly, definitely, she had not been.

Later, however, staring into the darkness, listening to the shrill whine of some mosquitoes which had escaped her, she wasn't sure that she had been so smart. Indeed, the major would have every reason to think of her as a presumptuous fool who felt her charms so irresistible that she must announce her engagement to marry. Her cheeks felt hot with embarrassment.

There was nothing to be done about it now; once said, it could not be unsaid. But then, in spite of herself, her thoughts shot back to that long-past ball.

They had danced, she and John Farrell. It was a waltz, which some old-fashioned people still considered all but immoral. The lilt, the swoop and beat of the music and their steps, the swish of lovely silk dancing dresses, wide hooped, caught up with lace and flowers; the grace of the young men, the drifting odors of perfume, the warm air coming in through the long windows—she remembered so clearly that all of it might have happened to her the previous night. When they had stopped, it was John Farrell who had suggested champagne. She hadn't even noted his name when her hostess had introduced him.

The champagne had been cold and delightful, and they had walked together down the wide steps to the first floor and then through a conservatory smelling of freesias and carnations. Here there were several other couples—girls who had quietly escaped their chaperons and handsomely dressed young men. The moist air of the conservatory had been too warm; there were open doors leading into a garden where paths of clean-cut turf wound through pleasant shadows of pines and willows and shrubbery. The path went down to a bench below some willows, which made a curtain around them.

There after a long silence John Farrell had turned to her. The shade of the willows, fully in leaf that April night, softened the moonlight, which fell gently, almost caressingly, upon them both. She was drawn by the knowledge that he was looking at her, and turned to meet his look. For what seemed a very long and strangely important moment, they simply looked into each other's eyes; it was as if they saw something new, deeply serious. Then, without a word, as if he didn't know what he was doing yet couldn't help it, he had taken her into his arms. She had gone to him without the least hesitation, as simply and yet urgently as if there were nothing else she could do. He had held her; neither had spoken for a long, long time. But not long enough, for all at once the music from the ballroom stopped. The sudden silence broke an incredible, wonderful spell. She tried to say, We must go in, and instead had whispered, "What is your name?"

Silly. He had laughed, deep in his throat. "John Farrell. You must remember it, you know." He had drawn her back into his arms, and she'd have stayed there forever if some-one hadn't come along the path, lifted a sweep of willows and said crossly, "Oh, you found that bench." There was a light giggle from near them and the sound of footsteps departing.

Marcy knew she must return to the ballroom. Tante Julie was a lenient chaperon, but not that lenient. "We must go back," she said.

John Farrell had laughed again, softly.

But she forced herself to move away from him and stood smoothing her hair. At last he took her hands, both of them, and put one on each side of his face. "Remember my name, John Farrell. I'll see you again tomorrow. And—think always, always..." It wasn't very coherent, but she thought he had said that.

They returned to the house. It was like a dream. By good luck, she had thought absently, she had escaped Tante Julie, who had found some cronies and was playing cards in a big library off the hall. But then, oh, then the dance was over.

The musicians had not merely stopped to rest; they had concluded the dance.

John Farrell had bowed over her hand and over Tante Julie's hand, which clearly Tante Julie had not remembered, for she had greeted him today as if she had never seen him before.

The day after that, the next morning indeed, messengers and dispatch riders had surged up to the house. Carriages had come; packing had been done; clothes had been hurled swiftly into trunks; and Tante Julie and she had been bundled out and away to the cars and home, for Fort Sumter had been fired upon, and war was now almost certain.

Sometime in that bewildering succession of emotions, a cold little voice had reminded her that she was formally betrothed to Armand. It had been settled, really, long ago, almost agreed upon by their families when they were children, formally arranged in January, when Louisiana seceded from the Union, barely three months previous to the Washington visit. No date had been set for a wedding, she reminded herself, and she believed that reflection ought to relieve her conscience; but the fact was, her conscience didn't hurt, not the smallest little stab. She had never felt anything like the moments with John Farrell, in his arms, when she was with Armand. Indeed, in Armand's cool and formal embrace she hadn't felt anything at all.

She was not likely, she had believed, to see John Farrell ever again. North and South would be separated, perhaps forever. She and John Farrell could not meet again. In the tumult and haste of those days, she had been like a doll, she thought now. Yet she *had* tried to induce her father to break off her engagement to Armand. The few moments under the willows had been, in a strangely deep sense, a revelation to her; she did not dwell upon the nature of the revelation, but she knew she could not marry Armand.

Her father, however, was adamant; children obeyed their parents. He had exerted all his familial and strong authority. Armand was a fitting *parti;* everyone, especially her father, believed their marriage a suitable one. She and Armand, she thought suddenly, had really never had much to say about it. Certainly she had felt no antipathy toward him; he had seemed reasonably attached to her, and at least had gone through all the motions of a loving fiancé—formal motions, naturally. But she couldn't, she wouldn't, nobody could make her, marry him now. Luckily, the marriage itself was far in the future.

Many things could happen.

The days preceding the war had been full of confusion, trouble, worry; her father had been distraught, concerned with a thousand anxieties, but mainly concerned with the inevitable departure of his son, Brule. Later, thinking of those strange and nightmarish days, it had seemed to Marcy that her father had almost a premonition that his son would be killed in battle.

When the news of Brule's death in the battle at Sharpsburg came at last, overnight her father had turned into an old and beaten man.

Later, he had furiously refused to take an oath of allegiance to the enemy which had killed his son, cursing the Federals when they had come to take him away.

Claudine had retreated to her room. Tante Julie had turned helplessly to Marcy; somebody had to keep the household going, find food, find wood for winter fires—and later sell whatever could be sold, because, like most Southern men, her father had put all the cash he could raise, even with the mortgages Gene had reluctantly reminded her of, in Confederate bonds. There began the long period when they lived somehow from day to day. The routine was changed only when Marcy defiantly brought Brule's little son home to live.

But now looking back, she knew that in the depths of her being there had existed far too strong a memory of the man who had arrived that day, had said cheerfully but distantly that he remembered her, and had clearly felt no particular significance in that brief memory.

Indeed, it was all too likely that the major was thinking, That fool girl: because I once paid her an easy compliment she feels she must warn me, hands off; she is to marry that man who tried to quarrel with me. It was a humiliating and embarrassing reflection; but tomorrow we must somehow see to it that Armand made no excuse for challenging the major to a duel. Gene might help about that.

Someone was in the courtyard below her open windows.

FOUR

There was the faintest rasping of the tiny shells in the driveway.

In an instant she had disentangled herself from the cobwebby folds of mosquito netting and got to a window.

She went without a sound, she was sure. Yet nothing, nothing at all moved in what she could see of the courtyard. The gallery itself made a heavy band of shadow. Anything, anybody could stay hidden within that band of shadow. But it was a clear starlit night. Eventually, whoever was there must show himself.

Perhaps he had moved into the house. No; the house doors were bolted. She waited, almost afraid that the thudding of her heart would alarm that night prowler.

Perhaps it was one of the family. M. Lemaire came and went as fancy seemed to dictate. He wouldn't move so stealthily. He wouldn't shrink out of sight within the band of shadow.

All at once, the ugly feeling of being under observation from somewhere—by someone—caught her again. She waited.

But time went on; the scent of flowers was sweet; nothing moved below—yes! Something did move out from the shadow and start across a starlit open space.

It was only a dark, shapeless figure, and even as she watched it crouched down and ran, lumbering awkwardly toward the stable entrance; that led to the mews behind the stable and out the door to the barnyard and street.

Then, almost before she could be sure that her own eyes were not deceiving her, the creature shambled with a lurch into the darkness of the stable entrance.

Nothing else moved in the starlit courtyard.

Presently she almost began to believe that she had been having a nightmare. But it was a peculiarly real nightmare. There had been the spattering of the tiny white shells below.

But nothing, nothing more happened.

She went back to bed. The night visitor had to be a prowling soldier.

Eventually she must have slept, for it was late and hot when she awoke and decided to tell no one of the stealthy intruder. She would, however, make very sure that the door to the mews was bolted hereafter.

New Orleans had been subdued by Yankee forces the previous spring. Civic government, the mayoralty, police, all utilities, were supposed to continue. The army ruled, in fact, yet New Orleans was by no means a completely conquered city.

There was the same vivacity, the same love of beauty, of music, of food, of its own special *joie de vivre* that had always been the heart of the city; these were merely banked, like fires with the heart still glowing, barely covered with ashes. There were outward changes of necessity; nothing had changed inwardly. It was like a temporary, hated, even dangerous spell laid upon the city, but there wasn't one Orleanian who did not feel that eventually the usurpers would be thrown over, out, away, and New Orleans would resume its own enchanting life.

Unhappily, when General Butler had been sent to command the city, he only aroused the deepest hatred: nothing was too bad a way to describe him, in the view of any

Orleanian. Whether or not he actually stole the silver that earned him the popular nickname Silver Spoons Butler, few people knew. It did appear that he and his brother, A. Butler, a so-called colonel not so formally appointed, had contrived to line their pockets with anything that struck them as lucrative. So, it was quite natural that his soldiers followed the example set by their superior. Things simply vanished, the horses and the carriage, the little chaise, odd objects within the house—even the huge piano, enameled yellow and decorated with a floral design which had been ordered long ago from New York, had disappeared. The Yankees seemed to take whatever they chose. Frequently a few soldiers, detailed to search a house for someone who had aroused a superior officer's ire (or envy of his worldly possessions), also lifted and pocketed whatever trifle appealed to them, and often it was no trifle. "Like master, like man," Marcy's father had said bitterly when Tante Julie had informed him of the disappearance of an entire set of Dresden plates.

Butler was also called Beast Butler, after his famous and infamous Woman Order, so vicious that it had aroused Lord Palmerston in faraway London to address the House of Lords concerning it. It was an order to the effect that any woman who expressed scorn or disdain of any United States soldier should be taken to be a woman of the streets and treated accordingly. In fact, the order aroused so much anger that it may have been a blessing in disguise. Certainly Mr. Lincoln must have known of the storm it stirred up even in England, and no Northerner wanted England to throw her weight in with the South. In December General Butler had been removed. When General Banks arrived to take his place, the whole city breathed a sigh of relief. The churches that Christmas were crowded.

When the city had fallen in the spring of 1862 to Admiral Farragut of the United States Navy, Marcy had not rushed down to the levees to see the bales of cotton and the sugar supplies, which might have been of some benefit to the conquerors, burning there. It had been tragic enough to see the dense clouds of smoke rising over the city.

Later, the conquerors had sailed upstream, and no Chastain

knew what had happened to the plantation there. Marcy had been born at Nine Oaks on the Bayou Reve Road. Its bluffs overlooked the river itself, and its acres spread widely behind it. Many slaves were needed for clearing, planting, seeding, chopping out cotton, and repairing the levees, which had been built against the greedy Mississippi, which nevertheless did eat away ruthlessly at the land below the low, long plantation main-house.

Marcy's dowry, as set forth in the articles of her betrothal to Armand, had been considerable then. No one knew or could guess what it might be now.

Liss brought Marcy a small cup of what passed for morning coffee, but was good enough to prove a real triumph of Liss's ingenuity. No Creole could enter the day with equanimity without that tiny cup of coffee. Formerly it had been black and strong; now it was, at least, a hot drink.

Liss said, "Look." She held out a miniature. It was the portrait of a lady, very stiff in her tightly laced dress, its skirt billowing below; her neck was rather long and slender; her eyes an extraordinary dark gray.

"Where—?"

"*M'sieu le Commandant.*" Liss dropped occasionally into the French tongue, as most people in New Orleans still did.

Marcy, being part American and part Creole, had spoken both French and American as long as she could remember. The English language was always explicitly called American, for it came to New Orleans with the influx of Northerners.

"His wife, *sans doute*," said Liss.

Something in the gray eyes suggested Major Farrell. "No. *Mère.*"

Liss shrugged. "*Ah, bien. Peut-être.*"

Marcy was recalled to her duty. "You shouldn't have taken this from his room."

Liss glowered. "*Mais il est parti. Ce matin là.* Early. I clean, make things neat. This was on a table."

Liss took the miniature in her strong hand and went out of the room.

When she was dressed, Marcy went to the locked drawer

of the enormous and rather ugly Empire chest; the sphinx heads at each side looked blankly into space. It was exceedingly difficult to clean, for the sphinx heads and the trimmings were brass and easily became cloudy and dull. The key was enormous too, with a red silk tassel. She kept the key hidden merely as a precaution against an unexpected visit of looting soldiers; no one in the house would be likely to search that drawer, and in any event, until Major Farrell had arrived the previous day, there was no money or anything of much value in it.

She pulled the drawer open and for a moment lingered over one keepsake that she liked, for it had been her mother's. It was a round box, perhaps two inches across; it was silver gilt, another cleaning problem, but set with a ruby (rather shallow to accommodate the lid of the box, but a good color) and numerous rubies interwoven in a pattern with tiny turquoises, some of which had dropped out. She let herself lovingly finger the box, then took one of the gold pieces—which really seemed heaven-sent rather than provided by a Yankee officer—and then locked up the drawer again. She paused for a second or two before opening the enormous armoire, now sadly almost empty. Her one ball gown, pale pink silk with laces, had taken the eye of a Yankee corporal.

She had gone to a few balls in New Orleans, but only a few—never one for which she had been permitted a real grown-up gown. She was not old enough, her father had said, to attend many balls. During Mardi Gras maskings, she had been permitted to attend private parties and watch the maskers from some convenient balcony. Then had come the invitation to Washington City, to visit the senator's home. And she had worn the pink dress and danced—it was no use brooding over that. She closed the door and went down to the kitchen.

Liss got out two big rush baskets. Her formidable face did seem to brighten. This was likely the effect of being able to procure food to cook; it was also barely possible that Liss would rather welcome an opportunity, should it occur, to take issue with any Union soldier unfortunate enough to cross her path.

Jason was not so willing, but he brightened when he saw Liss pick up the heavy kitchen poker and weigh it thoughtfully. She was a big woman; her white headscarf was tied firmly; she had donned a snowy white apron over her print dress. "Coffee, ten dollars a pound, last time I saw it," she said dourly, with a kind of eager anticipation. It had been a long time since she had had so much money to spend on food. "Sugar was nine dollars. Corn meal twelve dollars."

"The prices may have changed since General Banks came to New Orleans," Marcy said hopefully, but Liss's underlip protruded. "More likely got bigger. Come along, Jas."

They went out the kitchen door and through the wide arch of the carriage entrance, which led to the now deserted stable and the mews behind the house. For a chill second Marcy thought of the figure shambling swiftly into the protective shadow of that arch. In the light of day it seemed a nightmare—yet a remarkably vivid nightmare, endowed with the slight rasp of shells under its feet. She wouldn't think more of that now.

She could trust Liss to get the best food available and to keep an eye on Jason, who just might slide away for home at his first sight of a blue uniform. Luckily, Liss was made of sterner stuff.

Breakfast, such as it was, was on the long mahogany buffet in the dining room. No one was about. She helped herself to a rather gluey mass of rice and went out to the gallery; it was shaded by the second-floor gallery, but already the sun was hot. Little Brule was busy pulling some petals from the *Maréchal Niel* rose. He had little to play with; Marcy did not check him. Tante Julie was taking a late rest; she laughingly claimed to have been hopelessly Creolized, which only meant that she liked to be lazy when she chose, although when she didn't choose, her small feet danced like a girl's, unheeding her plump and corseted figure. Claudine was sitting on a bench in the shade of an enormous unpruned mock orange, looking coldly at Brule. But then it could never be expected that Claudine would take kindly to Brule's son, born of his alliance (Claudine would have called it *mésalliance*) with his gentle, beautiful Angele. Marcy knew her name and had caught a glimpse of her once, with Brule, near the French Market. So she knew that the girl was beautiful. Certainly Claudine was Brule's legal wife; as certainly Angele had been his beloved wife. During Brule's last leave, he had often disappeared for long hours and returned looking contented and happy. That was due to Angele and little Brule and the tiny house Brule had provided for them.

Could it be barely possible, Marcy thought, that Claudine would undertake the onerous chore of trying to spy upon John Farrell's assignments?

No. Armand was right when he said she would refuse. Beneath her Dresden-doll face and the Dupre charm and elegance with which she and Gene went through life so gracefully lay a complete, determined selfishness. Gene and Armand, Marcy thought again, were alike as twins—in their attitudes, their reactions to the world, their light-hearted but firm determination—yes, they were alike. It was only recently that Armand had changed owing to his war experience, his wound, some viewpoint of the war which Gene did not share. Gene had taken it in the beginning as a tremendous lark. It had not proved to be such a lark, for he had a slightly withered, never-to-be-quite-healed left arm; yet it had not embittered him. Armand's nature was essentially different: his Spanish blood perhaps gave him a somber touch of character which Gene, all French, had escaped. They remained, however, the closest of friends. And Defenders.

That organization was supposed to be secret, but naturally was not. Yet Marcy, while approving the activities of the Defenders as a force, actually found that her strong vein of common sense questioned their purpose. What good did it do, conspiring, carrying out small acts of vengeance which were really like pinpricks to the controlling Federals? Even when occasionally they were blamed, probably rightly, for an assassination, it only stiffened the Federal rule.

Marcy sighed, looking at Claudine. There was no use at all in trying to enlist her help in spying on John Farrell.

As if she could read Marcy's mind, Claudine rose, gave Brule an icy look, and passing Marcy, said, "That child you insisted upon bringing here is ruining the flowers." With that she went back into the house.

FIVE

Marcy watched her pass through the belt of shadow on the gallery; the door closed smartly.

A bee hovered around, buzzing indignantly when she waved her hand to frighten him away.

"Spy" was a despicable word. "Mortgage foreclosure" were not nice words, either. Gene would never have considered it himself; he was under pressure. So Marcy was under pressure too.

How *could* the Yankees have injured the whole South, New Orleans, the Queen City, so completely, so devastatingly, in what seemed a long time but really was not! A wave of helpless fury caught her. They had killed her brother. They had sent her father away; she had not heard any word of him. By now he might have died without care, without his family, away from his home.

"Spy" might be an ugly word, but the Yankees deserved any contribution she could make toward even a slight revenge.

Vicksburg was an important bastion for the South—only Vicksburg held the lower part of the rich Mississippi; New

Orleans was, of course, now in Yankee hands, but the entire Confederacy would be cut in half if Vicksburg fell.

Was it really in her power to help to defeat the Yankees threatening Vicksburg?

Grant's strategy was of vital significance to the South. Perhaps she was being worse than a spy, almost a traitor, in fact, in stubbornly refusing to do her best to extract Grant's plan from Major Farrell. Yes, she thought gloomily; she was wrong.

In another way, stubborn, too, she was right. Let them find out Grant's plans for themselves, she thought rebelliously.

But there was no getting around the fact that—given sufficient will, means and charm—it was a conceivable notion that she could succeed as a spy.

Patriotism was the strongest argument. Mortgages were no weak argument as well.

Again, suddenly she knew that someone, somewhere, was watching her. It shocked all her senses. She turned with a jerk toward the huge gates. A figure—man or woman, she couldn't tell—swiftly moved out of sight behind the wall.

Getting her breath, she ran for the gates. She was not afraid, as she had been in the night. The house and garden, all sunlit and alive, surrounded her. She removed the bolt, pulled open the small door, and darted out, with what even then she knew was a kind of false courage, onto the banquette. There was no moving figure, man or woman, anywhere.

But she hadn't fancied a watching figure, she hadn't dreamed it. It had been there, looking through the iron traceries of the gate.

Whoever it was had shot swiftly around the nearest corner, the nearest vine-covered wall. She turned back, closed and bolted the small door, and went to a bench where she sank down, trying to control her rapid breathing and trying to reason with herself. She had seen what she had seen the night before. For some time now—certainly it had started in recent weeks—she had been oppressed by the sense of covert watching from somewhere, by someone.

But this—this is the broad daylight—oh, no, she told

herself, it was some Yankee merely peering into the garden, some curious passer-by. Nothing else.

But she must remember to tell Jason to bolt the mews door.

Liss and Jason returned. They came through the mews and carriage drive toward the kitchen, the baskets on their arms, heavily laden. Liss permitted herself a triumphant jutting out of her chin in Marcy's direction. So that day the table would be well supplied; today and for as long as the gold pieces held out. They would be replenished as long as Major Farrell remained.

She rose, warded off another bee and went to the kitchen to gloat with Liss and Jason over the stock of provisions. Real coffee; she smelled it. Real cane sugar. Yellow cornmeal. Flour. Chickens—good heavens—okra, snap beans, squash. Down at the bottom of the basket was actually a large smoked ham. There would be a feast, and later there was, but the delectable dinner Liss prepared was not enjoyed by the major, who did not return until night.

After an equally lavish supper, Marcy caught Jason in the kitchen happily scooping up the remains on his plate with a crust of bread.

"Jason, did you lock the door last night? I mean the door from the stable."

"Oh, yes'm." Jason crunched at his bread and looked furtive.

Marcy glanced at Liss, whose lip was curled skeptically.

"Well, then, Jason, you must bolt it every night. Understand me? *Every night.*"

"Oh, yes'm."

She wasn't at all sure that he would; however, she told him he could go to bed, and she would wait up to open the gate for the major. Jason, happily gorged with food, said, "Yes'm. Yes'm." But she went with him, inexorably, as far as the cavernous black door to the stables; she listened as his footsteps padded along through the stables; she heard the heavy thump of the great iron bolt on the door that led to the mews.

Only then did she walk slowly back through a garden which was tenanted by flowers—and mosquitoes—and sat on a garden bench. She was oddly alert to any sigh of the light breeze and to any sound from the house, yet she felt, at least for the moment, safe from any sort of intrusion. At last the major came. He gave a single short rap against the small door in the carriage gate, and Marcy went to open it for him.

He passed through the clear starlight, tall, broad-shouldered, his epaulets shining. "Thank you," he said, sweeping off his black slouch hat. I hope I didn't inconvenience you. I was delayed." She murmured something and closed the gate; he reached out to fasten the big iron latch.

She turned toward the house, and he said softly, "It is very beautiful here. Even under the stars the garden is . . ." He paused and repeated, "Beautiful. Do you mind if I just sit here and enjoy the night?" He was polite, but that was all.

"There are mosquitoes." She seemed always to be warning him of mosquitoes.

"Pests, aren't they?" he said agreeably, and somehow, without meaning to, she was sitting beside him on the bench. He put back his head, and sighed. "I'm not accustomed to the heat here yet."

"It's nothing compared to August. We always went to Nine Oaks in the summer." There must have been a wistful note in her voice, for he turned his head sharply toward her. "Nine Oaks?"

"The Chastain plantation. On the Bayou Reve Road. Just off the River Road."

"But why—?"

"We didn't go last year because you—the Yankees—I mean, we can't be sure what is happening there. In any event, we can't leave the city without"—she swallowed hard—"without taking the Ironclad Oath."

He was silent for a moment. Then he said, "Ah, yes. The oath of allegiance. I take it that you refused."

"Only my father was asked to take it. They sent him away. I don't know where."

There was a pause. Then he said soberly, "Then your aunt—is it?"

"Tante Julie. Yes. She is my father's sister, widowed some years ago. Naturally she lives here."

"And Mrs. Chastain—"

"Mrs.—Oh, Claudine. Yes. My brother Brule was killed in battle. She is his widow."

Again there was a pause. Then he said soberly again, "You've had a hard time. I'm sorry. Is the little boy Mrs. Chastain's son?"

"No," she said shortly. He'd have to know sometime, and besides, it was no real disgrace, no matter what Claudine thought. "Brule's mother was my brother's *placée*—"

"*Placée?*"

"Well, mistress. A quadroon. The little house he bought for her was confiscated, taken over by some Yankee. Angele— that was her name—died before Christmas. The good sisters took care of her and the little boy. Then one of them wrote to me and asked me to take the little boy. So I did."

He digested that in silence before he said, "That was a very kind thing to do."

"It was the only thing to do. Angele had been like a wife to him." She felt she must defend Brule. "Many of the young men set themselves up before marriage. No one speaks of it, of course, but it is known. Claudine must have understood that. It isn't as if she hadn't known of Brule's first—I mean his other—household. But Brule—Brule loved Angele."

He said thoughtfully, "It took considerable courage on your part to bring him here. What did your sister-in-law, your aunt . . ."

It was oddly easy to talk to him. "They didn't like it. That is, Claudine didn't like it. But Tante Julie is always practical. She told other people that it was our affair—oh, she did it sweetly but very firmly. We hadn't the money to support my brother's son in any other way. People understood that. And Brule—that is, Angele and the little house and—it is almost a custom here."

The major pushed at the tiny white shells below a polished boot. "It happens, of course, in my home city. That kind of arrangement. However, it is not exactly accepted.

Not a custom, certainly. People pretend not to know. Such a connection is usually cut off when a man marries.''

''That is true here, usually. Sometimes it is impossible. With my brother, it was impossible. Claudine doesn't like the boy. She has no child. But she had accepted that situation when she and Brule were married.''

''But then why—''

''The marriage was an excellent one,'' she said shortly. ''Both families agreed to that. She has beauty, good family and a dowry. It was time Brule settled down properly with someone of his own sphere of life.''

''That's a practical way of looking at it.''

''Both families had money—then. It was a suitable marriage.''

He was smiling a little. ''Suitable. Very practical, indeed.''

''It's the French way,'' she said sharply.

''I'm sure. Yes. New Englanders are practical too. Not quite fond of arranged marriages, however. When I marry— ah, well . . .''

So, in all that time he hadn't married! The possibility had not occurred to her. Even then a kind of chill crept along her body. But she reminded herself that there had been time for many a dance and many a romantic interlude in many a garden since the few moments she remembered.

If she had any notion of complying with Gene's request— and, if she looked at it coldly, Gene's threat—perhaps now was a time to begin. She made herself say, as if idly, ''Your home is in Washington, isn't it?''

''Boston.'' She knew that he gave her a suddenly alert glance. ''I'm a lawyer by profession. That's why I was in Washington, where I had the pleasure of meeting you. I had been sent down to see about some bill that was coming up in the Senate.''

He said it too lightly, too formally. He added as lightly, ''I called at the senator's—my duty call, of course—the day after I met you. They said you had gone.''

''There was the news of Fort Sumter that morning. Everyone felt it meant war. Tante Julie and I were hustled back home as fast as they could send us.''

''So a servant at the senator's house told me. You see, I

really called on you. A duty call—but it was you I wanted to see.'' That, however, was said too coolly, too formally.

A mosquito was whining somewhere near; it gave her an excuse to lift her fan so he could not see her face in the clear starlight, or note any possible tightening of her lips. He said, ''And so, now I find you again.''

He rose unexpectedly, paced up and down, scattering the tiny white shells for a moment, and returned to sit beside her. ''This war ought never to have happened.''

''But you enlisted! You're an officer!''

''I don't like war. I keep thinking that it is a tragic waste. I keep thinking that Southern—wait a minute, I'm not blaming the South—but I do mean both Southern and Northern hotheads got us into it. It's all wrong.''

''You Northerners only want our property!'' She couldn't help that.

He sat down again, leaning his elbows on his knees, his profile strong against the starlit garden. ''We could disagree about that, and I expect each of us would have some truth. But the fact remains we are in the war and we—I mean the North now—have got to win it. And we will.''

''Don't say that!''

''Please—I remembered you, you see. Don't let us disagree.''

He put up his head, clasped his hands round one knee and leaned back against the bench. The stars looked strangely clear and near. It was hard to believe that somewhere, perhaps only up the river, too near Vicksburg, other soldiers were watching the same tranquil stars, not one of them sure what the next day would bring to him or whether indeed he would see another starlight. If Grant attacked Vicksburg . . . perhaps this was time to make a cautious inquiry?

He said, ''Mr. Lemaire? Another relative, I suppose?''

''Cousin—second cousin—of my mother's. He has lived here—oh, for years.''

''What does he do?'' the major asked, almost idly. Too idly, she thought suddenly. No—M. Lemaire was harmless.

''Nothing, really. He just—just lives here. He has had the same room up there''—she nodded toward the now darkened windows—''for years. Since I was a child.''

"Isn't that rather unusual?"

"Why, no. It's like that in the South. Some relative or friend comes for, say, a weekend and may live for the rest of his life in whatever house his friend or—relative owns."

He considered and shook his head. "That's what they mean by Southern hospitality?"

"I don't know." But suddenly she was overcome by an untimely giggle. It *was* a Southern custom, that generous hospitality, but also absurd. "Monsieur Lemaire is part of the family."

"Then his political views are Southern, too." There was a slight, slight question in his voice. Was he afraid of M. Lemaire discovering too much of his plans and of Grant's plans? This gave her a brief wave of something like triumph.

He said, "By the way, I met your fiancé again today."

"Armand! Again?"

He gazed up at the stars, his face rather too firm. "I'm afraid I disappointed him."

"*Ah, le bon Dieu!* He wanted a duel!"

"How did you know?"

She shrugged but was angry. "It's like him. He has a fiery kind of temper. Are you going to fight him?"

"No," he said lightly.

"But he struck you. He ought not to have done that but—"

"No reason why I should kill him. Or for that matter," he said lightly again, "let him kill me."

After a moment, she said, "Armand is a very good duelist. Before the war—"

She stopped, but someone had told him. He said, "I can't say a word against your fiancé, not to you, naturally. But I really don't like dueling. Your fiancé didn't like my refusal today. He seemed to consider it an insult, blaming his wounded leg and blaming me for deferring to what he considered his own weakness."

"Like Armand."

"May I ask . . . when are you to marry?"

She wouldn't say "Never," not now. She evaded. "It hasn't been settled."

There was a long pause. To avoid his steady gaze, she in

her turn scraped at the tiny white shells with her slipper toe. Her one good pair of slippers, she thought absently, donned tonight because—well, because a guest was expected at supper? Or because the guest was John Farrell, whom she had thought of far too many times and never expected to see again? She almost put her hand on his arm to assure herself that the miracle had happened. But no, no! It was not, it couldn't be, a miracle. Certainly he did not so consider it.

"Why are you marrying him?" It seemed a coolly impersonal question.

"Because—because—we are betrothed. It is a settled thing. The families—"

"Oh, the families. But what about you? Are you in love with him?"

She shot up. "You must not ask such things."

He caught her wrist and pulled her down gently beside him. "Forgive me. But I think I have every right to ask"—he mimicked her—"such things. You see, I came here because I wanted to see you again. If you are to marry this Monsieur Armand Whatever-his-name-is—"

"Ortega," she said helplessly, confused. At least he had said he wanted to see her again.

"Ortega." It diverted him. "Sounds Spanish. Is that all of it?"

"No, that is—it's Henri Pierre Armand Etienne Picot y Ortega."

He gave a little gulp like a chuckle. "All of that?"

"A French custom. His mother was Creole, his father of Spanish descent."

"So I gather. But you speak English."

"My mother was part American. My father is Creole."

"American. That's what you call English."

She nodded.

He said, "Your mother—"

She interrupted him swiftly. "She died of yellow fever. I was eight. I remember her." Even now her throat seemed to swell and ache at the thought of her lovely, graceful mother, laughing and happy one day, dying and dead in a matter of hours. She said, "She's buried in the Chastain family mausoleum. That's one blessing. So many died that terrible year of 1853 that graves couldn't be dug for everyone. There were rows of—''

"Don't think about it," the major said.

But she remembered. The stars had quietly vanished, almost as if they too mourned, and a thin layer of clouds had crept its way across the sky. As she looked, it grew heavier until all the stars began to disappear. That means rain tomorrow, she thought.

The major put his hand upon her arm. It was a large, firm and comforting hand. "You are very young."

"I was named for her, you know. Her surname. Marcy."

"I wondered about that. Is it a French name?"

"No. Only her family name."

"Lemaire," he said thoughtfully. "Close to Marcy. Sounds—'' he stopped.

She said, "You mean it sounds as if he adopted it because of the resemblance. Perhaps he did. It doesn't really matter, does it? Nothing," she said suddenly, "nothing seems to matter since the war, since everything—'' She felt a sob rise in her throat so it ached. "Everything is so different," she said low.

He put out one hand toward her, then quickly withdrew it, but said, "You've had more than your share. It seems to me that you have undertaken the care of this entire household. Some one of them ought to have helped you."

He had seen too much and in too short a time. She said, "Tante Julie was and still is completely dear and lovely. Of course Claudine—one must not expect much of a widow."

"Your fiancé must be a great solace and comfort to you?" It was said so softly that for an instant or two she did not feel any possible sting. Then she pulled herself distantly from him and rose. "Good night, Major."

"Don't go. I didn't mean to be—to hurt your feelings. Your Armand is determined to put me where he wants me."

"No! No, you must not duel with him."

"I don't intend to if I can avoid it. I have more important things to do."

Now—was it *now* a time to ask "What things?" He went on slowly, "Your Armand is not going to give up, you see. Apparently he has taken exception to me. The moment he saw me, yesterday, when we met. The young gentleman with him—"

"Gene Dupre."

"—tried to restrain him, which added fuel to your fiancé's wrath. The only explanation is—" He paused, obviously changed the course of his words and said dryly again, "*An* explanation is that he does not wish you to show any politeness or hospitality to a Yankee. It is quite comprehensible. Indeed he told me, on the street, as a matter of fact—I think he must have been waiting for me to come from headquarters—in any event, he told me that your marriage is to take place immediately. And thus, he said he had every right to tell me that I am not welcome in this house, and that I must leave at once."

SIX

"But that isn't true! We have no—*no* plan for immediate marriage!"

"Then," continued Major Farrell thoughtfully, "he struck at me again. I saw it coming. I dodged. And went on my way. Unfortunately, we were in a very public place. A number of people saw the incident."

"Then—but then they'll expect you to fight him."

"I don't believe in settling disagreements that way. I told you."

"But I don't understand."

"What don't you understand? Your fiancé's dislike for me, or the thought of your coming marriage?"

"Not immediate marriage! It can't be true."

"What can't be true?"

"I mean that Armand would say it was to be at once. We haven't talked of it at all. There is no such arrangement."

He stood. "That's your business. I'm afraid I have intruded. I did so because his attitude puzzled me. Even yesterday—well, good night and thank you for staying up to let me in."

He walked across toward the gallery. His tall figure disappeared into the shadow. She heard his footsteps on the stairs.

Well, she thought dazedly, what's the matter with Armand? Certainly there was no plan at all for their immediate marriage.

It must be late. She had sat there willingly, as if mesmerized, lingering on every word from a man who barely remembered her. All those nights when she couldn't sleep, when she thought of him, when even his name, John Farrell, seemed carved into her heart.

Stupid! A silly, silly woman putting a serious face upon a perfectly ordinary little flirtation. Yet he had said, hadn't he, that he had wanted to see her!

When she reached her room, Tante Julie was there, comfortably snuggled into a chaise lounge with a mosquito net wrapped prudently about her generous little body in its ruffled pink peignoir. She sat up sleepily, peered at Marcy through the net and thrust it aside. "I'm only your chaperon," she said, then giggled and added, "Whatever were you and the major talking about so long?"

"Nothing much. That is, yes. Armand is being difficult."

"Armand always was difficult, wasn't he?" She rubbed her eyes and began patting her chin upward in what Marcy knew was a habitual exercise in the hope of reducing that charming but very plump chin.

"Not—oh, I don't know."

"You're betrothed to him."

Marcy said rather desperately, "I honestly don't feel that I know Armand very well."

Tante Julie thrust away the entangling fold of thin net and began to struggle out of the cushions. "One understands Armand's reason for all this nonsense. He saw Major Farrell. A very handsome man, yes. He knows that you met him in Washington before the war. He knows or guesses that the major asked to be billeted here. You ask me, it's plain jealousy on Armand's part." She moved smoothly in spite of the bulk she carried, and put a dimpled hand on Marcy's shoulder. "Don't fret yourself. Just be sweet and patient with Armand. *Bonne nuit, chérie.*"

With that she went away, her fluffy peignoir like a pink cloud around her. Marcy heard a barely suppressed yawn as she disappeared and closed the door.

Armand *couldn't* be serious, talking of immediate marriage.

She thought angrily, Marriage! At such a time.

But then a light broke upon her. Armand had not been serious at all; he had merely vented his dislike for the Yankee officer, as Tante Julie, wise in the ways of the world, and Marcy surmised, of men, had explained it. Armand simply and directly intended to advise the major of his claim upon Marcy herself (and what property she might sometime have, her French sense of money reminded her); Armand meant to warn off the major so he would make no gestures of any special friendship on the excuse of once having met and danced with her—and remembering her, she thought, and wanting to see her again.

Under General Butler's regime, Armand would not have been allowed to live in New Orleans. The old Ortega city house had long been confiscated by the Federals on the score of Armand's having been a Confederate soldier. But then General Banks took command, and Armand returned, wounded, paroled and in Confederate uniform, as then required. He had been permitted a lodging at the St. Charles Hotel, where some of the occupation Union officers lived, and where they could keep an eye on and hopefully through him and some of his friends—possible members of the Defenders. Gene Dupre was one of them, but Gene was smarter than most, or at least more prudent. Responsibility for the bank and his associates, as well as for the clients of the bank, combined to give Gene a kind of reserved caution which some of the other young men did not share. Gene would never have tried to quarrel with John Farrell.

The Ortega family place was in Assumption parish, but Armand now had no immediate family: his father had died long ago, his mother more recently. Two sisters had married and gone to Natchez to live. There were, of course, cousins, uncles, aunts, scattered through the Bayou Teche country; this was a part of French and Spanish life.

Yes, Armand had been merely exploding. Tante Julie was right.

She smiled a little at Tante Julie's idea of proper chaperonage. She had installed herself in Marcy's room, not far, it was true, from the bench in the garden below, where Marcy had sat and talked to John Farrell; but she had then quietly gone to sleep. Of course, Tante Julie was, as always, a realist; she very much wished Major Farrell to find his billet pleasant enough to remain in the house.

Marriage immediately! Oh, how foolish Armand could be! But Armand could also be as Tante Julie had said, difficult. She must reason with him, dissuade him from his absurd quarrel with the major, or, rather, Armand's attempts at a quarrel into which the major refused to enter.

She folded the mosquito netting closely around her bed.

That night, if a visitor had contrived to enter the garden, she did not know it.

But she dreamed, and as usual in her bad dreams, she was helpless and in difficulty. She dreamed that she was riding, uncomfortably jouncing, in a carriage along the River Road, winding in and out as the river turned; then there was the great water oak, darkly vivid in her dream, which marked the turn into the Bayou Reve Road and toward Nine Oaks. But here, all at once, she was riding a horse who didn't know the way and who picked his feet uncertainly over the patches of corduroy which extended over the swampy land; and then she knew, as one does know in dreams, that there was danger somewhere, danger ahead, danger around her; the horse's hooves clopped unsteadily along the corduroy, and she woke, shaking with something like fear.

Fear of a dream! But fear it was. She rose and lighted a candle; she looked around at the familiar room, the dressing table with its rather shabby flounces and the mirror where her own face looked, for a moment, strange in the wavering candlelight, strange and white, and she was a fool!

She blew out the candle, remembered the stealthy figure

of the previous night, looked down into the rather misty darkness of the garden, listened, heard nothing and got back into bed. After a time she shook off the impression of danger along the peaceful, lovely Bayou Reve Road leading on to Nine Oaks.

But on the very edge of sleep at last, she thought of the major's saying that he had wanted to see her. If Gene knew that, he would consider it an opening to the program of coaxing and friendliness from which he hoped to derive some knowledge of General Grant's intentions. Gene had not heard the cool and impersonal way the major had spoken.

Morning dawned cloudy and gray and very humid. It was in such weather that there were cases of yellow fever—yellow john, some called it, or yellow jack. As a rule it was most prevalent during August and September. Everyone in the city dreaded the fever; there had been frightful occasions when deaths from it occurred all over the city, so many that crews to bury the victims could scarcely collect their tragic cargoes. At these times, in one of the futile efforts to ward off the fever's onset, barrels of tar were burned, covering the lovely city with a smoky pall. That spring, thus far, Marcy had heard of no cases of yellow fever. But it was the kind of morning when anything at all seemed ominous; in the humid air there was almost a foreknowledge of something to fear.

Perhaps everyone in the house felt that heaviness of spirit, for even Liss went about her tasks slowly; her thick underlip stuck out. Jason prudently stayed out of her way.

The major had apparently departed early, whether to the Union headquarters or to ride up the river and rendezvous eventually with one of General Grant's staff, no one knew.

Bébé Brule had a sore throat and a cough. Marcy found some camphor and wrapped his throat in a soaked handkerchief which had belonged to his father. She herself had embroidered the handkerchief, and it gave her another pang of sick incredulity. To keep busy she went about wiping mirrors; they always misted in this kind of weather. The mahogany in the stately dining room had a bluish haze which nothing could have polished away but for a moment; with the heavy, warm humidity, it would return. The sphinx heads on the Empire dresser were dull with moisture too, and looked green instead of golden. Even the parquet floors lost their shining glow. The flowers in the garden were drooping, the green leaves heavy. This misty, weighted silence was usual on a warm, hazy day, but this day seemed freighted with some kind of significance. Liss, in the kitchen, didn't even try to cook appetizing meals, and when Marcy went to talk to her about marketing the next day, Liss shook her head. "This no time to talk. Them is around," Liss muttered. "No use them hear us—"

Them? Marcy knew enough of Liss's moods to understand, or at least accept, "them," although Liss never explained precisely what she meant. Liss had come originally from an island in the West Indies; perhaps she knew things that most Negroes and probably no white people understood. "It's the weather," Marcy said stoutly.

She left the kitchen, knowing from previous experience that when tomorrow came and the sun came out, Liss's dark mood would vanish. She hoped that, this time, Liss's mood would not result in one of her disappearances. Fortunately it didn't, although it sadly affected Liss's cooking.

The day passed slowly. The major did not return.

The breathless humidity became fog and then turned to a slow, disheartening drizzle. The banquettes were shining with it, and the lamplighter was going on his rounds, carrying his ladder and his long lighter, when Armand came.

He was both stately and dashing in his fawn-colored trousers, his ruffled cravat, his embroidered satin waistcoat, his black coat. He was handsome as always, smiling as almost always, thin and white but altogether a desirable young *parti*. Marcy went to meet him. He bowed over her hand and then asked for Tante Julie.

Marcy's heart sank. He did not ask for Tante Julie because she was the chaperon for Marcy; it was because Tante Julie was the titular authority in the family.

So Armand had meant it when he told the major they were to be married soon!

Marcy sent Jason for Tante Julie, who also gave Armand one swift look and knew. Her dark eyes flashed a note of warning toward Marcy: Gently, he can be difficult.

He was not at first so difficult as he was authoritative. He stood below the portrait of her father in the long salon with the French clock ticking away as merrily as if there could be nothing in the world but pleasure. He lifted his rather sharp chin and informed Marcy that the time had come for their marriage; their betrothal had lasted too long; he did not expect to go back into the army; indeed—he said this rather bitterly, so Marcy could not help feeling a twinge of pity—indeed the army would not take him, crippled as he was. Tante Julie made a sad and sorry little gesture with one of her white hands. Armand went on.

"Your father signed the contracts. You signed and I signed. We are almost married now. It is best all around to take the other vows."

"But, Armand, those were only betrothal vows. Not marriage—not serious."

Armand's eyes flashed. "Not serious? What do you mean? All such contracts are serious. I have talked to Father Carlos. Next Monday is the date we have set. At ten in the morning. He says in the cathedral and I agree. Of course, in these times we cannot have the usual formalities of a wedding. I'm sure you agree about that—"

"*Armand!*"

"This is not a decision of the moment. The decision was made when we were betrothed. Now then, next Monday . . ."

Tante Julie gave Marcy a deeply troubled look; Tante Julie for once lost her usual *joie de vivre.* "But, Armand—" She faltered. "Why must it be so soon? So sudden! You have waited all this time—I can't see why you want an immediate marriage!"

Neither can I, Marcy thought. She said, "*Why*, Armand? What is the reason for such—such haste?"

Armand's eyes flashed. "Haste, you call it? After a two-year betrothal—over two years. That is not haste."

"But—but, Armand," Tante Julie said again. "Marcy—perhaps she does not wish marriage at this time."

Armand paid no attenition to that. "It is all planned. Tomorrow I shall send what few articles of clothing I still have."

"You mean, send them here? No, Armand, I—" She got it out. "I won't marry you," said Marcy, going against tradition, against her marriage contract, against all the mores of their life.

Tante Julie straightened up.

Armand simply stared, his eyes almost obsidian black.

"You will," he said after a moment. "I am master here from now on."

He limped toward her, reached for her hand, dug in a pocket and fetched out a ring set with diamonds and an enormous emerald. "This has been the Ortega ring for brides for many years. It is now your ring. See that you honor it," said Armand coolly. He slid the ring on her finger, kissed her hand and swiftly limped away.

She heard his irregular steps along the parquet floor of the hall, out the door, onto the gallery.

Tante Julie took a long breath. "Dear God, he means it!"

"I won't. He can't do this! He can't!"

"How are you going to get out of it?"

"Nobody can be married against her will!"

Tante Julie pursed her lips. "What can you do?"

"I can refuse. That's all. I will *not* be married—"

Tante Julie thought it over. Marcy sank down into a chair and stared at the heavy ring on her hand. She resisted an impulse to tear it off and fling it somewhere—out on the street. No, no, she couldn't do that. She must have some regard for Armand's pride. But not enough to make this marriage, so sudden, so lacking in suitable preparation. So lacking— Why, Marcy thought, surprised, there are times when I don't even like Armand!

"I told my father I couldn't marry him—" she began.

"He is away. Perhaps—if you are certain you won't marry Armand, we might go to see Father Carlos. If anybody can talk to Armand, he can. We could go to see him tomorrow morning."

Marcy had a wave of compunction.

"But we must be very careful, Tante Julie. Armand—poor Armand, wounded and lame for all this life. His pride—"

"Yes," Tante Julie agreed. Sometimes as now she could lose all her innate feminine art of pleasing and become very serious. "But this is a very suitable marriage, *ma petite*. Your father arranged—"

"But I didn't know—"

"Know what?" Tante Julie's dark eyes were as sharp as steel. "Didn't know what?"

"Didn't know then, at the time of the betrothal, that I don't want to marry him. I won't."

Tante Julie thought for a moment, fixing Marcy with her relentless gaze. It was rare to see Tante Julie becoming, in a moment, all serious, practical, French and too perceptive. "You haven't taken a liking to this Yankee major, I hope. You know nothing of him, nothing. Why—why, he may have no money at all! No background! No family heritage, no—"

"Darling," Marcy said, "I love you. But don't!"

But Tante Julie's eyes were very bright. "So it *is* this major."

"No!"

"What happened at that ball in Washington City?"

"Nothing. That is—nothing."

"Something," said Tante Julie. "I can see that. Two years ago! I should never have let you out of my sight."

"Tante Julie, believe me, he remembers having met me, that's all."

It was a mistake. "So something did happen. You! *Une jeune fille. Bien élevée.* You permitted—"

"I didn't. That is, there was nothing—oh, this has nothing to do with Armand. I simply am not going to marry him."

"This major. *Eh, bien,* you'll forget him. Now, *ma petite,* Monsieur Lemaire told me—"

"M'sieu Lemaire—oh, that!"

Tante Julie nodded. "Yes, that. Gene has asked you to act as an informant concerning Major Farrell."

"I can't!"

Tante Julie debated, but her eyes were like needles in the sharpness of her gaze. "I think you must try," she said slowly. "Otherwise . . ." She gave another entirely French shrug of her plump shoulders. "Gene is no featherhead. Besides, there are others who can bring pressure upon him. He can take over this house, your plantation, everything. We would have no place to go. There must be ways to—to watch the major, you know. Merely to watch. And please Gene. That is not much to ask of you, is it? When one thinks of the consequences, *ma petite!* And you do have ways of becoming most charming. Most delightful. To men."

She said it flatly: a truism, a fact of life; it was, her attitude made it unnecessarily clear, the first and foremost objective of a woman.

Not this woman, Marcy thought rebelliously, and just then Jason touched the gong for supper.

It sounded, that heavy day, dull and somehow fateful. Only the little French clock ticked happily and cheerfully.

Tante Julie shifted to a half-coquettish yet all-dignified old lady. "*Alors,* don't cry. Don't let anyone see—well, anything. Smooth your hair."

She patted Marcy's hair herself, smoothing it with a firm hand, the hand, Marcy thought defiantly, of a stern and unyielding matriarch. Tante Julie was going to force her to marry Armand; she didn't know how, but she knew the old lady would try; it would be a battle.

She followed Tante Julie as far as the dining-room door, where the odor of burnt potatoes and the precious ham, fried hard as bones, all of it placed helter-skelter on the table, discouraged her. Claudine said softly, "We'll have to serve ourselves. Liss is sulky. Jason says he's got a misery in his back. Really," said Claudine, sighing and patting her lovely curls, "I do think Marcy could manage better since she's taken on the authority in this house."

Tante Julie sighed too. "It is her house."

Marcy went to her room. Later she'd slip down to the kitchen if she felt hungry. Just now she had to give Armand's plans some very serious and careful thought. She knew as well as Tante Julie that her decision not to marry Armand would cause shocking waves of consternation through the entire family and community. For all her later life there would be disapproval for violating one of the most firmly clung-to conventions of that closed society.

But I won't, she said to herself. He can't make me. Father Carlos must see my point of view.

He wouldn't. He might, however, counsel Armand to wait, to be patient, something.

But why on earth had Armand come to a decision for an immediate marriage? After a while, she told herself practically that he felt he might be more comfortable in the Chastain house and obviously more certain of any inheritance Marcy might have from her father.

She would never wear the ring; she put it away thoughtfully but definitely.

That dark and dreary night all of them went to bed early except Marcy. This time she did not need to remind Jason of the mews door, for he went at sundown to bolt it; she had made sure of that. She was leaning against a window in her room, thinking she must blow out the candle lest it attract innumerable insects of the night, yet listening for the major's return in order to open the gate, when Gene Dupre came with his dreadful news.

She heard the knock at the gate. Thinking it was John Farrell, she hastened to wrap herself in a brocaded blue and silver peignoir (which had been ordered in Paris for her mother, who was dead before it arrived; she never wore it without a pang) and went hurriedly down through the wet garden. The iron latch was moist and heavy; later it seemed to her that even the gate was reluctant. "Marcy," Gene said, "it's Gene." He slid quickly in, closed the small door behind him and reached for her hand. His hat was pulled down; his dark cape swung around him. "Come," he whispered and drew her swiftly into the house, into the salon. "Don't make a sound," he whispered, released her and groped through the darkness. "Light! Candles?"

"On the mantel. Wait."

She groped along the mantel; the little clock ticked close to her face as gently as if there was nothing like fright or menace in the whole world. She found the vestas in the small dish where she kept them. She found the nearer candelabrum; she managed to get a wavering light in one candle, and Gene whispered, "That's enough. Not too much light."

He went to close the door; he who was never ruffled was now strangely disheveled; his light hair was flattened by his hat, which he tossed toward a chair; his whole, usually fastidious attire looked wrinkled, loose; an enormous pistol stuck out of an inner coat pocket. No Confederate was permitted to carry a gun of any kind.

"What is it?" She whispered too, but her throat had gone suddenly dry.

"I've been running. I had to reach you before anyone came here." He caught his breath hard. "Listen, Armand is dead."

"No!"

He caught a hard breath again. "Shot. Your major did it."

She sank down in one of the delicate armchairs. She felt as if she had fallen from some height and all breath had been knocked out of her.

"Murdered by this major," Gene repeated and sank down into a chair, drew out a handkerchief and mopped his forehead. She caught another unmistakable glimpse of the huge pistol he carried as his cape fell away from his shoulders. "Armand said so himself. He didn't die at once. There was time to call Father Carlos. He told Father Carlos that Major Farrell of the Union Army had quarreled with him and shot him."

After a long moment with only the brisk ticking of the little clock to be heard, she whispered, "But he didn't."

Gene did not seem to hear her. "God knows Armand gave him provocation. The whole world, at least our world, knows that. The major refused a duel. Then he shot Armand from ambush. Cowardly. Unbelievable."

She caught at the word, and it stiffened her spine. "It *is* unbelievable. I don't believe it."

"Armand told Father Carlos—"

"I can't help that. Major Farrell did not kill Armand."

He stared at her. "Then why would Armand say that?"

"I don't know. Oh, poor Armand."

He eyed her again, closely. "I wondered when you were going to say that. Oh, Marcy, I didn't mean that! I know that your marriage was arranged. It may not have been a love match. But Father Carlos told me that you were to marry him at once. Armand persuaded him to waive formalities since your contract was entered into so long ago." He sprang up, crossed the room lightly and swiftly, parted the heavy curtains and listened. His tall figure was outlined against the silks in their faded splendor of gold and rose and pale blue. Then he turned, came quickly back to her and leaned over the table to take both her hands. The candlelight was mellow upon his handsome face and his troubled eyes. "There isn't much time. There's something you must do for us. For me—no, for all of us. I've got to say it quickly before they come."

"Who—"

"Somebody from Yankee headquarters, of course. They are supposed to keep order here. Oh, we still have some of our own police, but it's the Yankees who are really in control. Now then, General Banks will not permit this murder to go unpunished. One of his own officers killing a man of respected standing in New Orleans, a returned soldier of the Confederacy, wounded, paroled and permitted to remain in the city—no, General Banks must seek out Major Farrell and have him tried for murder."

"He didn't kill Armand." She said it from a deep certainty.

Gene's glance was sharp with inquiry. "Was he here at the time?"

"I don't—when was Armand . . ." She couldn't say it. She had too vivid and touching a memory of Armand putting the ring on her finger, limping away full of plans for their wedding. She had put the ring in a drawer of the enormous Empire chest in her room. Perhaps she ought to have been wearing it.

But no. That was false. She was shocked, grieved, sorry, sorry for Armand, but she could never have been his wife.

Gene said, "You will say that the major was with you.

You will do that. It will be proved a complete—they call it an alibi, you wouldn't know that. It means merely—"

"I'm not a fool. I know what it means. But the major has not been here. You haven't told me when Armand was—was—"

"Tonight. About eight o'clock. It happened on the street, lower Royal Street. Not far from the river. Father Carlos thinks that Major Farrell intended to dispose of the body in the river. Jean Begley saw Armand lying in the road. He thinks that Major Farrell must have been frightened away. Begley helped Armand to the St. Charles Hotel; then he saw his condition was serious and called Father Carlos. He called a doctor, too, but it was too late for that. Armand had a few moments of consciousness, recognized Father Carlos, talked to him, told him only that Major Farrell had waited for him at the street corner and shot him. He was almost unconscious when Begley came along. Father gave him extreme unction just as he was dying. Armand didn't seem to know he was dying. If he did, that merely makes his accusation the more believable. You must tell them that the major was with you all evening, make it from seven o'clock on. Where is he now? You'd better call him. Tell him what you propose to do to clear him."

"He isn't here. He hasn't been here all day and—no, no, he didn't kill Armand."

"You've got to *say* he was here. Please, Marcy, say that he went out later on some military duty. They will assume—oh, there'll be some excuse. The point is that I want you to tell them he was here at the time Armand was killed."

"Nobody in the house will believe that. They know he wasn't here."

"We'll think of something. The military police will be arriving at any time. They know, of course, that the major is billeted here. You must have your answers ready. Major Farrell was with you. So he couldn't have killed Armand."

"I tell you he wouldn't have killed Armand!"

"Armand is dead. He was murdered. Marcy, can't you see what a hold this will give you over Major Farrell? This is our chance."

There was a short rap outside, loud and demanding.

Someone knocked at the small door in the gate. Marcy got to her feet.

"They are already here," Gene said. "Compose yourself. That is, not too much. This is a great shock to you—your fiancé! But don't let down for an instant. Major Farrell was here with you."

"But, Gene!"

Gene's face was tight and drawn although his cheeks blazed red and his eyes were brilliant with excited purpose. "You must see, Marcy. The major will know what you've done for him, saving him from a hanging, perhaps—sometimes the Yankees are very scrupulous, even about the crimes of their own men. This is likely to be one of those times, now that General Banks is so eager to make an improvement of the relations between his men and the Orleanians. It is almost certain that the general will wish to make an example of justice, even if it involves hanging a Union officer. You can save him. And then you'll have put him so much in your debt that the major will be very grateful to you. So you can easily find out all we want to know of General Grant's plans."

Tante Julie swung the door open. "What has happened, Gene? There are Yankee soldiers at the gate. What has happened?"

Gene swiftly replied, "Armand has been murdered. The major shot him. Armand told Father Carlos just as he died. Now, you too must say that Major Farrell was here and could not have killed Armand. We'll find some explanation for what he told Father Carlos later. But just now, all of you in the house must tell the same story—"

"*Tiens!*" Tante Julie pushed back her thick curls. "No. *Non. Ce n'est pas bon.* No *histoires, comprenez.* Too many people to keep a secret. Marcy did not come to the table tonight. She went away. We'll say we didn't know where she went. She'll say that she—oh, went out with the major for a walk—"

"In this weather?" Marcy said and was suddenly aware that the room seemed to sway, the delicate pinks and greens and blues of the Aubusson carpet flickered as if the candle flame was about to go out; she reached blindly for a chair, and Tante Julie said swiftly, "That's right. Faint—or pretend to. I'll go and let them in. Your reason for being here, Gene, is to tell her the sad news."

She whisked away. Marcy's head almost stopped swimming; the room almost became steady again. "But the major is not here now," she said.

SEVEN

"He may come in while they are here. Surely he'll have the sense to understand what you are doing for him. Surely—"

"I'll not do it."

Gene did not appear to have heard her. He whisked the pistol from his coat and tucked it below the dark cape he had flung over a chair. He ran his hands over his hair, he adjusted his cravat, he gave himself a kind of shake and was all at once a neat, composed young Frenchman. Even the excitement in his eyes seemed to have vanished. He said calmly, "You must. Unless you want to see the major hanged. An Orleanian killed, murdered on the street. A man of an old and honored family. Oh, yes, General Banks, whether he wants to or not, must make an example of this man. Remember young Mumford."

How could anyone forget the young man who had been hanged only because he had pulled down the Federal flag!

"But he was an Orleanian."

"They can do it. Even one of their own men, if they think they must make an example. Where is the major?"

"I don't know. I haven't seen him since last night—"

"But yes, you did! Remember. He was here, with you. You went to see—oh, to see the cathedral. There are a hundred places you might have taken him to see. Beauty spots, historic spots. Yes, you were together from six o'clock, say, or seven until ten. It doesn't matter where you were. Even in your room."

Entertaining a man in her own room was the very height of folly, and everyone in New Orleans would know of it. There was a grapevine which the Yankees had not been able to cut off.

"Gene! I can't say that."

"Well, no, perhaps not. But you were in this room! The others were at dinner. There's nobody to say you were not here."

Tante Julie was coming along the hall again, her wide skirt swishing. She was speaking in exaggeratedly French accents interspersed with a few French words. "*Non, non, messieurs, le commandant n'est pas ici maintenant. Il était ici*—he was here until about ten o'clock. *Oui, oui.* I remember—ah, yes. *Il a parlé*—that is, he said he had a military task, something he had to do. He left here shortly after ten. I heard the clock strike."

She had entered the room by then; two men in blue uniforms followed her, both looking a little blank and confused, which, Marcy reflected with a wry twist of humor, was precisely what Tante Julie had intended. Her eyes were sparkling; she was all coquettish femininity. She pushed up her black curls and looked beseechingly at the two men. "*Vous voyez*—I mean, you see, he was . . ." She glanced at Gene, whose eyes merely flickered once; his hand made a circular motion, brief, but Tante Julie, whose wits were of the sharpest, understood. She widened her dark eyes. "You see, he was here. In this room. So he couldn't have—have shot . . ." Here she blinked rapidly and passed a white hand over her eyes; she even contrived a suggestion of sobs, courageously withheld, in her voice. "Ah, poor Armand! Set upon by some street thief! Poor dear Armand!"

One of the men seemed to recover somewhat from the wash of words and womanly charm Tante Julie had produced. He introduced himself and bowed. "Captain Sargent, sir."

Gene acknowledged the introduction. "My name is Dupre. I came to inform Mademoiselle of this tragic occurrence. She and Armand Ortega were betrothed."

Captain Sargent bowed again, this time toward Marcy, but turned to his cohort. "What do you think, Lieutenant?"

The lieutenant was young, broad-shouldered, broad-faced and tired-looking. Perhaps Tante Julie had more or less stunned him. He shook his head. Tante Julie said, "Poor Marcée." Her accent was so heavy it could be cut with a knife, Marcy thought irrelevantly. She came to Marcy and put her arm around her. "Thees 'as been a terrible shock, n'est-ce pas, ma chérie. Terrrrible—"

The pressure of her arm forced Marcy to speak, and indeed she could tell the truth about that. "Yes," she said.

Tante Julie went on. "To think that he was here, votre commandant, making the speech, telling about his life in—in Washington, wasn't it?" She rushed on without giving Marcy a chance to speak, if indeed Marcy had felt that there could possibly be any sensible kind of speech for her to make.

The extreme gravity of the situation was becoming clearer and more urgent. These men meant business, no question of that. Gene's and Tante Julie's course became the right course, for the wrong reasons. Her own decision, therefore, became Jesuitical, perhaps, but mandatory.

She was spared an outright lie, however. Tante Julie and Gene seemed to have convinced both the Union soldiers. In a last but really formal request, they asked to search the house.

Tante Julie assented. "But of course. Mais—mais—we have a small child here. He is sick." Tante Julie paused thoughtfully. "We do not think it is yellow fever. Indeed, we hope not. It spreads so rapidly—"

Marcy believed her ears; Tante Julie had actually spoken the dread words. The two soldiers obviously had heard of the horrors of yellow fever; they exchanged a swift look. The captain said hesitantly, "Well, perhaps it isn't necessary to search the house. I feel sure we can take your word for it, Mrs. . . . ."

Tante Julie did not bother to give them her name. She pulled a lacy handkerchief from somewhere in her voluminous peignoir and held it close to her eyes. "Ah, we hope it is not that! Indeed, it is rather early for yellow fever. Still, in such warm and humid weather—not that any of us are afraid, are we, Gene?"

Gene also was quick to understand. "But if the child— then this entire house—"

"Perhaps it is *not* yellow fever. One hopes . . ."

But neither soldier evinced any desire to linger in the possible vicinity of yellow fever. They exchanged one serious look; they thanked them, then clanked away, for both were wearing swords that were cumbersome and awkward. In their undoubted haste, the swords contrived to strike the walls of the hall as they departed. Tante Julie went with them out through the garden. Gene stood quite still, staring at the Aubusson carpet. Marcy sank down in a chair again. But Brule had not yellow fever. Or had he? It was too ghastly a suggestion to allow it to take seed in her mind.

Gene was troubled too. He shot her a piercing glance. "Is that true? Has he yellow fever?"

"No!" she replied stoutly, but she was frightened.

Tante Julie came quickly back. She was half smiling, smug, perfectly composed. "I thought that I would get rid of them. No use in their searching the house."

"But you said the major is not here," Gene said.

"No, he isn't. I looked in his room before I came downstairs. But we must keep up this pretense—"

"Lies," Marcy said, but in a low voice.

Tante Julie heard her and smiled a little more smugly. "In a good cause, *ma petite*. I am sure that everyone in the house knows of Gene's request to you to discover what your major knows of General Grant's plans."

Marcy was entirely accustomed to the fact that everyone seemed to know everything about everyone else in the house. "Tante Julie, *has* Brule got symptoms of . . ."

Tante Julie gave a pleased, musical laugh. "Not at all. I

looked in Liss's room. The child was asleep. No fever at all." But her plump and merrily pretty face became older, not drawn but somehow sodden, as if it had been left out in the rain. "No, it is not yellow fever. I know the symptoms. Be at ease about that. Now then, Gene, I promise you we will do everything we can to protect the major. At least until—well, until."

Gene took Marcy's hand, lowered his head over it, lifted his face to give Marcy a direct and pleading look, and said, "It remains with you, Marcy. You can help your country . . ."

Marcy stiffened her spine. "I cannot act as a street woman."

Gene and Tante Julie both uttered truly shocked exclamations. Gene cried, "But no! Never! It should take much less than—than—"

Tante Julie said, suddenly very directly yet rather demurely, "That."

Gene said gravely, "Surely you can win his friendship so that he'll talk to you."

Tante Julie said practically, "We can search his room together."

Gene took up his cape and pistol. "Then search it. But stick to your story about tonight and about Armand's murder: a street thief killed him."

"What about Father Carlos?"

"He was mistaken," Gene said flatly. "He was mistaken . . ."

He went away into the drizzling rain.

Tante Julie said with a sigh, "The major may return tonight. He must have warning of this. Come, child."

But on the stairs she said, whispering, "Just for now, it is as well to let the Yankees think that the baby boy does have yellow fever. I'll suggest it to Claudine and—"

"She'll know the truth."

"Yes, but only the Yankees need to be frightened away. Now then . . ." Coolly she paused for a moment, evidently planning a campaign. "You must listen now for the major's return. While he is not here we can search his room. It may amount to nothing—"

Marcy interrupted. "He is not such a fool as to leave any military secrets written out on paper or—"

"One never knows," said Tante Julie serenely. "Come with me. When he does return, you know, you must tell him the situation. Come along."

She moved along the hall, paused for a second before she opened the door to the room Major Farrell used, listened, her pretty head quirked on one side, then went into the room.

Marcy followed her. Tante Julie swiftly explored drawers, a writing table, the saddlebags that lay in a corner of the room, the armoire where the major's clothes were hung. Her little hands sought through the pockets.

"Tante Julie—you know, everyone in the house seems to know what Gene asks of me. Only because I happened to have met the major before the war."

"Ah," said Tante Julie over her shoulder. *"Met . . ."* She left it there. "I can't find anything of interest. Now go to your room, Marcy. Try to sleep. If the major comes back tonight—whenever he comes back, remember what you must tell him. Things will seem much better in the morning."

Things were no better in the morning. For the most part of the night Marcy had lain awake, thinking of Armand, whom she had known all her life, who had been so delightful and gallant, so charming and full of life until he was frightfully lamed by the war. She had known him always, it seemed to her; even if she had not understood him, at least she had been familiar with his fiery temperament. Looking back, it now struck her as remarkable that the betrothal had meant so little to her. An agreement to marry Armand sometime had seemed an act of formality, something which did not touch her. Stupid, she told herself; but that was the way it must have happened. And when she *had* tried to withdraw, she had weakly yielded to her father's command.

Yet she had simply never conceived of their marriage as an actuality. She had liked Armand; she had pitied him. She could never have married him.

Poor Armand; some street thug, some quarrel, perhaps, of which none of them knew anything, was the cause of his murder. It would have been very easy for anybody to quarrel with Armand. He had tried to quarrel with the major.

The major had not killed him. She was completely, entirely certain of that.

The drizzle and fog turned during the night to a slow, steady rain, so that through the open windows Marcy could hear the light patter on the garden and the white shell driveway, the drip from the garden foliage; there was a rather indignant little murmur from some bird disturbed in his nesting place, probably in the honeysuckle vines. There was no sound of the major's return.

There was, too, no indication of the mysterious night visitor. There was no reason to connect this sense of being watched with Armand, yet once, remotely, it did occur to her to question her own sense of covert surveillance—when had it begun? A few weeks ago, surely not more than that. So there was no reason to consider whether or not Armand himself had set someone to watch her, thus, perhaps, intending to guard his interest in the Chastain fortune. All her common sense refuted that vague surmise. Sunday came and went; only Tante Julie attended early mass.

The major did not return at any time during those days, which was an unreal yet curiously occupied period of time for Marcy. There were many, so many details to settle, and she, as Armand's betrothed, if not in fact his widow, was obliged to make all decisions.

We look like three black crows, she thought, glancing at Tante Julie and Claudine, and rustling in her own black dress, almost suffocating in the black veil Tante Julie made her wear. They had started for the cathedral to hear the mass to be said for Armand.

Three black crows, she thought again after the services were over and they were able to leave the cemetery, which here was called the City of the Dead, an ominous title but a fitting one. In order to avoid the ever-present threat of rising muddy waters, almost every family had its own mausoleum, a white, usually marble structure decorated with carved figures of flowers or anything that struck the living owner's or the sculptor's taste. The Ortega mausoleum was built like a miniature Greek temple and was one of the oldest in the sadly crowded City of the Dead.

There were very few friends in the cathedral. The Ortega clan was widespread, but there had not been time or means for them to travel to New Orleans.

However, the scattered friends offered her kindness. She was assumed, naturally, to be in great grief; she was to have been Armand's wife. So she was accorded the deference due a widow, though she felt like an impostor.

I'm *not* a widow, she thought rebelliously, yanking at her heavy veil in the welcome privacy of her own room; I was never going to be Armand's wife. She debated removing the stifling black dress but realized that this would deeply offend Tante Julie and her decorous observance of custom.

Liss brought Marcy coffee. Marcy drank it thankfully. Then, greatly daring, she got out of the black dress and put on a pink and faded but still good poplin.

She went slowly down the stairs; they were all gathered in the salon, sipping sherry from a bottle which M. Lemaire had produced. He, too, was garbed in what could pass for mourning—a dark coat, a dark silk stock, a broad black band of crepe around a sleeve. He poured her sherry. Tante Julie said, "Oh, Marcy! Pink! Not so soon—" and stopped. Claudine's lovely face froze. Marcy said shortly, "It's too hot for black."

M. Lemaire said, sipping sherry, "Of course, now is usually the time to read the will. Armand could have left no will."

"Dear Armand," said Tante Julie. "He had nothing to leave."

The major still did not return that night or the next day. The days were dreamlike, the nights quiet, so quiet that again Marcy found herself listening, listening for any strange sound, any unwary footsteps, and heard nothing. She began to hope that if anyone had been watching the house, watching her, watching, he had given up. Once she awakened at some sound, went to the window again and heard only the light patter of rain. She waited until the sound was repeated; it was only a slight clatter of someone passing along the banquette outside the gates. She wondered vaguely why he paused and then continued his light but audible tread. It was nothing, however, she told herself and went back to bed. That night she had another confused dream of Nine Oaks and the Bayou Reve Road. Nine Oaks meant safety in her dream, but the Bayou Reve Road was unfamiliar and subtly frightening. She shrugged it off angrily; she did not intend to be haunted by such nonsense.

The drizzle, punctuated by showers, and the heat continued. The humidity put a sticky, dull surface upon everything. Even her thoughts, it seemed to Marcy, were as dull, as clogged of action, as the weather.

No Yankee soldiers returned to inquire about the major or to search the house. On the sixth day the major returned.

It was dusk and the others were at supper when he came to the gate and rapped upon it. Marcy heard the rap, which even so soon had become familiar. She went hurriedly to open the gate, warding off Jason, who followed her.

The major looked dark and tired; a horse snorted and whiffled at his side. "Good evening," he said as coolly as if he had not been away for nearly a week. "I do beg your pardon for disturbing you just at this hour."

She shook her head. His horse sighed gustily, and the major said, "Am I mistaken in thinking that you have a stable out beyond the kitchens?" He nodded toward the driveway and the wide arch leading to the stables.

"We do have a stable. It is not in use."

"May—that is, with your permission . . ."

Why not? Marcy thought. "Certainly. I'm not sure there is any feed for him."

"Thank you."

The horse, too, looked tired, and drooped as if he had had a long and weary ride. The major hooked the reins over his arm, and the footsteps of the man and the horse crunched slowly along the white shells of the driveway. She watched as both disappeared within the further carriage arch.

She waited for a moment, then went toward the stables too. It would be simpler to have the conversation with him, which she had concluded she must have, away from the house. Since it was the supper hour, probably no one would see or hear them in the garden, but it was safer to talk to him in the stables. It had become her custom to glance at the door to the mews and make sure that it was bolted; she did so then, and the great iron bolt was securely in place.

When she entered the stable, she found that the major had discovered some forgotten lantern which still held a little oil. He had lighted it so it cast a soft, yellowish glow over the stalls and feed boxes and remains of trodden hay. He had removed his saddle from his own horse. He glanced at her, said, "He needs water," and went off toward another part of the barn, the room that had been called the tack room. He came back presently with a battered wooden bucket which he had filled with water from an old and recently unused pump. It had not been oiled; it was rusty and it squeaked.

The horse thrust his nose into the pail gratefully.

"I think there may be some feed." She went to the small granary and scooped up what oats she could, sacrificing her wide pink skirt to carry them, inwardly cursing the hoops without which no polite Southern woman ever dressed. The hoops insisted upon bobbing up and down, disclosing her ruffled white petticoats with every motion she made. However, the dress itself was already worn, and a few oats wouldn't hurt it. The major came to her assistance, and the corners of his mouth twitched a little as he observed her swooping hoops.

He held his black slouch hat upside down. "Here."

She filled that too with oats. "I'm sorry there isn't more. But the Yankees—"

"It's enough. I'll get him more tomorrow. I didn't stop anyplace in the city. I have had a long ride."

From General Grant's headquarters, she thought. But no, that would indeed be a very long ride. It was more likely that he had met some emissary at an intermediate point.

The horse was slobbering over the pail; they couldn't quite fill the feed box. The major shook some remaining oat grains out of his hat. "Thank you."

"Wait. I've got to tell you something. You didn't stop in the city?"

He shook his head; in the light from the lantern, however, she saw that his eyes were instantly alert. "What is wrong?"

"Everything. No—no, not everything. I told them you didn't kill him. I told them you couldn't have killed him—"

His hands shot out and grasped her arms. "What are you talking about?"

"Armand was shot. He said you had done it. He died. They came to arrest you. But they think that you were with me."

"Tell me," he said tersely.

EIGHT

The horse ate greedily; the lantern light made a mellow glow; there was the faint, combined smell of hay, ammonia and old leather.

The major waited as she told him; Armand had been shot at night on the street. "But before he died, the man who found him had sent for Father Carlos."

"Father Carlos?"

"The priest. Our priest. Armand told him that you had shot him."

"*I* had shot him!"

"That's what he told Father Carlos."

"But I—Good God, I didn't. I never thought of such a thing. Oh, he tried to quarrel with me. But—Good God," he said again and wiped his forehead with the back of his hand. "I never would have killed him! I wouldn't even have consented to a duel."

"I know that. I told them—"

"What did you tell them?"

"Why, I—naturally knew you couldn't have killed him. But I'm not sure that anybody really believes me."

"I see—that is, I don't see, but—wait a minute, when was he killed?"

"About eight o'clock. Last—" She had to stop and think; it seemed like a year, but was only a few days. "Last Friday. The day you went away."

His eyes narrowed, but he shook his head. "Go on."

"Gene Dupre came that night to tell us."

"He was the man who was with your fiancé the day I arrived here, and your—Armand—he really did try to force a quarrel upon me."

"I know. I saw. And then after that—"

In the pale light his face showed rather grim lines. "Then what?"

"Then . . ." She couldn't explain why Gene had told her that she must say he was with her at the time Armand was killed. She couldn't tell him why Tante Julie had taken so swift and active a part in the deception; she wouldn't tell him that she had been delegated to act as a spy. She said, "Some Yankee soldiers came to arrest you. The feeling is that General Banks must make an example of Armand's murder to show the people of New Orleans that he will have justice even if one of his own officers must be—must be—"

"Hanged? But I didn't kill him."

"Is there any way you can prove that?"

He stood for long moment, one hand resting on his horse. Then he said absently, "This fellow has got to have a rubdown. I think I saw . . ." and disappeared in the direction of the tack room.

He returned with an ancient and smelly horse cloth. "What did you tell the men who came for me?"

"I—that is, Tante Julie—they believe you were with me at the time."

He rubbed and rubbed until the coat of his horse began to shine. He was no fool, she thought dismally. He would ask why Tante Julie had agreed to this deception or if Gene Dupre had known about it. He might even ask if they had suggested it. Instead he asked, from the other side of his horse, "Why did you let them think that?"

That was easy. "Because I know you didn't kill him."

She couldn't see his face now; he was stooping behind the

satiny smooth withers of his horse. "How did you know that?" he said at last.

"Why, I—I just know. You wouldn't have killed him like that. You wouldn't have killed him at all."

There was another long pause. She heard only the even swish of the horse cloth and the horse's steaming breath. Finally he came around into the lantern's light. "How do you know?"

"I just know. Good heavens! You *didn't* kill him, did you?"

He gave a laugh which was not quite a laugh. "No. It's true, however, that twice your Armand tried to inveigle me into a duel, and I wouldn't fight him. Everyone knows that. General Banks must have been informed of it. What of your police?"

She shrugged; it was a sufficient answer.

He gave an absent stroke or two with the horse cloth, spread it out neatly and hung it over the wooden partition to the adjoining stall. "I didn't kill him. But all the same I am grateful for your—I suppose we must call it an alibi. I can use that. So—so, I am asking you to continue it."

It was a curious kind of anticlimax. What had she expected? Resistance on his part? Efforts on her part to induce him to accept her explanation? Some kind of positive reaction, certainly. Instead, he seemed almost grateful for what was in fact a lie.

He must have seen something of her surprise, for he said slowly, "There are reasons. I can't tell you just now, but reasons. Even General Banks does not know the reasons. But I am most grateful to you. You have saved me considerable . . ." He hesitated as if groping for the words, and finally said, "—considerable problems. It is a military matter. Now, since you have been so very kind, I must ask you again for the further favor of continuing to lie in my behalf."

She herself hadn't literally lied; it had been Tante Julie who had done what lying had been done. Yet by accepting it—yes, it was a lie.

His own acceptance was unexpected. She ought to be pleased about it; she was perfectly sure that he had not killed Armand. She was almsot sure the lie had saved him from hanging, or at the very least, summary court-martial and trial, and who knew what verdict there would be from that?

But she was oddly disappointed. He hadn't seemed the kind of man who would ask a woman to lie for him, especially a woman whose sympathies were against everything he represented.

He said, "I do thank you. Thank you for informing me, too. It would have been difficult to walk into this affair without knowing anything of it." All at once, it seemed to her, he had withdrawn. He had become again a pleasant stranger, not the man she had remembered. He said, in that new and remote voice, "I am very tired. I ate supper at an inn somewhere out of the city. But I'm sure a bath will be waiting for me in that very delightful room you have so generously permitted me to use."

Dismissal. Nothing else. He took the lantern. It was now fully dark outside. At the door of the stables he carefully lifted the glass chimney of the lantern and blew out the flame. She had an instant's glimpse of his face, weary and more lined than she remembered, with a growth of beard. His eyes were in the shadow. He put down the lantern, and she went with him into the damp dusk of the garden with the scents of flowers heavy and sweet all around them.

When they reached the gallery and their ways separated, she said, rather sharply, "Don't be afraid that I shall tell them the truth."

It apparently did not touch him. He said coolly, "I'm sure of that. Thank you again." But then, unexpectedly, he looked down at her in a more natural, kind and troubled way. "I am sorry about your fiancé. Really sorry—"

Armand, the happy playmate she had known all her life; the charming, handsome young man she had once professed herself willing to marry. She did not, just then, remember the later quarrelsome, bad-tempered Armand. She felt tears come to her eyes. Major Farrell put his hand gently on her hand. "I am sorry," he said again and turned away.

She listened as his boots made thuds of sound up the

stairs and then along the gallery. She listened until she heard the door of his room open and then close.

But all the same, there was something coldly disappointing in his ready acceptance of the lie. Perhaps her instinctive belief that he was not a man who could waylay and kill anybody as Armand had been killed had been wrong. She had to dismiss that unwelcome thought. She went to tell Jason to see to hot water for the major.

Tante Julie was waiting for her in the hall and drew her into the salon. She lighted a few candles and then scrutinized Marcy's face. "You told him?"

"Yes."

"What is he going to do?"

"You won't believe it, Tante Julie—he asked me to keep on lying. The way I told him about it, he thought that I was the one who told lies. It never struck him that it was in fact you and Gene Dupre. That is—" She remembered a very perceptive something in the major's eyes. "That is, I *think* he believed it was my idea. I know he believes that the Yankees have accepted my—our story."

Tante Julie lifted her thick eyebrows. "So long as he believed. And he wants us to keep it up—h'm—well, thanks be to *le bon Dieu*. It is what we want too. Now, *ma petite*, we must occupy ourselves. Where has he been?"

"I don't know. He said he'd had a long ride. He's eaten something outside the city. His horse was tired too and thirsty and hungry."

Tante Julie thought and nodded. "The major was with General Grant, *sans doute*. Or in communication with him. But why does he wish to keep this a secret from General Banks? *Hein!* Because it *is* a secret! That is why! It must be kept a secret even from Union General Banks. So that means that there is a plan for Grant's attack. So secret that it must be contained by a very few people. Ah!" She nodded her head briskly. "We must find out just what this secret is. You must help, you know."

"I don't see how."

"Ah, nonsense. It is a *folie* you speak there. *Certainement, c'est possible*."

Tante Julie's mind was very quick and very devious.

Marcy said, "No, there is a flaw there, Tante Julie. The major is here as a liaison officer between General Banks's command and General Grant. This must mean that General Grant plans to use men from General Banks's command whenever or if he makes a move toward Vicksburg. So, General Banks would have to be informed at every moment."

Tante Julie thought that over but then shook her head. "No. No. I think not. Not, that is, until—say—the last moment. Yes. That is the answer. It must be—"

"Perhaps. I don't know but—oh, Tante Julie, I don't know!"

"We will know," Tante Julie said briskly. "Now that the major is back—"

The door opened and Claudine came in. Claudine's eyes were sparkling, her pretty lips smiling over small white teeth. "Your major has returned. You were in the stable for a very long time. I saw you go. I saw you return. The major held your hand, didn't he?"

"He is polite," said Tante Julie sharply.

There was a moment while the three women stood in the lovely room with its great mirror reflecting them—Tante Julie with her thick, curly black hair, done up so expertly and neatly, and her round, still-lovely face and secretive eyes; Claudine with a malicious smile on her delicate face, and her neat, blond curls framing it; Marcy herself in her faded pink dress, her dark hair ruffled, her eyes too bright.

M. Lemaire had strolled into the room when Gene was proposing his preposterous plan to Marcy, and Armand was angry and opposed it. It seemed fitting that M. Lemaire should come into the room now and say, "The major has returned. Jason took hot water to his room. Perhaps he is in need of supper."

"He said he has already had supper," Marcy said.

It wasn't late; it only seemed late because so much had happened. Yet as Marcy thought of it, over and over again, nothing much really had happened except John Farrell's acceptance of the alibi she had given him.

His acceptance of the alibi was unexpected, too ready, not what she might have known of him. He had been kind, speaking of Armand. He had taken her hand in a kind and friendly way. But it was only kind and friendly.

With the major in the house, the troubling sixth sense of surveillance from somewhere, even of danger from somewhere, relaxed, so she finally slept. Morning came quietly, hot and humid. She was accustomed to the fragrance of the garden and also to the smells of the city, which were not exactly fragrant. Everyone had to give General Butler grudging credit for having had some of the streets cleaned. He had not succeeded in clearing the city of renegades or of drunken and insulting soldiers, who lounged along the streets and visited the many brothels, most of which, Tante Julie once said, had sprung into existence since the army of occupation. No one was very sure of that; it was a closed topic for the gently bred girls; the married women whispered of it.

But the usually stench-laden gutters below the banquettes were cleaner that summer, and that was a mercy, the only mercy, Marcy thought crossly, that anybody in the world could claim from General Butler's reign.

However, in the misty, heavy morning light she found that her mind had made itself up; Major Farrell's reaction to the lie was not what she had expected. But there was still a firm conviction in her mind: he could not have murdered Armand. So she would continue the lie.

She gave Liss more gold and saw her set forth with baskets, without Jason this time but with her enormous iron poker, toward the French Market.

The major had gone early in the morning. Marcy spent the morning keeping Brule—now mercifully free of his sore throat—out of the untended flower beds, where, however, he could have done no harm, since most of the flowers were growing wild and drooping in the heavy, humid air.

About noon two men in rather sagging blue uniforms came reeling to the gate and frightened her until she realized that they were staggering under sacks of food they carried for the major's horse. She showed them to the stables. After feeding and watering the horse, they went away, and at about four o'clock, as the whole household was emerging from the siesta, which was still an ironbound custom in any

New Orleans house, Gene Dupre came and asked Marcy to accompany him to the St. Charles Hotel.

"Armand's effects," he said. "You must see to them."

"But I—there are his relatives—"

"In the Assumption parish; not here. You are his widow."

"No! Not his widow—"

"No." Gene's eyes dwelt slowly upon her. "But this is for Armand. I hope you'll accompany me. Perhaps it would be *comme il faut* to put on a black dress and veil."

A flare of anger caught her. "I'm tired of doing what is expected of me," she said irritably.

Gene ignored the irritation and merely waited.

She went to her room, dressed in black and put the thick veil over the black bonnet Tante Julie had lent her. Gene had procured from somewhere a quite new and smart carriage; she didn't inquire how he had gotten it. A Negro driver slapped the reins of the horse. When they reached the famed hotel and entered the enormous lobby with its high dome, it was crowded with Federal officers. Blue uniforms and gold bars and buttons were everywhere; the lounge chairs were almost all occupied. Every one of the officers, it seemed to her, paused in whatever he was doing—reading a paper, smoking a long black cigar, merely lounging—to stare at her as if those cold Yankee eyes could pierce her thick black veil. To her astonishment, Gene nodded and spoke to several. He knew the way to Armand's room and had possessed himself of the key. "They gave me permission to remove Armand's effects or, rather, to permit you to remove them."

"Gene, you seem to know so many of them."

"Naturally. They could close my bank. We must all yield to necessity in a conquered city. Now then, Armand had a portmanteau, I think."

There was no portmanteau anywhere in the room. There was, indeed, nothing to pack into a portmanteau. Armand had left almost nothing in the room, which bore hardly any evidence of his ever having used it.

NINE

This was puzzling.

Gene looked through the armoire and through the drawers of a small writing desk. Finally he shook his head.

Marcy had merely waited, wishing the mirror did not reflect Armand's handsome white and bitter face, which had once been so fine and spirited. At last Gene said, "I cannot understand it."

He had found a small heap of such nondescript articles as brushes, some boots and a few pieces of clothing, none of which suggested the dandy Armand had always been. "He must have had more than this. I can't understand it," Gene said again. "It's as if he had never lived here."

She thought back to her last conversation with Armand. "But he said he would send his clothing and such possessions as he had to my home."

Gene stared at her for a moment. Then he made another little tour of the room, opening the doors of the huge armoire and its drawers. She stood by the bed, looking down at the pitiful few garments Armand had left behind him. Yes, it was puzzling. Gene made some motion behind her, and she turned in time to see him remove his hand from his pocket.

"You found something?"

"No. That is—oh, nothing. Only a—a hotel bill." He came quickly to the bed, where they had put together the few of Armand's possessions they had found. "The poor boy, he had nothing," Gene said rather rapidly. Certainly, she thought, he was moved by the shabby, pathetic little heap. He bundled it all together, tied it with some shirt-sleeves and then said, "There is nothing of value here. I'll leave this for the clerk to dispose of. Do you agree?"

She nodded. "I have his ring, the Ortega wedding ring. I wish to send it to some—any one of his relatives who wants it."

"Quite correct. Shall we go?"

They went down the broad stairs. At the foot of them, a Union officer, a captain, by his bars, stepped forward. "Sir."

Gene became polite, remote, obviously on his guard with a representative of the Federals, who could seize on the slightest excuse and take over his bank. It was a sensible reaction, yet Gene's determined self-control turned his face into a mere handsome mask.

The captain said in a very low voice, "You've heard . . ."

Gene nodded once.

"There are several cases . . ." The captain spoke in such a low voice that Marcy barely heard scraps of it. "Down near the river, the brothel district . . . the general . . . nobody knows what to do. You as a resident of the city . . . some advice . . ."

Gene's face was very white. Yellow fever was the dreaded scourge of the city. Marcy's heart began to thump. It was true that the river area was far from the district where the Chastain house stood, but yellow fever knew no barriers. Nobody knew how it traveled, and everyone knew how fast it could travel.

The Union officer continued, still whispering but clearly enough to permit Marcy to hear. "I thought perhaps you . . . some remedy . . ."

"There is no remedy," Gene said flatly.

"But there must be something we can do! Some way of

protecting ourselves. And, of course,'' the captain added with a glance at Marcy, "the citizens of New Orleans.''

"We've tried everything,'' Gene said.

"And nothing—*nothing* stops it?'' the captain asked.

"Nothing. Oh, sometimes barrels of tar burned in the streets may drive away the air in which yellow fever seems to breed. Nothing much helps, really.''

"But doctors—''

"Know nothing about it. They've tried everything. However . . .'' Gene himself had lived through some of the worst epidemics. There was something tragic, something strange and terrible about yellow fever, since no medication, no remedies, nothing could stop its course. Gene said, "Not everyone dies of it. Some recover.''

The Union captain fingered his sweeping blond moustache. "But I, myself—this morning—I heard . . .'' He lowered his voice again. "I saw some wagons. They said something about the dead . . .''

Gene nodded. "The dead wagons. They'll make their trips daily.''

Suddenly Marcy realized that the conversation had attracted the attention of all the men lounging, standing and smoking around the lobby. Only the man at the desk pretended not to hear.

Marcy had an almost overwhelming urge to run, run for home, run for any refuge.

Gene bowed formally to the captain. "I'll do everything I can. Meanwhile, barrels of burning tar—I'm afraid if this goes on, the doctors will be busy. This is only April. The worst of the yellow fever periods have occurred during August or early September.''

"Oh, my God,'' said the captain and then, remembering his manners, bowed and said, "If you think of anything, sir—''

"Yes, yes, by all means, sir. Now I must escort my—my cousin,'' said Gene, preserving Marcy's dignity by way of Claudine's relationship to her.

There was a heavy silence through the entire lobby as they passed by. It seemed to Marcy that their footsteps, even the slight rustle of her sweeping black skirts, all but echoed in the dome far above them.

Gene said, "I'll just speak to the clerk at the desk. Pay—Armand's bill. Excuse me?"

Marcy nodded. She didn't wish to look at the clusters of Federal officers; she watched Gene at the desk speaking to the swarthy little Creole behind it, who stroked his neat, shining black moustache and shook his head and replied.

Gene came back.

"You didn't pay him," Marcy said.

"That—oh, no. There was nothing to pay. I asked him when he had seen Armand—all that. He didn't seem to remember precisely. Head in a whirl among all these Yankees. This way . . ."

They emerged upon the banquette.

"Scared?" Gene asked as he gave her an arm into the carriage, which stood waiting.

Marcy settled herself, uneasily aware of the heavy thumping of her heart. "If only we could go to Nine Oaks! Nine Oaks would be safer. We always went there during the summer."

"But you haven't forgotten the Eagle Oath."

"I—good heavens, I think I'd even take that if the provost marshal would let us leave."

"I don't know. I have a few—well, they pass as friends among the Federals. But I am not sure that they would permit you to leave the city."

When they reached home and the carriage gates, he sighed heavily. "Keep on trying to make friends with the major. If you succeed, I may be able to procure a pass for you. Stop, boy."

The Negro driver had been listening, Marcy was sure; the Negroes always knew everything.

Yellow fever, oddly, did not attack the Negroes as viciously as it attacked white people. Indeed, someone had once told her it was more likely to attack strangers to New Orleans than native Orleanians.

Yet her mother had died of yellow fever.

Gene alighted and put up a hand to help her descend. She gathered her full black skirts around her and remembered to control her hoops, which could tilt so treacherously. Gene went with her into the garden, but instead of permitting her to enter the house, he led her to a bench, the bench where she had sat one night and talked to John Farrell. Gene sat down beside her. "I haven't told you this," he said. "I'm not sure I ought to. Yet I must warn you. The Federal captain in the hotel apparently didn't know. Their doctors will know soon, if they don't already and are simply trying to keep it secret."

It was a misty, yet warm day; in spite of the heat, a kind of chill crept over her, almost as if she guessed what he was about to say. Cholera!

The dreaded word. It was dreaded even more than yellow jack. Sometimes people recovered from yellow fever. She had never heard of anyone recovering from cholera.

Gene said slowly, "I am a little—a very little—in the confidence of the Federal authorities. They don't trust me. They suspect me and watch me. But they know that I am not without a certain standing in my own city, and therefore, if they want to restore peace to New Orleans, they hope that I will help. Last year there was anything but peace here. Stabbings, brawls, assassinations. They don't like feeling, when they turn around some corner at night or eat some specially prepared dish, that the corner may shield an assassin or the food conceal poison."

"I know."

There was swift comprehension in his face. "Armand told you."

"No. I only knew that the Defenders—"

"Don't. Don't even whisper of anything you may know or guess. We can't do much. What has been done has been sometimes without any value whatever. Too often it is merely a harassment which brings about even harsher treatment from our conquerors." The bitterness in his voice reminded her of Armand. "I and a few others are trying to control senseless acts, hoping, trying, to save what and whom we can, but as quietly as we can. Sometimes it seems hopeless. But it isn't." He lifted his head as if bracing himself. "We've got to wait, seem to bow down, but always—wait. Now then, I've got to tell you about something else. I don't want to, but—you have been living a very sheltered life. You haven't known of all these things. Well, now you must know that another danger has come upon us.''

"Cholera," she whispered. Even her lips felt cold.

He nodded. ''A ship came in from somewhere in the West Indies. Out of Shanghai originally, it is said. Some say she was ridden with cholera. In any event it was ascertained that a rather large number of her crew died during the sailing. Those that were left scattered as soon as they could from the ship. So they may be anywhere in the city, carrying cholera with them. You and your Tante Julie, Claudine, all of you really ought to get away, go to Nine Oaks. Away from the city, you will be safer. If I can convince the provost marshal and if you will take the Ironclad Oath—''

"Oh, I'll do anything to get to Nine Oaks!"

"Good. One of our—our number has managed to ingratiate himself with the provost marshal. Once I give him any information at all you can find out about Grant's plans, I feel reasonably sure that he can induce the provost marshal to let you leave the city."

"Oh, Gene!" All her scruples had vanished at the word "cholera." "I'll do my best."

His face grew troubled. "I don't know how you feel about the major, Marcy. I know you hate the task we've asked you to perform. But really, I wouldn't ask you to do anything—well, anything that is not fitting or dignified. Surely, merely a friendly-seeming interest in his affairs." He took out a snowy handkerchief and touched his forehead with it. "Believe me, Marcy." His eyes were almost pleading. "I would never injure you or cause you the slightest feeling of—of embarrassment."

"Oh, I know that, Gene. I know. I promise to help. If I can."

"That's enough, then." He took her hand, lifted it briefly to his lips and went away, his slender figure moving gracefully amid the colors of the garden.

Through the iron gates she saw him stepping lightly into the carriage. Apparently he said something to the Negro boy, and the boy was frightened; he had heard enough to terrify him; she could tell that by the way he lashed at the horse and the carriage jounced away over the cobblestones.

She herself was terrified; for herself, Tante Julie, Claudine, Brule, M. Lemaire, Liss and Jason. The entire household. Cholera! Escape was now urgent. So she *must* find out what General Grant was planning to do.

Tante Julie came out onto the gallery and then approached her. "You look very stuffy in all that black," she said with candor. "But of course you must wear it."

"It is hot and too big for me." She pulled at the stifling bodice, buttoned up close under her chin. She took off her black bonnet and heavy veil.

"Where are Armand's possessions?"

"There weren't any."

"Nothing! But that is impossible!"

"Only a few things, nothing important enough to care for. Gene left them for the hotel to dispose of."

"But—why, that is impossible! Armand was so rich. That is, not now; no one knows what may be left! But he must have had a gun. A sword. Whatever he intended to use to fight this famous duel with the major. Everyone knows about that."

Marcy felt a little shock of surprise. "Why, there was no gun! No sword! Oh, of course, I see. He was not permitted to bear arms. That must have been one of the conditions of allowing him to remain free in the city and not thrusting him into jail or a prison camp. Yes, it must have been that."

"He could have borrowed from someone," Tante Julie said thoughtfully.

"Perhaps." Still, it was odd that Armand had so confidently tried to force a duel with Major Farrell if he knew in his heart that he would be obliged to borrow a sword or a gun or whatever the choice of weapons would be. That choice, as she remembered in dueling customs, would have been the major's, the challenged man.

"Someone would have borrowed for him. Perhaps it is as well the major would not duel with him," Tante Julie said.

Marcy said shortly, "It is against the law. It has been against the law for some time."

"Oh, that! Who paid any mind to that? Where is the major, I wonder. He's been out all day."

"At headquarters, I suppose." She had to get out of her stifling black dress. She stood, and Tante Julie said sternly, "How are you getting along with your spying? You seem to make no progress. Unless last night . . . that long time in the stables. Surely you didn't waste such an opportunity to—"

"To what?" Marcy said crossly, knowing perfectly well what Tante Julie affected to hesitate in saying.

She did not hesitate further. "Why, to make him your special friend." There was an unmistakable emphasis on the word "special."

"I didn't try. I'm going to change my dress."

"Perhaps that would be best." Tante Julie, suddenly agreeable, reversed herself.

Marcy made an escape. Yellow fever. Cholera. Even in Marcy's thoughts she seemed to try to skirt around the terrifying words.

Then act, she told herself.

She would change first; she couldn't drag those suffocating folds of black around another moment. She met no one as she went along the gallery to her own room.

Cold water, talcum powder—not much left, she thought absently; no way to purchase more. A clean, crisply starched blue muslin. Surely it would be cooler if she had no hoops; she untied the tape that held them around her waist. She did have a nice waist, she told herself. The crinoline and wires fell around her feet, but unhappily, when she slid into the blue muslin, that fell around her feet, too, for it had been made wide and long to accommodate the fashion of hoops. Fuming, she resumed the hoops.

She did take a long look at herself in the mirror; it was just a face she was accustomed to, but she decided that it was really not a bad face. She looked rather like the portrait of her mother: blue eyes, black hair brushed smoothly back to a heavy chignon at her neck. No, she really wasn't too bad to look at. She stiffened her neck and took a swift look down toward the garden, out along the gallery and then the hall. No one was about.

She knocked at the door of the major's room. There was

no answer. She entered the room. Now for it. Papers, letters, anything.

It occurred to her fleetingly that there ought to be a school for spies; they ought to be trained in some fashion. Perhaps the real spies were trained. She didn't know where to begin. The door of the great armoire swung open, showing his neatly pressed and handsomely tailored uniforms. Coat pockets?

Tante Julie had already searched, but she might have missed something. Marcy, too, went through the pockets, not forgetting those inside the tunics. She felt rather like a pickpocket but found nothing, no scrap of paper, no tag ends of string, no penknife.

Major Farrell must be inordinately neat. Or afraid of a spy?

Well then. She went to the escritoire, which had been her father's. She could see her father sitting there, his pen in his hand, writing one of his long, polite letters.

Writing paper was scarce in New Orleans, as it was everywhere in the South, but there were still a few sheets in one of the small drawers.

They were blank. She searched the shallow drawers, and there was simply nothing to find. The narrow pigeonholes looked empty too. She was groping into one of them when without warning the door of the room opened.

It had grown dusk during her search. She whirled around, but even in the dusk she had too clear a view of John Farrell, who was simply standing there, watching her. She couldn't see any expression at all on his face. But after a thunderstruck moment, while her heart beat so hard it made her ears ring, he came into the room, closing the door quietly behind him.

"So," he said. "It was you."

"I . . ." In God's name, what excuse?

"I knew someone had been taking an interest in my possessions."

She couldn't answer; the pounding of her pulses all but choked her. She shoved desperately at the last drawer she had opened, and her move was so jerky that instead of falling back into its groove, the tiny drawer fell with a clatter onto the floor.

"I didn't think it was you," Major Farrell said. "Don't look like that. I'm not going to hurt you. Only tell me what you hope to find. Why have you been searching my room every day? Perhaps not every day but often enough. There is nothing here for you to see. What are you looking for?"

Tante Julie had searched that one time, but surely no one else.

If only she could answer, say something, say anything. She couldn't bear the direct, grave look in his eyes; she couldn't bear his voice, soft yet curiously inexorable. She looked down and the answer came.

It was a completely unexpected answer, but there it was, at her feet, gleaming dully in the half-light.

She pointed. "The wedding ring. Armand gave it to me. The Ortega wedding ring."

TEN

There was no time, no chance to wonder how it got there, who had placed it in the drawer. It was enough to know it was there. It gave her an excuse; it pulled her out of the morass of helpless shame.

The major stared at it silently. Then he tossed his black slouch hat on a chair, came to her, leaned over and picked up the ring. He turned it in his hands. They were good hands, she thought absently—firm, strong, very well tended; strong enough to govern a horse; sensitive enough, perhaps, to suggest that he might understand her own utter dismay. Oh, no! She mustn't hope that he would fully understand that!

He said, turning the ring, "It is a beautiful stone. Old?"

She found her voice. "Very, I believe. Armand said it had always been the Ortega ring."

He turned the ring thoughtfully; his dark eyebrows were level across his face. "Does this mean that you were in fact married to him?"

"Oh, no! He had only planned the wedding ceremony before he was killed."

"But he gave you this."

"Yes. The day he came to tell me that he had seen Father Carlos and the date for our marriage had been set—the time and place—but after that he was shot."

He took her hand and put the ring in it. It lay on her palm; the heavy gold claws of the setting, the huge emerald, seemed to accuse her of something. Unfaithfulness? But why, when she hadn't actually been Armand's wife?

The major said, "Aren't you going to wear the ring?"

"No. I don't wear it."

"Why not?" He asked it in a low voice, looking at the ring.

"Because I didn't intend—" She stopped herself. "Because," she said.

"But the wedding was planned, wasn't it?"

"No. That is Armand suddenly planned it. I knew nothing of his decision. I had nothing to do with that."

He frowned. "But I don't understand."

"There isn't anything to understand," she said shortly. "Armand just made up his mind—"

"Without consulting you?"

She could only reply, "Yes."

He looked at her seriously for a moment. "But that seems unusual. Was there any reason for this—sudden decision on his part?"

"No. That is—oh, Armand was like that. I think he simply made up his mind and—and acted." Yet it couldn't fully explain the sudden decision. But then, she thought again, she had not really known Armand.

The major let that question drop. He looked at the ring and said quietly again, "But of course you'll wear the ring. Keep it. A very precious—"

"Not precious to me at all," she cried, and then wished she had not spoken so impulsively. She tried to cover it. "I mean, since it is an Ortega ring and I was not married to Armand, it ought to go to his people."

He looked up now, fully into her eyes. Yet the room had grown so dark that she couldn't fathom the expression on his face.

"You came here to my room to look for the ring? Is that right?"

"Yes." Go ahead and lie, she told herself. Nothing else to do.

"Has it been missing long?"

"I really don't know. I only happened to notice that it was gone"—she swallowed hard—"today. It was not in my room. I couldn't think—"

"So, you came to my room to look for it. I can't feel that you believe I took your ring."

"Oh, no! Nobody took it. I mean—"

He interrupted. "But obviously somebody did take it. That somebody put it here in my room. Who?"

She shook her head. Who, indeed? "Nobody in the house. We have no thieves."

"Is the little boy old enough to search my room?"

"Search?" she said blankly, but she knew full well what he meant.

"I mean pockets, desk, papers, all that?"

"Have you lost anything?"

He turned away, walked over to the window and stood there, his back turned to her. Over his shoulder he said, "Yes. But only temporarily."

"Temporarily?"

He swung around. "Merely a few letters. Papers. Nothing of importance. They were gone and then seem to have been returned. They were of no interest to anybody. But I don't understand it."

She did understand. Everyone in the house felt the importance of learning everything there was to be known about his activities. Tante Julie, trying again? Claudine? Perhaps even Liss?

The major said unexpectedly, "I've been wondering a little about M'sieu Lemaire. It did occur to me that as a loyal Southerner he might be inclined to hunt around through my effects in the hope he might discover information that could be turned to advantage. Not his advantage, but the Confederacy's."

"But he—oh, no. He'd never do that!"

"How do you know?"

She paused, faced with the difficulty of explaining to this Northerner, this lawyer, this man who dealt in black and white facts, just why good-natured, idle M. Lemaire would not bother to investigate anything about the major.

"You don't understand."

"Try to make me understand."

"I'll ask him," she said. "But he wouldn't be interested in searching your room or any papers or anything," she finished lamely. Perhaps M. Lemaire *had* searched his room. In his wandering about the city, M. Lemaire did manage to bring home odd facts, news notes, gossip. Sometimes she suspected that he did not tell all that he heard, but she was sure that nothing born of simple curiosity could have provoked M. Lemaire to anything as active and as purposeful as searching for news of any kind in the major's possession.

The major said thoughtfully, "There was nothing in my papers that was of the slightest importance to anyone. I saw to that. You must know that anything of military value is something I would guard very carefully. If, that is, I had such information. Indeed, I doubt if I would put anything on paper which could be of any use whatever to anybody at all."

Especially not in a Southern household; especially (she felt her cheeks grow hot) if by any chance he had guessed that there existed such an enterprise and she was supposed to be its main tool.

She grasped at something he had said. "But you say the papers you missed were returned."

He nodded. "I told you. They were of no interest to anybody but me. A few letters from my mother. Only news from home." He smiled slightly. "A warning not to get yellow fever."

Did he know, then, that yellow fever had arrived? Or cholera? Her pulse quickened again and also her determination. She must get them all away from the city, up the river, to the peace and safety of Nine Oaks, and hope that it had not been taken over by the Yankees.

"Also," he added lightly, "a letter or two from my banker. Nothing that could be of the least interest to anybody."

She swallowed hard again. Her throat had gone dry at the mention of yellow fever. "Of course, little Brule just might go poking around drawers or anything that attracts his interest."

"He wouldn't be likely to take letters and return them."

"No. Really, I don't understand it." But she must settle this in her own mind; she thought swiftly again: Tante Julie or Claudine or Liss—or just possibly M. Lemaire. First, however, she had to discover some kind of fact of such value that Gene might secure the permission of the provost marshal for their escape to Nine Oaks.

She said, "Yellow fever does strike during the summers." She wouldn't speak the dreaded word "cholera." "It's best to be prepared." A notion shot into her mind. Suppose she begged his assistance in procuring that necessary pass.

At second thought she dismissed the impulse; it remained, though, in the back of her mind. But just then the major said, oddly, soberly, looking very straight at her, "I'm grateful to you for providing me with an alibi. I want you to know that I told the general the same lie you were kind enough to tell for me."

Again she was surprised, not quite believing his ready acceptance of her lie. He said, "He sent for me at headquarters. Sent two men, as a matter of fact. I believe they would have arrested me if I had not gone with them willingly."

"What did the general say?"

"About what I had expected. He had been told that I had had a public scene with your fiancé. He asked if there was truth in the account. I said yes. He asked why it had happened. I told him the truth—I said I didn't know. He told me of the murder. I said that yes, I had heard of it, but that I had been out of town later in the evening."

"Where were you, then?"

It popped out without any volition on her part. He gave her a startled glance. "Why, I—never mind that. I told him that I had known nothing of the shooting until I returned. Then I said that I had been with you at the time your fiancé was killed. I said he could ask you about it. I told him that you would substantiate my statement."

"Then—then what?" She had to insist.

"After a while we got onto more cordial ground. He admitted that he had sent men here, also, to arrest me. He said he was having great difficulty in New Orleans in trying to establish more friendly relations between his army of occupation and the citizens. He is a sorely troubled man. When he heard that Armand Ortega had accused me in so many words, speaking to his priest, the general said that he had felt under the heaviest requirement to have me arrested and stand court-martial. The result of that, he admitted frankly, might have been hanging. So, you see, you did save my life.''

''But at a court-martial, couldn't you have justified yourself?''

''Justified in killing Armand Ortega? Surely you don't mean that.''

''No, no. I meant, couldn't you have told him where you actually were and what you were doing and—well, saved your own life?''

He took her hand quietly, as if he didn't know what he was doing. His touch was warm and strong. He turned over the ring and looked at it. At last he said, ''Yes, if it had come to that, such an admission on my part would have saved me. It would have required proof, however, and that proof—no, I couldn't—at least I wouldn't. In any event, it is better this way. I am under real debt to you. Thank you again. I'm glad you have found your ring.''

It was a dismissal. No doubt of that. But once she reached the safety of her own room, after thinking it over, she came to the conclusion that it had not been a very satisfactory ending. Clearly he couldn't have believed that the little boy would have taken his letters and then returned them; and certainly he had caught her in the act of searching.

The Ortega ring had rescued her momentarily, perhaps, but it created another puzzle, too. She put the ring away again, in the small drawer of the great Empire chest of drawers, beside the ruby and turquoise box. Nobody was a thief in that house. Yet the ring had certainly been taken away by someone and as certainly left in the major's room. Why? There had to be some purpose.

It was all too likely that someone had decided she was too slow about carrying out the investigation Gene had demanded, and had taken matters into his own hands. M. Lemaire?

There was too short a list of persons in that house: M. Lemaire or Tante Julie or Claudine or Liss.

Unless, of course, the strange night visitor had managed to get into the house, unseen, and searched the major's room. For a moment she thought it over and decided against the likelihood that anybody could enter the house without being seen. That left the same short list of people living in the house.

She could, of course, inquire very carefully. It was almost as difficult to conceive of M. Lemaire's undertaking anything that required both enterprise and energy as it was to believe that Bébé Brule had not only taken the ring but Major Farrell's papers and then returned them. Besides, Brule could not have reached the small drawer in the Empire chest! It was far too high for his arms and his delicate hands.

Then who had dropped the ring in the major's room? Why? Tante Julie would never have tried to cast suspicion upon Marcy. Claudine was different; Claudine might readily have decided to search John Farrell's room; she could have taken the ring and dropped it in the desk with the express purpose of shielding herself in the event the search was detected, inducing the major to blame Marcy. Claudine had never liked Marcy; since she had brought the child into the house, there had been a cold dislike, almost hatred, in Claudine's lovely eyes. Yet in a sense Marcy couldn't blame Claudine; it must be humiliating in the extreme, seeing little Brule, her husband's illegal son, being cared for, being indulged every day.

Yes, it was possible that Claudine had reasoned that someone might be suspected of prowling through the major's room; that someone might as well be Marcy.

The major may have noted Marcy's surprise at the discovery of the ring. He had a very direct way of swiftly observing everything.

The troublesome point was that she had found nothing to indicate any connection with Grant or Grant's army. Thinking of the tired horse of the previous night and the major's own patent weariness, she wondered whether or not he had taken the trip to wherever Grant's army was then encamped.

But that must be almost opposite Vicksburg; it would have been too long and arduous a ride. If his errand were so secret that even the general in command of New Orleans could not be told of it, it was not likely that he would readily have taken one of the few riverboats. The only conclusion was that he had met an emissary of General Grant's somewhere nearer. She had no idea of the condition of the River Road or the Bayou Reve Road, and now she must find a way to go to Nine Oaks and take the entire household with her—even M. Lemaire, who would do whatever he was told to do.

She was standing at a window, looking down into the garden without seeing it, when M. Lemaire himself ambled out from the gallery opposite. She might as well satisfy herself that M. Lemaire had not been interested in the major's affairs. She went down to the garden.

ELEVEN

But M. Lemaire did not enlighten her very adequately.

Her inquiries were not very adequate either, she had to admit. She began tentatively, "You've lived here a long time, sir."

He lifted a dreamy gaze to her. "Why, yes, my dear. You were a very small child when your mother and father invited me to stay here."

She ventured further. "Because you were my mother's cousin?"

"Why, of course. You must remember when I came."

"No. No, really I don't. You were just always here."

His eyebrows lifted gently. "Still welcome, I trust."

"Oh, sir, yes. That is—you've lived here so long. You must have Southern sympathies. Where was your home? I mean, before you came here."

She imagined that his gaze sharpened, but she couldn't be sure. He had always been there, true; but he had vaguely seemed to her like an idle—and rather dingy—butterfly, ambling about the house, about the city, interested in nothing much save perhaps his own comfort.

He said now, mildly, "I thought you must know. *Eh bien,*

it doesn't matter. My home was in Virginia. But then..." He gazed out across the garden and said, as mildly, "From there I went to New York City. It was there the trouble— happened."

"Trouble—"

"The murder," said M. Lemaire pleasantly. "It became difficult. Very difficult."

"The—murder!"

He nodded. "I am an escaped murderer."

"A what?"

He nodded almost complacently. "Oh, yes. It happened in New York City. A duel. I didn't really mean to kill him. It was unfortunate. A law against dueling. They said I was a murderer. So I got away. And came here."

She felt her mouth opening and shut it quickly. He said vaguely, "My name was Marcy too. I am a cousin—your mother's second cousin. But I changed my name. The United States, or at least the New York police, were after me. I changed my name from Marcy to Lemaire. Here, in so French a city, it would seem natural. I believe it was your mother's suggestion. Your father, of course, agreed. So I have lived here ever since."

Well, she thought. Serves you right, Marcy, sticking your nose into his business. But an escaped murderer!

She moistened lips which were all at once rather dry. "But you had an income."

He nodded absently again. "Oh, yes. Small, but something. It was your father who managed to secure the capital, withdrew it from the Northern lawyer who was custodian. But then"—he sighed—"he told me to buy Confederate bonds with it. So I did."

And so, thus far during the period of the war, he had had no money.

He said, again unexpectedly, "The police in New York are said never to give up. They called it a crime, killing that man. Indeed, now that I think about it, I feel that it was a crime. An unintentional one, but a crime. At the same time I do not wish to be sent back to New York City. No." He said it with simple finality; that ended it, he seemed to think.

"Well," she began, and did not know what to say.

"Things will work out, somehow. Give it time. Meanwhile, of course, Gene Dupre is quite right. If you can extract any news of note from the major, anything to help the Confederacy, you will do us all a great benefit. Especially me, perhaps."

Good heavens, he had been there, cozily ensconced as a member of the family, for years. Nobody had told her; perhaps only her mother and father had known of his need to hide.

She said, "I don't think any Union official would question you about anything that happened to you so long ago."

He appeared to think that over; after a while he murmured, "Perhaps, my dear. But you must do as Gene asks you to do. Discover something, anything, about this General Grant. Time is passing. If Grant makes a move, he must be planning to make it soon."

He adjusted the black silk stock he had worn since Armand's murder. His chin was bagging a little below what Marcy considered elderly cheeks. Certainly he was over military age. He couldn't be expected to go into the army. He said now, surprising her again, "I understand there's yellow fever and also cholera—"

"Don't," she whispered. "If Gene can get us passes . . ."

His usually vague glance seemed rather perceptive. "You are right to be afraid. I have heard whispers of both illnesses in the city. What you must do, my dear, is get the information Gene wants." At that, he rose, gave her a slight nod and ambled off toward the gates. He had had a hat on the bench. She hadn't seen it until he put it on his head with a flourish. It was a rather battered hat, just as M. Lemaire always seemed—weary and battered.

And why not, she thought wildly. An escaped murderer!

But he was right in his advice. Get some information, any kind, from the major.

The major did not come to supper, although Tante Julie and she had met him in the gallery as he was leaving and invited him. "He said he was engaged," said Tante Julie and added with a sparkle in her dark eyes, "but I truly don't think with a lady. He hadn't that look."

Claudine drew delicate blond eyebrows up fastidiously. "What look?"

Tanie Julie shrugged. Jason came in with Floating Island in an enormous bowl.

During the hot and muggy night, however, Marcy, almost for the first time, began to question the circumstances of Armand's murder more closely and sharply.

It had been easy and logical to accept the answer that it was done by some street thug. The streets of New Orleans had become dangerous for everyone, let alone a handsome, prosperous-looking young man and paroled Confederate officer. Besides, she had told herself, it was easy for Armand to quarrel with anybody. So she had accepted the explanation that his murderer was either a street thug, a drunken Union soldier intent on robbery if the opportunity offered, or someone Armand had intentionally offended.

Now in the thick blackness of the night a shocking question asked itself: Was it possible that Armand's murderer was, in fact, someone she knew? Someone of the close circle of friends and relatives?

It was M. Lemaire's statement that had set off her new uneasiness. Could M. Lemaire have shot him? He had known that Armand insisted upon immediate marriage; he had known or could have guessed that Marcy herself was firmly decided not to marry Armand. Could he have known or guessed that Armand would have insisted with all his angry force?

The answer to those questions was yes. M. Lemaire had somehow always known everything that went on in the house. Could he possibly have shot Armand to prevent the marriage?

Her relative! A cousin of her mother's, kin. Taking a different name at her mother's suggestion, yet one which derived from her own. But the errant notion that he had murdered Armand to save her, Marcy, from an unwelcome marriage was too preposterous to accept for long.

It must have been toward morning when she roused to sniff at an acrid smoky odor that came drifting in: the tar barrels, of course. She knew the ugly odor and the uglier reason for it. Already they were burning tar across the city in the hope of averting yellow fever, which seemed to travel through the air with malignant speed.

They must get away somehow—it didn't matter how—to Nine Oaks and comparative safety. Neither she nor Tante Julie had, in fact, made as thorough a search of the major's room as perhaps they might have. She went back at last into an uneasy sleep, wondering what she could have overlooked and how she could gain the complete confidence of this too-sensible, too-alert, too-self-possessed Yankee. Yankee, she repeated. She hated the word.

The next day Gene Dupre came with not one but two thunderbolts. The first was Armand's will. Gene drew her and Tante Julie into the formal salon, and there in the gentle twilight of the room, with the jalousies and door closed, he told them that Armand had drawn up and left a will.

"Everything goes to you, my dear Marcy. Everything."

Marcy felt rather as if the breath had been knocked out of her. The elegant piano was long gone, but the silk-covered stool remained and squealed and swerved and nearly threw her off balance as she sank down upon it. "But he had nothing to leave," she said feebly.

Gene shook his head. "Ah, but perhaps he did. Once this war is over. His father bought all the Confederate bonds he could buy, yes. Now, really, one does not know . . ." He paused, his face very serious. He did not say, One wonders if the Confederate bonds will ever amount to anything; one wonders how this war will end, but the words almost said themselves in the quiet, charming room.

Tante Julie, however, was practical as always. "But he had land."

Gene nodded. "Land. That will always be of value, no matter what. He made the will himself, the day before he was killed. There is no likely way of challenging its legality. Not that any of his relatives is likely to challenge it. They had land too, but just now there are far too many Southerners with too much land and too little cash. He gave the will to me, and I put it in a strongbox. Actually, I didn't think of it until today. But I brought it with me. Read it, Marcy. And then, if you wish, I'll act as your—oh, man of business, however I *can* act in these times."

She took the heavy paper. She read the stiffly correct phrases. There was no misunderstanding it. The property, all that remained after the war or existed at that time, was the only bequest. It was worded rather oddly yet very specifically; there was to her no possible doubt as to his intentions. It read in one formal phrase, "To my wife, or Marcy Juliet Chastain—" She glanced at Gene. "Why, it's almost as if he was afraid of being killed that night!"

Gene shook his head. "It is merely the kind of statement that lawyers and bankers advise at the present time. During war one never knows. Armand wanted to be sure everything went to you either before your marriage or afterwards."

Marcy read on. There was his full name, all the Christian names in his own fine, spiky handwriting. Suddenly she remembered a dry half-smile in the major's face when he heard all those names. She gave Gene the will. "Please see to it, Gene."

"*Certainement*," Tante Julie said. "*Elle n'est pas une femme d'affaires.*"

But she had had to be a businesswoman of a kind, Marcy thought vaguely.

The will was exactly like Armand; even the formal phrases, the correct behavior, was like him. Gene folded up the paper and tucked it back into his pocket; then he took a deep breath, put one hand on a chair back as if to steady himself, and with obvious reluctance exploded his second thunderbolt. "Madame." He addressed Julie. "May I speak to Marcy alone?"

Tante Julie's bright eyes narrowed. She wasn't accustomed to being asked to leave; if anyone was asked to withdraw, it had been Tante Julie who made the request. However, she gave a neat, if haughty, bow and retreated. Marcy wasn't sure that, after she closed the door very smartly, she didn't open it again, the barest crack, and apply her ear to it.

Gene sat down, looked at the carpet, looked up at Marcy and said, "I asked your Tante Julie to leave because she would only make this harder. I don't know how to tell you. I have to tell you. But I can't think of anything you can do. It doesn't bear thinking of, I realize that, but a man came to see me and—well, it's this way. Claudine has had an offer to sell the little boy, and accepted it."

Marcy sprang to her feet. The piano stool whirled madly. "Sell the baby! Sell Brule's son!"

Gene nodded, miserably.

"But she can't! It's impossible! No, no! Not even Claudine could do that!"

"She has decided."

"No." Marcy wasn't shouting. Her own ears rang just the same. Sometimes people did faint, didn't they? Not, her innate common sense rather reluctantly assured her, when they were as healthy and strong as she was.

"The man who offered to buy him saw the child somewhere. He discovered Claudine's connection and made a good offer for the boy."

Marcy began to rally the same unwelcome common sense which forbade fainting. "Nobody wants a slave now! They're only an expense."

"The purchaser intends to take the boy, I believe, to the West Indies. It seems that so handsome a child and—I'm so sorry, Marcy, but it is Claudine's decision."

"No! How *can* it be!"

"You forget the circumstances of your brother's alliance with this girl Angele, Brule's mother. He bought her. There are papers to prove the purchase. Angele died just before Christmas. Your brother had purchased her in the regular way. So, as you can see, his property naturally went to his legal wife, Claudine, and consequently a part of that property is Brule—"

"I won't let him be sold!" She felt as she had felt when she refused to marry Armand. Yet even at the time when she was refusing her marriage to Armand, she had had an uneasy feeling like quicksand, as if the code she had been brought up in, the code she had lived in, would enforce her marriage to him. She had sprung up so fast from the piano stool that it was still whirling slowly. She was whirling too, she thought, and made herself look straight at Gene. "I'll never consent."

"The child belongs to Claudine. She does not need your consent." He rose, walked back and forth across the rosy garlands of the carpet, and finally said, "I know Claudine. She is my cousin. We don't agree about many things. There is nothing I can do to stop her when she has made up her mind."

"Gene! I'll take him to Nine Oaks!"

His look was compassionate. "Dear Marcy, you can't!"

She cried, "If I had a pass! The provost marshal's pass! Gene—if I do find out something, anything about Grant, you can get me a pass?"

"Oh, Marcy, I would try, I told you. You know I'll do my best. I can't promise success."

"But you will try, Gene. You knew my brother. You were all such close friends—you will do it."

"I'll try," he said again. "There's a problem of time, I think. Let's consider it." He sat down, frowning thoughtfully. "Grant is said to have encamped his army near Grand Gulf. There are twelve big guns at Grand Gulf, which, if properly used, should stop any attempt to cross the river. However, there appears to be a diversionary tactic the Yankees are employing. One of my Yankee friends"—he winced as he said "friends"—"was in his cups the other night and did some barroom talking, which came to my ears. A certain Union Colonel Grierson and his cavalry force are raiding down through Mississippi. His action is almost certainly designed to draw off General Pemberton and some of his army from Vicksburg. Grant is said to be a very tenacious man. Naturally he intends to get across the river and attack Vicksburg. It seems unlikely that he should try to get an army across the river at Grand Gulf. However, your Major Farrell might know."

"I'll try," she said. "Gene, I'll try again to find out."

"I'm sorry to ask it of you, Marcy. But it's our land—our way of living."

It left no argument. Gene knew that, but so did Marcy. After he had gone, she went out into the garden; Brule was sniffing at a red rose. He turned happy dark eyes toward her and smiled. Brule's face, Brule's firm chin, Brule's wide forehead, even Brule's thick black hair. The child leaned confidingly against her. Let him be sold—never! She hugged him so hard that he gave a startled little gasp, but then smiled up at her again in full love and trust.

She had searched the major's room. The major's horse was still quartered in the old stables but not, she thought wryly, likely to tell her anything.

However, she went to the stables. The horse was interested and turned his wise but regrettably silent face to watch her. He had water; probably the major had seen to that before he went out.

The major had taken his saddlebags to his room. Tante Julie had searched quickly through them and found nothing. His saddle was in the old tack room. The saddle was in no position to offer information either, but she went there, brushing away a spider web or two. The saddle smelled of horse; attached to it was a small bag, also smelling of horse. She felt for the clasp and thrust it open; the bag was leather, neatly made, designed perhaps to carry food, papers or firearms.

She couldn't believe that she might find anything of interest in it, left there so openly and so carelessly. However, she thrust her hand inside it, groped around and drew out a large pistol. Since she had had very little to do with pistols, she eyed it respectfully through the dusk, and it caught a gleam or two of light in what seemed, just then, a menacing manner. She let it drop back into the leather bag, and her hand encountered a crumpled bit of something that felt like paper. She withdrew it cautiously. In the dim light of the tack room she straightened out the folds and read a few words. They made no sense, yet when she looked harder, holding the paper nearer the light which sifted in from the wide stable door, she could discern words. "From the east . . . Bruinsberg . . . June . . . last week."

The rest was not decipherable.

If it meant what she thought it meant, perhaps there was an answer. Perhaps here was the saving of little Brule, all of them.

She didn't hear anything; her heart was pounding too hard.

She did hear Major Farrell's voice. "Give me that."

She whirled around. Her heart now jumped into her throat. He stood, an implacable figure in blue, in the doorway.

It was a repetition of the scene when he had found her searching his room, only the day before, and had stood like that between her and escape.

TWELVE

He repeated it and held out his hand. "Give me that."

All right, she thought swiftly, I can remember it.

She shrugged—lightly, she hoped—and handed over the crumpled and all but indecipherable scrap of paper. Indecipherable, but she had seen enough to report to Gene Dupre.

He took the paper; even in the dusk she could see how his face hardened. "So it *was* you who searched my room several times."

She didn't need to reply, for this time M. Lemaire saved her. He came ambling in through the dusty, musty scents of the barn, and stopped, blinking but gazing at them. Then, unexpectedly, he wagged one finger at them with roguery and cackled.

It was nothing else, a silly cackle. "So you've caught her," he said muzzily, addressing the major. "Caught yourself a prize, haven't you? Pretty as a picture, I always say. Like her mother. Mother the most beautiful girl in all Virginia. All New York, all Louisiana, that's what everybody said. Didn't this Marcy girl capture Armand? He was a catch. Every girl in New Orleans was after him. But this little lovely caught him. Did you ever see such beautiful

hair—soft, black, like a cloud. And her eyes as blue as
midnight if she's angry or upset, but dancing with mischief
when she's flirting. But now, Marcy, dear child, you mustn't
flirt. Just lower those long eyelashes and—the trouble with
her,'' he said seriously to the major, ''is that she's proud.
See the way she lifts her head, like a flower on a stalk. See
her nose: arrogant, some would say. I say it's right. What a
lucky man who finally gets her! Oh, yes, lucky—'' He
swayed a little, and the major, who up to then had looked a
little bemused, caught him.

Why, he's been drinking, Marcy thought.

But M. Lemaire had not finished. ''Never thinks of
herself, though, not since the war. Doubt if she's even
looked in a mirror. See how wide her eyes are now. Pink
roses in her cheeks. She doesn't want me to talk, but I'll tell
you this, sir.'' He leaned against the major's arm. ''She's
had too much on her mind since the war. Too much to see
to. All for us and—and . . .'' He paused to give forth a large
hiccup.

The major glanced at Marcy. ''Is this usual?'' he asked in
a stunned way.

''No,'' Marcy said, and then gave it a second thought.
Certainly M. Lemaire had produced wines sometimes, li-
queurs, brandy from some stock of his own. The wine cellar
had been broken into the preceding fall by some Yankees,
who departed with the bottles under their arms, but M.
Lemaire had clearly secreted wine or brandy or something
alcoholic; he had also imbibed them secretly. Hadn't he?
Perhaps he lived in a kind, friendly alcoholic daze. Escaped
murderer! Alcoholic, and none of them had guessed it!

M. Lemaire righted himself, but clung to the major's
arm. ''You ought to see her in a ball gown. She has to wear
rags now. All the ladies wear rags. Have to. But when she
wears a ball gown, you should see that!''

''I have,'' the major said shortly.

Something in the way he said it sent a warm wave over
Marcy's face. She said, ''I didn't know that he did this.''
She couldn't say, ''drank himself into a state of confusion.''
She said instead, ''He is confused.''

''No, not confused. Speaking the truth, if I may say so,''

the major said thoughtfully, but with a glint in his eyes, discernible even in the dusk of the tack room as complimentary. Oddly, even at that moment, it sent another wave of warmth along her pulses. "What shall I do with him?" he asked.

"He'll be all right, I think," she said, but doubtfully. "There's a bench outside the stable."

"Come, sir." The major supported the now almost recumbent man with a steady arm and took him out past the horse, who eyed them over one shoulder with what seemed to Marcy an air of long-nosed reproof.

Marcy followed. So this was the reason for M. Lemaire's customary fogginess, an alcoholic fog which none of them had ever suspected. On the bench, the major lowered M. Lemaire, who somehow managed to look very confused indeed with his hair tousled, his big cravat loosened, his mouth unsteady, his eyes—she caught herself there, for certainly there was something rather shrewd and alert in the one glance he shot at her before he closed his eyes and leaned limply back. It so surprised her, that swift but very shrewd gleam, that she leaned over him, thinking to rouse him, speak to him, something, and caught a violent aroma of liquor. Rum? Yes. Sickeningly, sweetly heavy; no gentleman drinks rum, her father always said.

M. Lemaire seemed sodden with it; even his ruffled white shirt was soaked. It occurred to her that he couldn't have got more rum upon himself if he had tried; and then, instantly, she wondered if perhaps he did try. Then—well, then his motive in all his praise of her beauty was clear; he wished to make sure that the major saw her—her hair, her eyes, her—she began to blush again. The major had a laughing gleam in his eyes. "He'll be all right here, I think."

"Thank you," she said in a stifled way.

But he hadn't forgotten the tiny scrap of paper. He had at some time during M. Lemaire's discourse slid it into a pocket. He drew it out again. "You read this, of course."

"Why, yes. I think I did. I didn't mean to. I don't know what it means. Is it important?"

The last question was daring. The major eyed her for a

moment, very seriously. "Do you remember what you read?"

She shook her head, pretending to seek back through memory. "I think, there was something about June—June?"

"That's all you remember?"

No, indeed. She lowered her eyelids quickly. "I'm not sure. I can't remember. You came in just as I picked it up."

"You were hunting through the dispatch bag in my saddle."

"Yes." She had to think quickly, if not very reasonably. "I hoped to find a pistol of some kind. And I did."

"Why? I mean, why do you want a pistol?"

That was easy. "Women alone in the house. Drunken Yank—I mean, no street, no house in New Orleans is safe. Yes, I wanted some kind of firearms."

"You put it back."

"I didn't know how to load it or fire it." She spoke with perfect truth at last. Then she had to embroider it. "And, you see, there's little Brule. He might have got his hands on it. So I decided not to keep it, after all."

M. Lemaire gave a sigh and wriggled his legs into a more comfortable position. Major Farrell looked down at him. "He's coming around, I think. Fresh air is what he needs. Unless a bucket of water—"

"Oh, no, please don't. He has so few clothes. None of us has anything to wear."

"You have your ball gown." He was half smiling.

She thought of the ball gown again, her only truly dressed-up ball gown. She had felt like a fairy princess in it. Pale pink *mousseline de soie*, the wide skirt hooped and flounced with Chantilly lace; the waist cinched in to a breathless eighteen inches; the bodice cut very low, too low, her father had said, but Marcy had got the dressmaker alone. The dressmaker had been only too willing to cut a low bodice, saying with delight that Marcy's shoulders must show; *"Si belle, si blanche,"* she had said over the pins in her mouth.

Marcy now said flatly, "One of your soldiers fancied it and took it. I expect some Yankee woman is now wearing it."

The major's face changed; it had been kind and friendly—yes, friendly at least; now it became too sober. "I'm sorry," he said after a moment. "Now then, that litttle scrap of paper you found."

So he still hadn't forgotten it, she thought in dismay; I've got to invent something for a reply. "Yes." She lifted her eyelashes as sweetly as she could contrive, and looked up at him, she hoped confidingly. She wasn't sure how successful either attempt was, but he did hesitate and finally say, "That is, you said you saw some words."

"I told you. It was so dark in the tack room. But I'm sure there was something about June. Perhaps July—no, June. I couldn't see any words." She risked repeating her question. "Was it important?"

"No. Not at all. Someone must have left it there in the dispatch case."

That last remark she believed. If he had known it was there, surely he'd have destroyed it!

She wondered if Gene's associates would accept this information, if information it was, and a pass for them could be procured. The major's next words drove that out of her mind. "I came to bring you some news," he said hesitantly. He was now very grave.

"News!" Her heart really did stop. All news lately had been bad.

He guessed that. "Yes, it's your father. But he's all right. I mean, I found out where he is, and he is in good health. I didn't mean to frighten you. I only meant to—to—"

"Yes, I know."

He eyed her seriously. "Sometimes good news is as much a shock as bad news. But I do assure you I had it from headquarters. A very recent report."

"Where is he?"

"In Texas. A place called Neuverte. There are others there. I am assured they are well treated. The point is, I believe I can get a parole for him. If he'll take it."

This was the man she was prepared to deceive. She felt a wave of shame. Yet what else could she do? *From the east . . . Bruinsberg . . . June . . . last week.* She repeated the words in her memory for fear she might forget them, and hoped that the man before her couldn't guess what she was thinking.

He said, "Do you think he will be willing to take the oath of allegiance?"

The Eagle Oath, again; the Ironclad Oath. "I don't know. He wouldn't do it in the beginning when it was required. Perhaps now—"

"He will be given time to think it over. I want you to know that there is a good doctor in the camp. They have plenty of good food. I truly don't think he is suffering. Physically, that is. Undoubtedly he would prefer being here, but if it's any comfort to you, he is not in any real need."

"You are so kind. So very kind—"

"Nonsense. In a way, he is my host. You have been very kind to me."

And if you knew why, she thought; if you knew why!

She must get to Gene before the small string of words went out of her mind. *East . . . Bruinsberg . . . June . . . last week.* She wished she could have read more of the message.

He said pleasantly but formally, "I'll try to get more news of your father. I may not be here for several days." At that he walked back through the heat and the blazing colors of the flowers, toward the stables. She went slowly along the shaded gallery to her room.

She had not properly thanked him for his great courtesy. She intended instead to betray him in a very real sense; surely the few words on the paper, crumpled up and thrust into the dispatch case by someone—who or why she could not surmise—could be important. She must see Gene.

Yet she lingered at her window until she saw the major leading his horse, saddled now, toward the wide doors to the mews behind the stable. So he was gone again on one of those mysterious journeys. There was no way of knowing when he would return.

Once the blue uniformed figure and the bay horse had disappeared, she started to reach for a bonnet, wondered how she could get some sort of conveyance to take her to Gene, and then stopped to gaze at herself in the mirror.

Actually, she had been so thoroughly occupied, so troubled and worried for so many months, that she had barely glanced at herself to see that her hair was neat and her collar fastened. Now she looked closely at her image. Drunk he might be—or might not be!—M. Lemaire had described her hair rather accurately, if fulsomely; her eyes were blue, yes; in her heart, perhaps, she had known that she could sparkle; that knowledge was born in a Southern woman. They were not trained to attract men, but every one of them was fully aware of the advantage of a man's admiration. It was a man's world; what could one do about it except please men?

Her skin was white, yes; but a Southern woman had been taught to care for that white skin, never to stay out in the sun. Glycerine, rose water and lemon juice; it was a standard recipe for the complexion, a little sticky sometimes, but pride knoweth no pain, Tante Julie had once reminded her.

Yes, she decided, M. Lemaire might have been drunk, or he might have been coldly sober beneath all that pretense, only determined in a peculiar way to impress the major with her charms. Suddenly and uncomfortably, it reminded her of the one slave market she had happened to catch a glimpse of; it was only a glimpse, for Brule had been in the carriage with her and had hurried her away. The auctioneer was describing the beauty of a young Negress—an octoroon, she had thought at that one glimpse, for the girl was almost white. M. Lemaire had sounded altogether too much like that auctioneer. No, no; he must have been drunk, and drinking would explain much about him.

She must find a way at once to tell Gene of the few words on that crumpled piece of paper. They *must* have significance.

She went to the window and saw M. Lemaire sitting quietly on a bench in the garden. She smoothed her hair, adjusted the tiny white frill around her neck and went down.

M. Lemaire looked up and his blurry eyes positively twinkled. He had changed his rum-soaked shirt to a ruffled white one; he was now clean and very, very perky, as if pleased with himself.

"Why, you—you weren't drunk at all!"

"Me? Drunk? My dear—"

"You are an old fraud!" She laughed.

"My dear! To speak to me like that! Your only uncle."

"Uncle! But you said you were a cousin of my mother's—"

"Oh! Did I?"

"And you said—"

"Did I ever tell you about my gold-mining experiences?" He appeared to inquire with honest curiosity.

She caught her breath with exasperation but also vast relief. "You *are* a fraud! You said you were an escaped murderer!"

"Dear me," he said gently. "How very confusing!"

"I want the truth—"

"Naturally. I'll say anything you please."

Might as well try to pin down a frayed but elusive butterfly. "You'll say anything that you want to say, is that it? Oh, never mind. At least you are sober."

"Never anything else," he said cheerfully.

"As to that—oh, pay it no mind. I've got to see Gene."

"Ah. So you did gather some news. I thought so from what I heard when I came into the stable. I'll take you."

"Take me—"

"To see Gene, of course. You can't go alone. And you can't go in that dress, either. Charming, yes, indeed. Put on your weeds."

"Weeds! I'm *not* a widow!"

"Same thing with us. Go on. All black."

Gene and M. Lemaire had the same respect for convention. "The dress is so hot—"

"And your veil," he said inexorably.

He was right, yes. She went up to her room again, got out the stifling black crepe and the more-than-stifling veil for the black bonnet.

When she went down again, M. Lemaire was no longer on the bench but waiting outside the carriage gates in a sagging chaise. She could see his figure through the tracery of wrought iron, and he was sitting erectly, a hat on his head, holding the reins of a rather worn-down horse with firm hands. She opened the small gate. He made a kind of salute with the whip and then restored it to its socket. "Can you climb in, my dear? I'm afraid to leave this mettlesome steed."

She climbed in, guarding her hoops lest they fly up.

"A handsome equipage," observed M. Lemaire. "Are you comfortable, my dear?"

For a second it reminded her of Mr. Barkis and his courtship of Peggotty; she and her father had laughed over that. But "mettlesome steed"! "A handsome equipage"!

He guessed her thoughts. "Never mind. I believe the horse will move if properly approached. Just a tickle, perhaps." He took out the whip.

"Where did you find him? And the chaise?"

"Oh, a boy down the street."

Probably, she reflected briefly, M. Lemaire had very rarely spoken a honest fact in his life. No, that was wrong. Once or twice he had shown good sense; even his motive, while he was parading her charms for the major, still had a certain, if unusual, logic. He tickled the horse with the whip, but the tickle had a remarkable effect, for all at once the animal, who had appeared to be in dreamland, awoke with a start and a jolt that sent them careening along the cobblestones. She clung to the handrail.

"Can't you stop him?"

"Better let the horse have his way. Try not to mind the odor of smoke."

Nobody could avoid the smoky, rancid odor left by the burning barrels of the previous night. Nobody knew—or at least if anyone knew, Marcy had never been told—why there was a belief in the efficacy of burning pitch to prevent yellow fever. It wasn't possible that clouds of smoke could clear the air.

The streets began to seem oddly deserted. They reached the business district and the street of Gene's bank. M. Lemaire halted the horse, which went back to sleep again at once. He leaped out of the chaise and tied the horse to a hitching post near the impressive doorway to Gene's bank.

He held up hands to assist Marcy's descent. *From the east . . . Bruinsberg . . . June . . . last week.* She repeated it to herself like an open sesame, and she hoped that the way out of New Orleans would be opened.

A man who seemed to have been lounging at the corner of the bank building moved, turned away and vanished into the side street. She had a fleeting glimpse of a tall, thin figure with a black coat, light trousers, a black slouch hat pulled low over his face. Then he was gone. He was almost the only person on the street.

M. Lemaire looked after the vanishing figure in a thoughtful way.

The bank seemed rather empty; there was a vaulted ceiling and a number of desks, but only one clerk, who, at M. Lemaire's inquiry, merely jerked his head toward an impressive flight of mahogany stairs.

"Gene's office is above," said M. Lemaire and added again thoughtfully, "I do believe that young man is leaving the bank."

He was. Over the bannister they saw the neatly frock-coated clerk making a kind of stately haste toward the doors. "Afraid of the fever, I expect," said M. Lemaire. "Explains the empty streets. Now then—ah, Gene. We've come to see you. Sorry. You seem to be busy."

Gene had risen as they entered his office. M. Lemaire had not taken the trouble to knock; he merely pushed Marcy ahead of him and smiled politely at Gene, but then gazed about him with dreamy eyes which never seemed to see anything but, Marcy was beginning to suspect, saw everything. Gene was blushing and wiping his forehead with a handkerchief. There were two bright splotches high up on his cheeks. But Marcy's attention was caught by a woman who sat gracefully in one of the big black leather armchairs. Even at her first glance, Marcy realized that here was a woman extraordinarily attractive in an indescribably exotic way.

She was small and very composed; she had thick black curls showing below a charmingly coquettish bonnet. She was dressed in very becoming black, showing a tiny waist and beautifully neat, if revealing, basque. Her face was small, too, with quite lovely curves; her eyes caught Marcy's gaze and held it. They were an odd color, almost topaz, and bright between sweeping black eyelashes. After a second or two which seemed moments, she fluttered the black eyelashes toward Gene and said, in a lovely, rather husky voice, "M'sieu, won't you introduce me?"

Gene swallowed hard. Then he said, rather loudly, "Certainly, madame. Mademoiselle Chastain. Madame Lorne."

Marcy murmured something.

Madame Lorne said clearly, "I thought so," gave Marcy a very deliberate look from her startlingly topaz eyes, then lowered thick black lashes, adjusted black lace mitts over slender white hands, and walked gracefully, her full black skirts rustling, out of the room.

Gene sat down, rose at once, motioned to Marcy to be seated, and applied his handkerchief again.

M. Lemaire said, "I suppose she's the one. Wants money?"

Gene said, "How did you know?"

M. Lemaire lifted his eyebrows. "I didn't exactly *know*, Gene. It only seemed likely. I happened to have a little chat with the clerk at the St. Charles. I understood from him that you found nothing in Armand's room to indicate that he used the room very often. Naturally I thought, where's the woman? I take it she's the one. Armand had good taste," said M. Lemaire mildly.

Gene gave him an angry glance. "Oh, yes. She's the one—"

M. Lemaire interrupted. "How did you find her, Gene?"

"I didn't!" He gave Marcy an embarrassed glance and wiped his forehead again. "But there was a letter. In a drawer—I took it."

And I saw you, Marcy thought; you told me it was a bill.

"It was only a note Armand had written but hadn't sent—or delivered."

"And what," said M. Lemaire, "did Armand say in this note?"

"If you've got to have the truth—well, all right. He said he could only repeat his decision not to see her again. He said he was fully determined, and that was all. She might as well accept it. He was to be married to you. He wrote that. You'll have to know sometime, Cousin Marcy. She was Armand's mistress."

THIRTEEN

Marcy sat down; her limp knees wouldn't hold her up.

M. Lemaire pursed his lips and moved to a window. "No escort," he said over his shoulder as he looked down into the street.

Gene pushed at his blond hair nervously. "Oh, yes. I believe someone brought her here. Some escort. Must have done. Wouldn't do to walk the streets of New Orleans just now."

"M'm." M. Lemaire was craning his neck to peer downward. "I thought so. Young man. Black slouch hat. He's back again."

"Huh?" Gene said inelegantly.

"He dodged out of the way when he saw us entering the bank. Didn't want to be seen. Who is he?"

"I don't know. I suppose some friend or relative." He gave Marcy an astonished look. "You are not surprised?"

"Why—why, yes. I never dreamed . . ." Her hands grasped the black leather arms of the chair, which felt sticky from the humid heat.

From the window M. Lemaire said almost idly, "By the

way, your young man at the desk downstairs must have remembered some urgent business elsewhere.''

Gene shot upward again. ''Do you mean he's leaving?''

''Gone,'' said M. Lemaire laconically.

''The rat!'' cried Gene, and all but galloped on his graceful legs out of the room.

M. Lemaire sauntered to a chair. ''Dear me,'' he said. ''So Armand—dear me.''

''I never knew. He *couldn't* have—'' Marcy began. ''I never suspected!''

''Of course not,'' M. Lemaire assured her cheerfully. ''It was not the kind of thing you were supposed to know. But I do wonder how much money she wants.''

''Money.'' Marcy was still feeling stunned. Not grieved, not shocked perhaps, but astounded. Armand had always assured her that she was his only love.

She said, ''I can't believe it. Not Armand—''

''Now, now. Remember Brule and his Angele.''

''I know, but—but this is different.''

''Because Angele was a lovely and a well-behaved girl. And this woman—dear me—I'm afraid is not well behaved!''

Gene came back and sat down, breathing hard. ''Rat,'' he repeated. ''All of them are rats. Afraid. Running for home. Trying to escape the fever, as if they could. I put a *'Fermé'* sign on the doors and locked them.''

''A wise move,'' said M. Lemaire in a congratulatory way.

Gene didn't glare at him, but almost. ''Didn't you notice the 'Closed' signs on the stores, on the restaurants?''

M. Lemaire shrugged. ''To tell you the truth, it needed all my attention to control our mettlesome steed. This is tragic and shocking news for Marcy.''

Gene made a stifled sound in his throat.

M. Lemaire said, ''The fever is worse, I take it.''

''Worse. Why didn't you stop my young clerk? You saw him leaving. You could have run after him. Are you afraid?'' Gene was thoroughly aroused.

''Certainly. Why should I stop any employee of yours? Besides, he may have been armed. How should I know!''

"But you're the man who told me that he rode shotgun on stagecoaches traveling the Western route."

Again the vague gray film seemed to come across M. Lemaire's face. "Did I say that? Dear me! How remarkable!"

Oh, yes, a consummate liar, too, Marcy thought.

Gene took a long, exasperated breath. "What's remarkable is how you can make up so many different tales!"

"You must be mistaken, Gene." M. Lemaire sat down, put one lank knee over the other, swung his foot, and eyed his shabby but neatly polished shoe reflectively. Then he lifted his eyes. "How much money does that woman want?"

"She doesn't—I don't know."

"Come, come, Gene." M. Lemaire shook his head reprovingly. "You can't make us believe that she only admired your blue eyes. Not," he added with an air of meticulous accuracy, "that they are blue. I'd say—gray. Wouldn't you say gray, Marcy?"

Gene made an explosive sound, then leaned his elbows on the desk. "Yes," he said soberly, "she came about money. She said Armand hadn't left her any, and she needs it." He frowned uneasily and looked away. "I really think that you might consider paying her off, Marcy."

"Why should I? I wouldn't think of it," Marcy said hotly. "Besides, I have nothing to pay her off with."

M. Lemaire said thoughtfully, "Not a helpless female, that one! Beautiful, yet somehow I'd hate to meet her on a dark night in an alley. Does she carry knives under all those silky black ruffles, Gene? Where'd Armand find her?"

"I don't know. She's not an Orleanian. Possibly Armand met her while he was convalescing, after he'd been released from the hospital."

"That would be near Richmond." Marcy thought of the letters she had tried to send to Armand when she learned that he had been wounded.

"And he brought her here?" M. Lemaire asked.

Gene nodded. "Must have. Or she followed him. Marcy, I didn't know this to be a fact. But frankly, when I found that note—naturally I began to suspect. I destroyed the note. I didn't want you to know. But this woman, this Madame Lorne—she told me before you arrived that Armand had told her he had left his will with me. So she came to me. Wants money, of course," he said again in a troubled and rather evasive way.

M. Lemaire sighed. "She looks quite capable of—shall I say, discovering money herself. With all these soldiers in the city," he said cynically. "You said 'Madame.' Where is her husband?"

"She told me that her husband was killed at Sharpsburg."

"Where Brule died," Marcy said.

Gene's face tightened and in a flash was older and sadder. "Yes. Of course, I'm sure when Armand met her she was already a widow. I don't like the woman, but I think it might be wise simply to pay her off and forget about her."

M. Lemaire looked into space. "I wonder," he said dreamily, "if she could be the reason for Armand's sudden decision to have his marriage to Marcy take place at once."

Gene picked it up. "You may be right! Yes, you just may be right. Armand's betrothal to you, Marcy, had gone on a long time, that is true. But still—"

Marcy said bluntly, "Still, just all at once Armand demanded the marriage ceremony. That *could* have been because this woman—"

"Made trouble," said M. Lemaire. "Ah, yes. He told her clearly in the note you found, Gene, that he was determined upon marriage. So—so he was trying to get rid of her. H'm. Yes. It does not explain Armand's murder. Oh, she could have done it, but surely it would have been more prudent on her part to let the ceremony go on and then—"

Gene cried, "Blackmail! But—no—what could she blackmail him about? A love affair, which he broke off? Nothing to blackmail Armand about. Besides, he was killed. She wouldn't have killed the goose—I beg your pardon, Marcy—she wouldn't have cut off any source of money."

"No," Marcy said flatly. "Armand left nothing. I have nothing."

Marcy's astounded disbelief had given way to belief. Yet she could not possibly summon up a feeling of jealousy of Madame Lorne. There were other, more urgent things to think of.

She cried, "Oh, Gene, I think I have a kind of message.

It was on a paper. In a kind of case—a dispatch case, I think, on the major's saddle. In our stables.''

Gene leaned across the desk. *"What is it? Tell me."*

"I couldn't read it all. The paper was so creased, the handwriting small, and it was dark in the tack room, but it said, 'From the east . . . Bruinsberg . . . June . . . last week.' ''

" 'From the east . . . Bruinsberg . . . June . . . last week.' Is that all?''

"There was more. I couldn't read it.''

"She didn't have time to read it.'' M. Lemaire wriggled his neat foot. "The major came in and found her.''

"What did he say?"

M. Lemaire replied. "We had a little talk about Marcy. He got the entirely erroneous idea that I had been drinking,'' he said without so much as a quiver. "It is possible that he didn't know that paper was there. Some messenger might have merely stuffed it into the dispatch case—for what reason, of course, I cannot say—and the major might then have failed to find it. On the other hand''—again M. Lemaire looked dreamily at nothing—"there could be other explanations.''

"One is enough,'' Gene said shortly. "What did he say to you, Marcy?''

"He asked me what I had seen. I evaded, or tried to. I asked if it was important. He said no. That was all, really. I pretended I couldn't read or remember much of it—''

"But you couldn't read the whole message?'' Gene asked.

"There wasn't time. Now, have I done enough? Will your friend procure our passes?'' She wanted to get out of Gene's office, which had witnessed her betrayal of a man who had tried to befriend her father and thus herself. She was ashamed and yet determined to extract the pass as her payment.

Gene went to a shelf of books and pamphlets and drew out a long paper, a map, which he spread out over the desk. "Now then, Bruinsberg. Where . . .'' He frowned and looked and finally said, "Grant *can't* cross there. If that is what the message means. He can't possibly cross there. It's a tiny place, scarcely a crossroad—no, it really doesn't seem feasible.''

"You promised! I brought it to you. I hated it, but I did."

"I'll do my best. But this sounds as if someone only wants us to believe that Grant is planning to cross the river below Grand Gulf and attack Vicksburg from the east. It may have been placed there for the purpose of confusing us. A trap! Has Major Farrell any reason to suspect you of prying into his affairs?"

Of course he did have reason to suspect her: her presence in his room, opening his drawers—even with the Ortega ring for an excuse—and the other searches of his belongings that he talked about.

"He believes that his room was searched before I searched it, as indeed I did. So did Tante Julie. But he said that some papers, letters or something, had been taken away and later returned. I don't know who did that—"

Gene broke in. "It wouldn't have been you, M'sieu Lemaire?"

"Me!" M. Lemaire's face was as bland as a baby's. "Why would I do that?"

"I don't know," Gene said slowly. "I feel, though, that you don't miss much."

M. Lemaire was unperturbed. "Don't flatter me, Gene. I'm too old to accept it."

Not so very old, Marcy thought, and smart as a fox beneath that dreamy air of detachment.

Gene sighed. "You said, Marcy, he found you in his room, searching."

"Yes. And just as I was trying to explain and didn't know what to say, Armand's ring, the Ortega wedding ring, fell out of a drawer I had opened. So I lied. What else could I do? I said I was so thankful to find the ring. I said that was why I was in his room."

"But he did find you in there. And now he finds you searching the dispatch case. Oh, I know you tried. Well, I'll report it to my associates. If we decide that such may be Grant's intention, then I am almost sure you will get the passes. Are you sure the major does not suspect you?"

"I don't think he does. I'm not sure. He did ask me about his room having been searched. I believe he thinks that Brule was hunting through it. Of course, he must realize that the baby is too small to reach any drawers or look through the armoire or anything," she finished feebly, and then leaned forward. "Gene, we must have the passes."

Gene swung around his desk and took her hands in his own. "Dear Marcy, I told you that I would try. I will try. I'll convince the—the others—"

"The Defenders? Or someone in the army defending Vicksburg?" Lemaire asked as smoothly as a knife slipping through butter.

Gene didn't so much as glance at him; his gray eyes were dark with anxiety. "I promised to help. And I will. I'll make them believe it. Or if they won't believe it, if they think it is only a trap—I'll get those passes somehow. I don't care how!"

M. Lemaire said, "No need to be too daring about it, Gene. Come, Marcy, we'd better leave while we still have our mettlesome steed."

Gene took them down through the empty, echoing bank. He unlocked and opened the door with its sign, *Fermé*, fluttering against it. There was no mettlesome steed. There was only steamy heat. "Gone," said Gene resignedly. "Nothing is organized. Nothing is safe. Take my horse. The chaise and the horse are in Hevert's livery stable."

"Ah," said M. Lemaire, and slid away.

"He'll not be a moment," Gene said, sensing her discomfort as a group of men in blue uniform, obviously drunk, lounged along the banquette.

Marcy shrank against Gene into the shadow of the columns which impressively flanked the big doors of the bank. The men laughed and looked at her, and one of them said something to the other which gave them more laughter. Gene's face was marble white, but to her relief he summoned up the self-control not to move. She reached for her veil and pulled it down over her face. The men went on, leaning on one another's shoulders, still laughing.

Up the street there seemed to be a group of people standing around something or someone on the cobblestones. There were women dressed flamboyantly, a few Negroes, some more men in blue. Suddenly the group broke up; it was like quicksilver, for the people scattered swiftly in every direction, calling out to one another. She thought she could distinguish a few words: *"Il est mort . . ."* "The dead wagon . . ." *"Vite, vite . . ."*

"Gene!"

"Don't look."

"But there's a man—"

"I know. Nothing you can do. Nothing anybody can do. Poor devil!"

At that instant M. Lemaire whirled around the corner again, this time seated in a chaise, driving what was truly a mettlesome steed, a gray. She recognized the horse and carriage which Gene had used to take them to Armand's hotel.

"Come, Marcy, I'll help you. Now then . . ." Gene almost lifted her into the chaise. "Just give the horse a slap," he told M. Lemaire. "He'll come back."

"Yes, yes. Hang on, Marcy, I'm turning." He took the whip from its socket and gave the gray a swift lick with it. The horse leaped and the chaise rocked.

"M'sieu Lemaire, there's a man in the street."

"The fever."

"He'll die."

"Probably dead. I heard them shout for the dead wagon."

They had whirled around a corner, hurtling along the cobblestones. She felt strangely hot and cold, shivery and suffocating.

When they reached home, she had to conquer trembling knees in order to climb down at the big gates. She felt as if her veil might be protection from the humid air and left it down over her face as M. Lemaire climbed down with an agility which she had not noted before in all those years, led the horse around by his bridle, hooked the reins over the whip shaft, and gave the satin rump a whack. This astonished the horse, who started off again at a leap, this time toward the bank.

She opened the small door in the gate.

It was safe here, inside the gates, inside the garden, the house all around her.

No, it wasn't safe anywhere, not from the yellow fever. A man dying in the street—oh, no, yellow fever could not be penned up, held within boundaries. She had to get Brule, all of them, to Nine Oaks. It might be no safer there, but it seemed safer. Gene must get the passes soon. Perhaps he couldn't!

M. Lemaire, after his display of energy, had sunk down beside her, mopping his forehead with a fine cambric handkerchief which she recognized as one of her father's. "You really behaved very well about that woman."

"What woman?" Had the man in the street yellow fever? The man from whom that cluster of bright dresses, bright turbans and blue-coated men suddenly dispersed, fled as if from a plague?

"Armand's woman, of course," M. Lemaire reminded her.

"Oh, that." She thought for a long but revealing moment, then removed her veil and her black bonnet. "At least he had some happiness before he died. He'd never have brought her home if he hadn't wanted her."

M. Lemaire turned toward her. She could feel a sharp scrutiny in those dreamy eyes. Perhaps he had always seen everything. "All the same, I didn't like her looks. Have you ever seen a young tiger?"

"Why, no!"

"Neither have I," said M. Lemaire in what, Marcy felt briefly, was an unusual moment of truth. "But I can imagine the lithe, destructive, utterly feral beauty. Oh, yes," he finished dreamily. "Like this woman."

"Well, it can't matter to us."

"M'm. I'm not sure. But I feel—yes, I do feel, Marcy—that Gene must hurry to get your pass. That woman is dangerous."

"She can't hurt me. Why should she? I'm not afraid of her! I'm afraid of yellow fever!"

FOURTEEN

The dinner gong rang from the lower gallery. Jason was there, standing in the shadow of a pillar, swinging the bell slowly.

Marcy went to her room, changed to a thin muslin dress darned at the elbows, flung her black dress and bonnet and veil into the armoire—deciding never to wear them again, no matter what anybody said—and went down to the dining room.

The meal was not very generous. She went to the kitchen afterward, bringing Liss another of the major's gold pieces, and found that a crisis had developed. Jason had decided that, at his age and considering his years of service, he was to be called Uncle Jason. Liss did not agree.

Both expected Marcy to decide. Jason was sulking, his lower lip sticking out. Liss's candidly ugly face wore a heavy scowl, which threatened trouble. Brule was at a table, placidly spooning up gumbo.

Marcy put down the gold piece. "For more food, Liss. Now then—"

"It's my place," Jason said.

"No more his place than a baboon's. Uncle!" Liss stirred

something in a big iron pot. "If you mean me to go to the French Market today, I ain't."

Marcy had never known Liss to refuse anything. Liss stirred and then said, "They's got fever. Won't attack us colored folk. But you—no telling what that yellow fever do. I'm putting garlic in everything. Much as you can eat."

"Garlic?"

"Yes'm. Chases away that old fever. Don't know why, but those folks take garlic don't seem to take much of that old yellow jack."

Could there possibly be some medical truth in Liss's pronouncement? Marcy didn't think so; surely the doctors, and not this tall, ugly Negress from somewhere in the West Indies, would have found this link. On the other hand, Liss did know curious things about herbs.

"Alors, donnez-nous beaucoup de garlic," she said, hoping to placate. If they did manage to get away to Nine Oaks, she would need Liss. She had always needed Liss, strong and never complaining.

Old Jason grumbled something under his breath, at which Liss turned around so slowly, so deliberately threateningly, that Jason shrank back and even Marcy felt a slight chill; she made a quick retreat. She knew that the slaves had all held Liss in a certain respect, as if she had some arcane power which none of them could describe definitely but which gave Liss an undeniable authority. Voodoo? No. Liss was too sensible to put up with barbaric spells of any kind. Perhaps that was the secret of her power; she was simply, completely, a woman of strong common sense. If that common sense provided her with a reasonable deduction and thus prediction of events to come, that was all there was to it. Liss was usually right, because she was intelligent and forethinking; she thought ahead. All the same, Marcy, too, felt a certain awe when she heard one of Liss's pronouncements.

Of course, it might be that Liss had a hidden sense of humor and it amused her to frighten others with her vague talk of "them" being around to hear. It was impressive, however; no doubt about that.

The major returned unexpectedly that night.

She had seen that Jason had bolted the big door to the mews; it was now a regular chore for her—she made the trip through the stables while it was still daylight. That night she heard the distant pounding on the big door and Jason's scramble from his room through the wide stable to remove the bolt. She even thought she could hear the remote sound of the major's voice saying something or other, thanking Jason probably.

Then she heard the horse being led into the stable, his hooves striking the old wooden floor. She had been awake, thinking, thinking and finding only problems with no answers. She always came back to Major Farrell as a possible means of rescue if Gene would be unable to provide passes soon.

She roused quickly, thrust aside the entangling folds of the mosquito netting and found her peignoir and slippers. She didn't light her lamp or even a candle; she knew every inch of the way.

She crept down the gallery stairs so swiftly that she met the major walking rather heavily along the shell path, his boots making little crisp sounds. The night was dark, cloudy and heavy. The smell from the burning pitch seemed to cling to everything.

She stepped out from the shadow of the gallery. "Major."

He stopped. "Oh! I didn't mean to wake anybody."

"I wasn't asleep." She came closer to him. She hoped that the dim light would be kind to her tousled hair and her worn-out, once-elegant silk peignoir. She held it close to her body. "I want to see you."

He looked down at her. He seemed taller somehow in that dim light, very strong and solid. "I hope nothing has happened."

"We have to get away, Major! There's yellow fever—"

"Yes. I know. I hope it has not attacked anyone here!"

She remembered with dreadful clarity the man dying in the street while the people around him fled. "It's everywhere, Major. I saw a man today on the street. He died—"

He took her hands. "I don't think it will reach you. People in what you call the Garden District seem to have less fever than the people down by the river."

"It can strike anywhere."

His hands felt strong and comforting, almost as if he could fight off the disease. He drew her to the same bench where they had once sat and talked with a certain ease and frankness. "Something has happened. Was it the man dying in the street?"

"Partly."

He held her hands with that strong, warm grip. "It's tragic, yes. I've read of the epidemics of yellow fever here. It does seem to strike more viciously around river or swampy areas, for no reason that anybody knows."

She decided to risk all. "Can you get us a pass to go to our plantation? It is upriver. Then along the Bayou Reve. It's called Nine Oaks. We always went there in the summers. Of course," she had to admit, "sometimes yellow fever strikes there, too. But here—and besides . . ." Get it out, she told herself. "Besides, there are some cases of cholera."

His grasp on her hand stiffened for a second. "I hoped you wouldn't hear of that. Who told you?"

Gene; no, better not quote Gene. "Everyone knows it. News—it's like an unseen telegraph. Travels all over the city."

"I expect the Negroes tell one another. Bad news always moves quickly."

She said, "We must have passes."

He thought for a long moment. Finally he said, "I can try to get passes for you so you can leave the city. I'm not sure that I can get passes for everyone in the house. You really are frightened."

Suddenly his kindness, which she didn't deserve, or merely the passing on of a burden which was too heavy for her to carry, broke down her carefully stored self-confidence, and she cried recklessly, "I'm scared. I can't tell you how scared!" She was also instantly ashamed. Only that day she had reported the message she had stolen from him and pretended to him not to know the importance of.

"Don't let anyone frighten you."

"Yellow fever! Cholera!" She whispered the words, as if even speaking them aloud might bring the scourge into the lovely garden, the loved house. "That man on the street! I know he died, right before our eyes."

"I am told that that happens. Darling, try not to think of it."

Darling. And she had stolen a scrap of paper, denied it to him and then taken it to Gene. But then, perhaps he used the word lightly; sweetheart, dear, darling, were all merely words of greeting, in her experience.

However, he took her moment of silence as a rebuke. "I only meant—I'm not taking advantage of you. You are in a helpless position, I know that—"

"You can help."

"You mean, by getting passes for you and the whole household? Even the servants?"

She turned to him. She was so close that she could detect a faint smell of horse and leather and surely, very faintly, some kind of drink. Bourbon? But he was sober as a judge. And kind.

It had always been difficult for her to surrender to tears. Yet now she couldn't help a betraying tremble in her voice. "We've got to get away. You don't understand. It's not only the fever and the—the other." She decided to risk the truth. "Claudine intends to sell little Brule."

He suddenly put his arm around her. She felt that he could see her face as clearly as if it were daylight. "Sell that baby?"

"Yes, yes. It's all arranged."

"But that's impossible. He can't be sold—"

"Oh, yes, he can be sold. He's Claudine's property, you see."

"No, I don't see. The Emancipation Proclamation—"

"That doesn't mean anything here."

"New Orleans is under Northern command."

"It still doesn't apply. There are all kinds of ways to get around anything the Yankees tell us we must do. Or not do."

There was a suggestion of a smile in his reply. "So I'm told." He became grave again. "But to sell that handsome little boy! Who would want to buy him?"

She felt so tired all at once that she wished she could

relax in his arms and put her head on his shoulder and forget everything. She said wearily, "Someone saw him, admired his beauty. He wants to take him to some island. I don't know where or—"

"This is very bad. You say he is Claudine's property?"

"Of course. Brule, my brother, made a—a purchase of his *placée*, Angele. It is not unusual," she said hurriedly. "Brule was truly in love with Angele. But then he died, and his property—"

"Went to his legal wife. I see. And she intends to sell the child."

"Yes."

His arm still held her. The fragrant scents of flowers almost conquered the acrid stench from the pitch barrels. He said, "We can't allow that. I don't know what I can do. But I'll do something."

"Oh, if only you can."

"I will. Trust me."

He had trusted her. She had lied about the scrap of paper, and he had believed her.

"I will," she said. "I will. Thank you." She turned in his arm and looked at his face. It was dimly outlined in the night, yet oddly, she seemed to know every feature, the way his eyebrows made a straight line across his face and above very steady, very observant eyes (she reminded herself); his nose, straight, strong, not too strong; his mouth . . .

He pulled her close against him and put that mouth down upon her cheek. After a moment he moved her face with his lips and found her mouth.

The night, the scent of flowers, the drifting smoke from the pitch barrels, the hum of mosquitoes, everything vanished. She was conscious only of his nearness, of his lips, of his warmth and—why, she thought, half aware of thinking at all, it's the way it was at the ball, in the midnight garden. He lifted his head, laughed softly, took her chin in one hand and lowered his face to her face again.

She couldn't check a suddenly whirling world. Her heart was thudding, her pulses were racing.

He lifted his face a little and said low, close to her, "That night at the dance. I remember what you wore. Pink something, with lacy things, and your hair was done up high so I could see your face, and your shoulders and arms were bare and white, and you danced and laughed, and then later, in the garden, I fell in love with you." Suddenly he was speaking in almost an objective way, as if viewing himself from the outside. "I couldn't get you out of my mind. Something—I can't describe it. Every time I met another girl, I kept thinking of you and that night." He seemed to come to a decision, as if he had argued with himself and reached a conclusion. "Yes," he said in that same, almost impersonal, objective way. "That must be what happened to me. When I saw the name Chastain at headquarters, it was like fate or—or because I still, after two years, so wanted to see you again and either know that I was deceiving myself, imagining something that wasn't so, couldn't be true—or that I wasn't imagining anything. Well, so—then I knew."

She meant to say *no, no*. She said, "You can't—you can't—"

"Don't pull back, darling. Time is so very important just now, you know. Time may not be very long for either of us. You do like me, don't you?"

"Yes." She pulled herself away from him, but only by battling her own wishes. She mustn't give way to feelings or—or anything, she thought; not just now. He was right in saying that time could be their enemy.

He laughed again, low. "You must have remembered me. You saved me from some serious trouble, to say the least."

"Oh, that."

"You were honestly afraid of my being given a court-martial."

"Yes. Yes, I was."

"You knew that I hadn't shot Armand."

"Certainly."

"So you lied for me."

But that was because I was told to gain your confidence, she thought swiftly; yet she had known in her heart that he was not the kind of man to waylay Armand and shoot him from the darkness of some street corner. "I knew you hadn't shot him."

"How did you know?"

"How?" She said helplessly, "Because."

There was amusement in his voice. "Because you had met me in respectable surroundings? Because you had danced with me? Because, just possibly, you remembered me?"

She couldn't stop it. "You acted as if you had only the very slightest, most unimportant recollection of having met me!"

"Well, naturally. What else could I do or say? You were so formal, so distant. And it had been two years. I couldn't possibly say, 'Do you remember' . . . anything. And then, of course, you said you were to marry Armand."

She was confused and happy and frightened, all at the same time. "I wouldn't have married him. Not really."

There was a long pause, but his arms seemed closer. At last he said, "I didn't know that. I only thought that you had—oh, amused yourself, been a little flattered in some feminine way by my own quite evident feeling and—but then after Armand was killed, you invented that alibi. It wasn't possible just then for me to tell—" He checked himself.

She said, "Tell what?"

He recovered swiftly. "Tell anybody anything. There are things I have to do. You understand that."

"Like . . ." If he couldn't get passes there was still the possibility that Gene might succeed. She tried to make her heart stop thudding. "Like meeting General Grant?"

To her surprise he put back his dark head and laughed. "My dear, I haven't seen General Grant—since, oh, I don't remember. Months ago." He stopped laughing. "How did you happen to speak of General Grant?"

How, indeed? "He is planning to attack Vicksburg."

"Why do you say that?"

"It's an open secret. Isn't it?"

There was a long pause before he said very quietly, "I don't know. Perhaps everyone believes that because he is stubborn, a good fighter. Yes, I am sure people must expect him to attack Vicksburg."

"But there's the river to cross."

"There's the river to cross. As I suppose you know, it has not been easy for General Grant."

"So people say."

"Naturally, you are very much interested in Vicksburg. It's a Southern stronghold."

"Everyone is interested. Is there great suffering there?"

"I don't know." He was all at once as formal again as he had been on a very long-ago night when he had been introduced to her and had bowed over her white-gloved hand. He added, as distantly, "Of course, you know it has been under heavy attack for some time."

"But Federal boats can't cross. Your army couldn't take Vicksburg! How could Grant attack?"

But she had spoken too swiftly, far too urgently. He withdrew the warm arms, which had seemed to promise her support for the rest of her life. Oh, what a thing to think, she told herself angrily.

He said obliquely, "You told me that you saw a man die on the street. That was today?"

"Yes."

"Where?"

"In the city. Not far from the bank."

Too late she saw where his questions were leading. "You went to the bank?"

"Yes. I—you see, the bank has a mortgage on the plantation and on the house. I had to try to—to get a . . ." What on earth did they call it?

He said, still distantly, "An extension. Did you succeed?"

"No. That is, I can't say yet."

"Why not? Wouldn't your friend Gene Dupre give you an extension?"

She made a quick effort to draw him away from her business at the bank. "I wish I hadn't gone." That was true enough.

"Why? Because you didn't succeed in getting the extension?"

"Because—because, for one thing, Armand's mistress was there." That ought to divert his line of inquiry.

It did surprise him. He turned toward her. "But I thought he was determined to marry you."

"Oh, yes. Of course, our marriage had been arranged for some time."

"Then this woman—is she another what you call a *placée*? Like the little boy's mother?"

"Not at all like Angele. Angele was sweet and dear and—no, she is not like Angele."

He waited. She plunged on; anything to draw him from too close an inquiry about her visit to Gene. "Armand met her, I think, somewhere near Richmond."

He thought for a few moments. "What did she want?" he asked then.

"Gene said money might be an answer."

"And you'll give it to her, I suppose."

"I have nothing to give," she said with sad truth.

"Besides," he said softly, "you didn't like her."

"No. That is—no, I didn't."

"Why not?"

"I don't know. Yes—perhaps because she—oh, I can't explain."

"I wouldn't have expected you to be jealous."

"I am not jealous. I was surprised, yes. But I think I'm glad Armand had her, someone he cared enough about to—to give him some interest. His life was so short."

"Perhaps he left her some money or property."

"Armand had nothing to leave."

"There might be something when the war is over."

"Unless you—" She bit back the word "Yankees." "Unless it is all taken away."

Again he seemed lost in thought. At last he drew away from her. "I'm keeping you in the night air. I'm told it is dangerous with so much yellow fever around. Now then—how much of that message left in my dispatch case did you report to Dupre?" His voice was suddenly different, alert and angry.

"I—"

"Don't try to lie. I might be such a fool as to believe you again. Answer me. Did you tell him 'June'?"

She couldn't, she wouldn't speak. He put his hands on her shoulders; they were not kind hands now; they were hard and tense. "What did you tell him? You saw the whole message, didn't you?"

"No. That is—"

"You saw enough. Just what did you tell him?"

"I can't—"

"You don't need to tell me. All you wanted from me is information about General Grant. What did you tell Dupre?"

She rose; she clutched her peignoir around her closely. She couldn't see his face clearly and was thankful. "Good night, Major."

His hand shot out and grasped her wrist. "Oh, no, you don't get out of this so easily. You did search my room. Didn't you?"

She took refuge in evasion. "I took no papers away. I know nothing of that."

"But you were searching my room when I found you there. You said you were looking for Armand's ring. But you were astonished when in fact you saw it there. Oh, I knew that at the time. I preferred to think something else. But then, the second time, you were searching my dispatch case. Well—you may have thought you deceived me. You did. Or at least I was only too willing to believe you. So I told myself that you couldn't lie and scheme. I told myself that you were the beautiful, truthful dear—the woman I thought of all this time. I wouldn't let myself question your honor. Don't ask me why. It's just something that happens once in a while to a man. It happened to me. So I believed you in spite of my doubts. In spite of what I now must acknowledge to be my better judgment. You are not the woman I thought you were. I can't respect a liar using her beauty to act as a spy. I was all wrong about you. I hope I'll never see you again."

She had deserved worse than that. She wrenched away from him. She ran for the stairs, her shabby slippers almost tripping her. At the top she nearly fell; she reached down, clutched off the slippers and ran in her bare feet along the gallery.

She didn't know what the major did; she didn't care, she told herself later, staring into the darkness. But she would get to Nine Oaks somehow, she didn't care how, but she was going to get there and take Brule with her.

Sometime later she heard the muffled, distant *thump, thump* of a horse's hooves.

FIFTEEN

The major was leaving again on one of his secret errands. He had barely returned. His too-quick, far too adept analysis of her own attempts to spy must have been the cause for this sudden departure. He had gone out, as usual, through the stable door to the barnyard and street. It would remain unbolted for the rest of the night, but she couldn't bring herself to go down through the darkness and bolt it.

After a while she swished the mosquito netting around sufficiently to dislodge any mosquito, hoped that Liss was right about garlic keeping away yellow fever and heard the deep roar of a gun, muffled by distance. That would have been fired down near the river; it was another custom she recognized. There were people who believed that the smoke of gun powder cleared the air of yellow fever, too; that and the smoking barrels of pitch.

She wondered how bad the fever was by now, and knew instinctively that it was worse by the hour, creeping over the city, by night as well as by day. She must get away. Now, of course, Major Farrell would never help get a pass.

Probably now he was pounding along the river road on an already weary horse, heading for some place where he could meet an emissary from General Grant. Then he could send a message to the general, warning him that something of his plans for attack had been discovered.

When he did it, he would think of her as a liar, a cheat, nothing that he had believed her to be. But he would carry out his intention to warn General Grant. Bruinsberg—she could almost see the map Gene had spread out on his desk. Grand Gulf, on the Mississippi side of the great, rolling river, had big guns. Little Bruinsberg, not even a dot on the map, would not be fortified. So, if that were really his plan, Grant could get sufficient numbers of his troops across the river, land at Bruinsberg, which must provide some sort of landing, however small—and then what? There was only one course anybody, even someone as unskilled in warfare as Marcy knew herself to be, could surmise with reasonable accuracy; his next move would simply be to march through Mississippi toward Vicksburg, and attack from the east.

The message had said clearly, "From the east."

It had also said, "June."

She got out of bed again, pushing back the netting, lighted her lamp and found a calendar. It was only the last week in April. There were weeks until June; if Gene and his friends believed her dearly bought message, there was time to warn the men defending Vicksburg. She went back to bed. The gun roared again, very far away. Perhaps some people took what comfort they could from the sound.

But Gene had not put much faith in the message; he had said it might be a trap.

If it was factual, and yet Gene and the others refused to accept it, then in a way her conscience was clear. Oh, no. That was specious reasoning; it wasn't reasoning at all. She had done precisely what Major Farrell had accused her of doing.

She closed her eyes firmly.

It didn't help, for when at last she drifted off to sleep, she dreamed and dreamed that arms were holding her, a man's face lay against her own, a man's lips covered her own, and she was lost in love with Major John Farrell.

She fought off the dream and yet, in some half-conscious way, welcomed it. Certainly it was far better than an absurdly frightening dream of the Bayou Reve Road. It did not return.

Neither did the major return; there was no sound of his horse's hooves on the floor of the stable, and no tall, swiftly moving figure came swinging up the gallery steps and along the narrow hall.

The next day was hot, sullen, very still and humid. Everyone in the house seemed still, as if waiting for something, not knowing what it would be but knowing only that whatever it was, it was going to happen. The heat was relentless. The humidity made it difficult to breathe. Only Brule seemed unaffected by the atmosphere of waiting, and played his quiet little games in the garden.

Once that morning, sitting for a few moments on a garden bench, Marcy felt herself again under observation. She turned swiftly to look out through the wrought-iron gates. It seemed to her that a figure of some kind, a man, she thought, moved quickly out of sight beyond the wall.

There was no reason to connect the figure with the man who, according to M. Lemaire, had been escort for Armand's mistress on her visit to the bank. She thought of it only because, whoever he was, he slid so quickly out of sight.

She wondered what Madame Lorne was doing and what she planned to do. She was reasonably sure that she would not give up quickly. Yet Marcy owed her nothing; she had nothing at all to give her. To propitiate the pitiful memory of Armand, she promised herself never to yield even the Ortega ring. Oddly and perhaps very wrongly, it struck her that a beauty like that could and would grasp successfully at anything she chose.

M. Lemaire apparently had quietly gone somewhere away from the house. Nobody inquired; all of them were accustomed to his elusive wanderings.

Dinner was sparse. Again Liss had refused to go to the French market. Her ugly face was set. "Not while the yellow jack is getting worse." When Marcy asked how she knew that, Liss merely shook her head, adjusted the brilliantly colored head wrap she always wore, and sliced more garlic into the rather thin, watery gumbo she was stirring.

Nobody complained either of the garlic or of the wateriness of the gumbo. The next day, Marcy resolved, she really must discover some way to buy more food; at the same time she didn't want to sally forth into what might be a fever-ridden district herself, and logically could not ask anyone else to do so.

After dinner she drifted out to the garden in the hope of getting some fresh air. It was the humidity, Marcy decided, which made her heart feel heavy—the humidity and the muggy air with its underlying stench of tar barrels burning. She really had to make up her mind to secure food for them. If she wore a heavy veil, perhaps it would protect her from yellow fever.

A great pounding at the gate aroused her. She looked and saw a petite and graceful figure, all in artfully draped black. She knew who it was even before the heavy black veil was flung up, revealing a lovely, triangular face and sparkling topaz eyes between heavy black lashes. She could not merely sit there and refuse that summons. She went slowly to the gate, pulled up the latch and stood aside as the charmingly curved small figure moved deliberately inside the garden.

"I came to see you," said Madame Lorne composedly.

Without hesitation, uninvited, she moved across to a bench. She sat down with the utmost composure and said, softly, "I came for Armand's ring."

Marcy remained standing. In a way she had been grateful to Madame Lorne, but only because she must have given Armand some interest in his far too brief life. She was not prepared to give her the Ortega ring.

Madame Lorne's lovely eyes were bright and determined. "You don't want to give it to me."

Marcy must have made a gesture of refusal.

"Why not?"

She had to reply to that. In another part of her mind she wondered if anyone was outside, close to the gate, listening to this conversation. She was instinctively sure that a shadow had slid out of sight. She said, "Because it is the Ortega wedding ring."

"That's why I want it," said Madame Lorne sweetly.

"You have come to the wrong person. I can't give you the ring."

"But you have it?"

Marcy tried to evade. "Why do you think that?"

Madame Lorne's eyes fixed themselves like those of a very pretty young cat about to pounce. "I tell you to give it to me. It belongs to me."

Armand must have promised it to her. Armand must have told her of the ring.

Madame Lorne added, sweetly and incredibly, "I was Armand's wife."

Someone inside the house said something indistinguishable to someone else and laughed. Tante Julie, of course. Finally Marcy found words. "That is not possible."

"It is true. I want my wedding ring. He promised it to me."

"But he gave it to me."

"I want it. Now."

"It belongs to neither of us. It goes back to the Ortega family."

"I am the Ortega family—that is, I was his wife. The ring is mine."

If only it was not so hot and humid; Marcy touched her face and was dimly surprised to find it cool. "I don't believe you! The ring belongs to his family. I can't give it to you."

"You've got to. It is my property. You have it here. Give it to me."

Marcy was slowly beginning to find a modicum of common sense. "You did not tell Gene—M'sieu Dupre—that you had been married to Armand."

"Certainly not," said Madame Lorne calmly.

"Why not?"

Lovely black eyelashes swept down and up again. "My own reasons. Nothing to do with you."

"You are mistaken. Armand was to marry me. At once.

He would never have committed"—what was the word? Oh, yes—"bigamy."

"I was his wife."

It was no answer. Marcy said slowly, "Armand planned our marriage. In the cathedral. With Father Carlos performing the ceremony. Armand would not have done that if he had already been married."

"My ring," said the woman.

"And besides—why, you told M'sieu Dupre that your name is Lorne. Why? If you had been married to Armand, you would have used his name—"

"That is none of your business." Again her eyelashes flickered; her eyes hardened. "But I'll tell you why. Armand said that I must meet his family, get to know them. We must have their approval before we told them that we were to be married. Again."

"Were to be married?"

"We had already been married. I told you. It was only a question of waiting for a few weeks, something like that, so his family could meet me. It was Armand's idea."

Marcy could have guessed that. In spite of herself, she began to believe Madame Lorne. No, no. If she had been married to Armand—Madame Ortega? No! It simply was not possible.

Yet had Marcy ever really known Armand? Curiously, in that second she realized that always, even as a child, Armand had seemed to erect a kind of wall around himself and his innermost feelings.

Madame Lorne said pleasantly, "I'll not give up. It is mine."

M. Lemaire—again, Marcy thought, but was not surprised—rescued her. He came through the small door, jauntily swinging the gold-headed walking stick which belonged to Marcy's father. He saw Madame Lorne, checked for a second and then came toward them. Madame Lorne's utterly beautiful face fixed itself for an instant. Then she said to him, "I came for some of my property. I am Armand's wife—I mean, widow. I want the Ortega ring—my wedding ring. She refuses to give it to me."

"Dear me!" M. Lemaire looked thoughtfully at the

gold-topped walking stick. "Then you'll show us your marriage certificate, no doubt."

There was a long moment of silence. Again someone in the house spoke distantly to someone else.

Madame Lorne (Ortega? No!) smiled. "It was left in—in a trunk. The trunk was lost."

"Too bad," said M. Lemaire gently. "Now, you see that even if my—niece had the ring, she couldn't possibly give it to anyone but a member of the Ortega family."

"I tell you, I was his wife!"

M. Lemaire said mildly, "Ah, well, we must see Gene about this, I fear, Marcy."

Madame Lorne's piquant, determined face was suddenly, delicately scornful. "That lawyer!"

"Banker," M. Lemaire said again, mildly.

Madame Lorne laughed, musically. "I'll see him again too! I'll find my certificate. But it doesn't matter. I want the ring."

"Really now, you aren't going to get it. Not now. Not by making such demands. Come." He took her elbow. It was unbelievable, but he turned her, flowing black veil, elegant black costume and all, toward the gate.

She took a step or two and stopped. "I know all about you, Mr. Lemaire!" This time the lovely topaz eyes turned fiery. "I denounce you! I spit upon you!" she said evenly, and did.

M. Lemaire, with the new agility Marcy had observed, saw it coming and moved adroitly. A tall tiger lily just behind him quivered as if insulted, as indeed it had been.

Then M. Lemaire grasped Madame Lorne's elbow again. He did not seem to exert pressure, but he must have done so, for all at once she was walking gracefully toward the gates. He opened the small door with his free arm; he quietly—yet forcefully, certainly—ushered her out. He closed the gate and turned the bolt. Madame Lorne, still self-possessed, vanished.

M. Lemaire came back to Marcy, swinging the walking stick again.

"Her escort was waiting for her," he said almost idly. "I do wonder who he is."

"Do you think—can Armand really have married her?"

He considered it. "Stranger things have happened. It does strike me that just possibly—just possibly, Marcy, she killed Armand."

SIXTEEN

Everything in the garden seemed to stop for a second and then whirl around Marcy. M. Lemaire eyed her thoughtfully. "Somebody killed him."

"But if she was speaking the truth, if he really had married her—"

"Yes, I know. She'd have been better off simply to tell of the marriage. Produce some kind of proof. It is possible that Armand himself had this wedding certificate she claims to have lost. Naturally, he wouldn't have permitted anyone to know of its existence. He was determined to marry you. He felt very strongly about that. He suddenly insisted upon an immediate marriage. Probably tired of her—or there could have been a more pressing reason." M. Lemaire swished the overgrown hedge of laurels below the gallery with the walking stick. "Yes, I can see what could have happened. He met her somewhere and either brought her here or she followed him. I'll try to get at the truth about it, although that part is not really important. The important aspect is Armand's murder. I never believed in a street thug. Did you?"

"Why, I—yes. Yes, I did. At least—"

"At least you wanted to. Much more comfortable for everybody. I understand that even the Union command has taken that view. They are no longer suspicious of our major. However, does he wish you to continue your alibi for him?"

"I think so. Yes. But—oh, he knows that I tried to spy. He knows I searched his room. He knows I found that piece of paper and accused me of passing on the information that Gene says cannot be accepted yet as fact."

"I see. He didn't like that."

"He said—he said that he had believed my explanation against his better judgment." She avoided M. Lemaire's vague, yet all too perceptive gaze.

"So he put two and two together. Did you admit the truth?"

"He knew it. He said . . ." She could feel color sweep up into her face. It was hard to meet M. Lemaire's gaze. "He was"—she swallowed—"very disappointed in me."

"I see."

He turned aside, sat down on a bench, rested his chin on the gold head of the walking stick, and sighed. She sat down beside him. Presently he said, "Now, my dear there are other men, you know. The major is not the only one."

"You see too much."

"I see that you are in love with him. At least you think you are."

"I don't want another man—" It was said too defiantly.

"M'm. Well, where is he now?"

"I don't know. He went away last night just a little while after he told me he knew that I had lied."

"Riding?"

"Yes."

"Probably riding to tell somebody that the message had been handed over to Gene."

"I thought that. I was afraid of that."

"I believe the message, you know. Gene still hesitates. Fool!"

"Did you see him today?" She was surprised. M. Lemaire had not, in her previous experience, exerted himself to do anything which required activity.

"Oh, yes. I wanted to find out more of this—woman now calling herself Armand's wife."

"What did you discover?"

"Not much. I found the house she and Armand must have lived in. A small house. Windows shuttered up. Closed. I thumped at the door with this." He gestured with the walking stick. "Nobody came. No servants, I'd say. Unless, of course, they did have servants who ran away. Yellow fever or—anyway, nobody answered. But the escort, the man—I'm sure he was waiting at the corner when I came home just now." He began to poke holes in the rose bed nearby with the stick. "I stopped at the bank. Gene is pigheaded. Still refuses to believe that Grant is planning to cross the river in June. Of course, now that your major—"

"Don't call him 'my major.' " She snapped it out and knew again that she was too defiant.

M. Lemaire apparently didn't hear. "Now that he has gone so quickly—I'm sure it is to send a warning to the effect that some of us here know of Grant's plan—yes, now Grant may change the plan. Depends upon time, of course. Your—I mean, the major must use a courier. I'm sure that there must be some chain of information based somewhere nearer than Baton Rouge."

He poked another hole beside a rose and said, "Armand's murderer ought to be discovered, and his identity proved. It was really very wicked of Armand to accuse Major Farrell. Yet I can see how that happened. My feeling is that Armand didn't believe that he was going to die. He merely had a chance to make trouble for the major, and did. I'm sure it must have been that way. Armand knew that he was wounded, yes. He even knew that he was being given extreme unction. Yet Armand was not of a nature to give up anything, especially life. So he saw a chance to accuse the major, and did, and then, poor foolish Armand, died. Impulsive. These young men in New Orleans who have been given paroles for one reason or another still make plots, conspire. They call themselves the Defenders, as I'm sure you know.

"Armand was full of hatred for Major Farrell, partly because you seemed to like him and had known him before the war. Armand must have been sure that Major Farrell had pulled strings to get himself billeted here in order to see you again. He may have felt that the major might have threatened his sudden determination for an immediate marriage. But the major is also a Union officer. Yes, I'm afraid that was poor Armand's intention. And then he died. And this woman may have killed him.''

"Oh, no! Not if she loved him."

"As Gene told us, Armand informed this woman that he intended to marry you. Since Armand really could not have meant bigamy, I can't believe in her marriage. She strikes me as the kind of woman who would refuse to accept his decision. But if he convinced her—yes, she might have killed him."

"Oh, no! Not in revenge," she cried again, incredulous.

"No—no. Not exactly—still in fury—I don't know. A difficult woman to understand." He went on: "Whatever her motive—yes. I think she might have killed him. It has been comforting in a way for us to blame a street thug, a drunken Yankee soldier, or even, knowing Armand's temper, somebody with whom he had quarreled. But I am beginning to wonder... On the other hand, this woman certainly might have been better off if he had lived and married you. Then she *could* have blackmailed him."

"If she really was married to Armand, he couldn't have married me."

"Not legally. I cannot believe there was a legal marriage. Here is Liss, looking like a thundercloud."

It was indeed Liss. Her chin was set, her ugly face was lined and angry. She marched across the garden in such a threatening way that Marcy had a wild notion it was lucky Liss did not happen to be carrying the heavy iron poker which accompanied her on her forays upon the market. She stood before Marcy. "It's got to stop. You've got to stop it."

M. Lemaire drifted quietly away. Marcy said, "Stop what, Liss? What's gone wrong?"

"She's going to sell that little boy."

"I know but—"

"Tomorrow."

"*Oh, no!*"

"The man comes for him then. She told me to pack up his clothes. As if he had any real clothes. I made his little dresses from some of Miss Claudine's old dresses when she throw them away—at least she put them away in a cupboard when she start to wear black all the time. So I took the old dresses and made the dresses for Bébé Brule. Miss Claudine very, very angry when she see them on him."

Unexpectedly, Liss grinned, showing enormous, square white teeth.

"What did—what happened?" Somehow Marcy had to know the end of that little episode.

"Oh, nothing," Liss said rather airily. "I just turn up my eyes like this." She turned up her eyelids and stared strangely, solemnly, yet wildly, too, at nothing in the world; Marcy could easily have convinced herself that Liss was calling upon some power, probably the powers of darkness. "And then," Liss said, resuming her normal gaze, "I say this." She jumbled up words, solemnly too, almost chanting.

"Liss! You're scaring the daylights out of me!"

"Scared daylights out of Miss Claudine," said Liss with some satisfaction. "But . . ." She sobered. "She a wicked, mean woman, Miss Marcy. But I can't see how she could have shot M'sieu Armand."

"Can't see—Claudine—oh, no! *She* didn't shoot him!"

"Could have," Liss said dourly. "Mean enough. Maybe she afraid after you marry him he manage to take more property than Miss Claudine want to lose. Your father gave your brother half of the house and the money and Nine Oaks when he marry Claudine—at least that way it look to me."

"Why—why, yes. It does. That is, only half. My father owns the other half." But Marcy tried to rally her scattered wits. "She couldn't have shot Armand. She was at the supper table when he was killed."

Liss sighed. "Yes'm. That I know. But she a wicked woman, just the same. She got no right to sell that baby."

Tomorrow, Marcy thought desperately. It left no time. No time at all. Liss said again, "He your brother's son. She got no right—"

"Liss, yes. I'm afraid she does have the right."

"You say that! You!"

"Wait, Liss. You see, she owns him."

"Can't. You brought him here!"

"But legally—by law, you see—he is her property."

Liss took a hissing breath. "Then God help the Yankees," she said. Marcy thought, God help—oh, for claiming to free all the Negroes held in slavery in the states that had seceded. Nowhere else. It was a curious provision, Marcy had always thought. Liss showed her square white teeth. "I don't let her sell him." She whirled around and stalked back toward the carriage entrance and the kitchen. What would she do to stop the sale? What could she do?

What could Marcy herself do? Tomorrow!

Gene couldn't have stopped it. Gene had admitted he could not do so legally. M. Lemaire? Hopeless. As if anticipating problems, he had discreetly vanished the instant Liss bore down upon them.

She must try to reason with Claudine. She had not much hope of success, but she must try.

She found Claudine sitting in the salon, stitching calmly at a lacy handkerchief. Marcy's approach lacked tact, perhaps, but there was no other way; she had to be direct. "Claudine!"

Claudine's smooth blond head lifted, as if she had not been aware of Marcy's entrance. The long festoons of blond curls dangled on either side of her pink-and-white face. Her lovely gray eyes showed no expression whatever. "Yes, Marcy."

"You can't sell Brule!" Marcy cried. "You can't do it, Claudine. It's inhuman. It's—wicked. You can't do it!"

"Dear me, Marcy. Why not?"

"Surely you don't intend to—not really. Surely Liss was mistaken."

"So Liss told you!" Her eyes hardened.

"And Gene told me. But Liss said tomorrow."

"That's quite right." Claudine assumed her sewing.

"You can't! I won't let you. I . . ." Marcy advanced upon her so swiftly that Claudine sensed some physical danger.

She sprang up, dropping her needlework. "How do you propose to stop me? How dare you try to stop me!"

"I'm going to stop you. I'll never let you . . ." Marcy

must have made some threatening gesture without really knowing it, for one of Claudine's hands shot out and struck Marcy savagely across the face. "Take that, you little fool! Pretending to act like a patriot. Spy on the major, and all the time so mad in love with him that you hang around him like a lovesick girl, which is what you are. You—"

By this time Marcy had got her breath, and her own hands involuntarily shot out and grasped at Claudine's curls, and all at once it became a struggling, scratching brawl. A real brawl, for Claudine had one of Marcy's arms turned painfully behind her and was pulling it up, while Marcy's other hand had got a long blond curl of Claudine's and was yanking with all her force. Oddly, neither of them knew she was making any noise at all, but they must have been screaming, for suddenly Tante Julie was with them, dragging them apart. Stopping them.

"For heaven's sake," Tante Julie gasped.

Marcy, panting, put her hand to her face where Claudine's fingernails must have left scratches, for it stung.

Claudine, her face screwed up with pain, was pushing and stroking at her curls. "She nearly killed me," Claudine cried.

"You hit me first," shouted Marcy and instantly realized how very childish she was.

She turned around and went out of the room. Tante Julie had not yet got her breath after her herculean efforts in pulling the two girls apart.

Once in her own room, Marcy straightened her tousled dress and examined her cheek, which did indeed show three red scratches.

But in a deep, altogether unladylike way, she felt better. She wondered vaguely how long it had been since she had felt so strong a desire to pull Claudine's dangling blond curls. Shocking!

But satisfactory. She hoped Claudine had got the worst of it. Her arm was only a little sore.

She sank down on the bed. Nothing was settled. Merely an indecent but strangely gratifying brawl had taken place. Tomorrow the buyer would come for Brule.

Well then, she would have to appeal to the major again.

She had little, if any, hope for that. But something—something had to be done. All sorts of wildly impossible suggestions surged through her thoughts.

The day dragged on, stiflingly hot. She saw nothing of Liss or Brule. Claudine sat at supper, pretty and cool, but her fair curls, which had always hung down on either side of her face, had vanished; for one fantastic, savage instant it occurred to Marcy that perhaps she had pulled one of them entirely out. She was mistaken, however; Claudine had merely coiled them all very neatly above her ears. Out of reach, Marcy thought in another triumphant instant, and at the same time knew with terrible clarity that she had probably only increased Claudine's determination to sell Brule. She could have pulled Claudine bald-headed, and still Claudine would have sold the child.

Only once did her feelings take control again, and that was when M. Lemaire looked at her face and said with a slight gleam in his eyes, "What happened to your face, Marcy? It looks as if it had been scratched."

"A cat did it," Marcy said before she could stop herself. Tante Julie swiftly made conversation.

It struck Marcy, as it had before occurred to her, that it was a pity Claudine had inherited the Dupre blood, good looks and charm, but not the good nature that Gene seemed to have. She wished that Claudine had shared at least a little of Gene's warmth and compassion. He had felt genuinely sorry to tell her that he could not accept the message she had found until at least he had consulted his associates. She could only guess at the various identities of the young men who made up the Defenders. It was better not to know.

After supper Marcy went out to the garden again; from there she could hear and intercept the major if he did return. If he didn't return that night—well, what could she do? For the moment she forgot what had become an automatic glance around the garden and the galleries to make perfectly sure that no pair of eyes were anywhere near, watching her.

Again, a hundred mad schemes crossed her mind, only to be dismissed as impractical and, indeed, impossible. She couldn't ask Liss to take the boy to her friends, wherever or whoever they were. He would be found; Claudine would see to that, and Liss and her friends blamed.

The night grew darker; the smell of burning pitch began to waft through the wrought-iron gates. She had snatched up a fan from a table as she went out upon the gallery, and she carried it with her down to the bench from where she would hear the major, if he returned. She waved away a whining insect. For the first time in her life it occurred to her that some laws seemed to have been made to protect the guilty, not the innocent. Brule was guilty of nothing but being illegitimately born.

It was an unusually quiet night. The sky seemed low and black; not a star showed through. The shapes of the shrubbery lining the galleries were almost obscured; she could barely detect the slender white pillars which supported the gallery opposite her. She began dismally to believe that it was unlikely that the major would return that night. She had waited, she acknowledged at last, a very long time as the shadows around her deepened and the scent of flowers grew so heavy that it almost masked the acrid tinge of burning pitch. It was strangely lonely in the garden below the windows of the house she had known all her life. Unheralded, it came again, an atavistic sense of menace. Someone was watching her.

Oh, no! There was no one in the garden except herself; there were no eyes peering at her from any deeper shadow. She could not help looking hard at the surrounding shapes of flower beds and shrubbery and the house itself. The white shells of the driveway made only a faint, lighter tracery. The shrubbery hugging close to the house, close to her, was just the same. But as she watched, a massive clump of crepe myrtle changed its shape entirely.

SEVENTEEN

Had someone been standing in its shadow, taking advantage of the darkness of the night? No, she must be mistaken. The shadows had confused her. But then she heard distantly the gentle rattle of tiny shells in the driveway.

So someone *had* been there, watching her. Waiting? Why?

Where had he gone, then? Worse, where had he come from?

She was suddenly afraid. There had been somebody there. Whoever it was had guessed her alarm and tiptoed stealthily, lightly toward the stables. And toward the carriage entrance to the mews.

She had to move. There was no reason for terror. She must move—find Jason, find someone. Suppose she screamed. Everyone could hear her.

Whoever had watched and waited—for what? her senses clamored again—in the shadow of the great clump of crepe myrtle had now gone. Hadn't he?

The image of Liss—strong, battling Liss with her poker— was the only inducement that could have moved her. She sprang up and then thought, no, no, move carefully. Don't let him know of your alarm.

But, of course, it was only—only a prowling Yankee, seeing the carriage door open, as Jason must have left it and she had forgotten it. He had crept into the garden, waiting for a chance to—well, what? Loot the house? Anything!

She clutched her skirts around her and ran, not along the shell-made driveway which would rattle and betray her, but carefully along the grass edges of the flower plots to the kitchen door. There was no light there; as she cautiously opened the door, Liss said hoarsely in the darkness from her room beyond the kitchen, "No, you can't take him. I'll not let you!"

"Liss!" Rather to her surprise her voice shook. "Liss, it's only me. Liss, someone was in the garden."

For a long second, there was silence. Then Brule piped up, *"Qu'est-ce que cela?"*

"Nothing, little one, nothing." Marcy could never have dreamed that Liss's voice could become so gentle, so soothing. A vesta flared beyond the kitchen, outlining Liss's room and Brule's small bed. Claudine would never permit him to have a room anywhere near her own; Liss had offered the child protection, for Marcy herself had been conquered by her own recognition of what Brule's presence must mean to Claudine, a pricking, sharp sting every time she looked at him. It was Claudine who had refused to permit him to share the table with the family. Yet, again, Claudine had a certain justification.

"Who is there, Miss Marcy, who—"

"He's gone, Liss. Whoever it was. He was in the garden. I heard him on the driveway, running toward the stables." The light became steady as Liss lighted a lamp; she then came into the doorway, a tall, gaunt and incredibly welcome figure. "Who was it?"

"Oh, I don't know. I don't know."

"You're scared."

"I'm terrified. He must have been there in the garden for a long time just—just watching me. Or waiting. Oh—oh, I don't know, Liss."

"You'd better come in here." Marcy almost fell across

the kitchen with its heartening odors of Liss's good cooking, and went into the big woman's room; it was small, but adequate. Her father had always seen to the comfort and care of his slaves. Brule was sitting up, dark eyes wide with excitement at this, to him, delightful break in the night's sleep.

Marcy caught her breath. "Liss, I don't know who it was in the garden. I don't know how long he was there. But I think, I'm sure, he ran away, out through the mews. I didn't see about the bolt." How could she have been so dangerously careless! "Jason—"

"Jason's an old fool. I'll look."

"No, wait. Some Yankee. He might still be there."

"Better not be," said Liss grimly as she snatched up a cloak and the poker and went out. Marcy knew that she ought to follow her, give her help if she needed it. Not that Liss ever required help. She went out into the still blackness of the night again and heard Liss tramping through the stable.

She knew her when she returned, a tall, stalwart figure, vaguely darker than the night. "Gone," Liss said abruptly. "That old Jason. Can't ever remember to bolt those doors."

"Then, if he's gone—oh, Liss, it *must* have been only some prowling Yankee." They moved back into the dimly lighted kitchen. "What you sitting out there in the night for?" Liss said sternly. "Catch your death."

"Not on a night like this." All the same, there was a curious chill up her back. She replied as obediently as a child. "I've been waiting for the major. But, Liss, he didn't • come."

"Why did you wait?"

"Because I hoped he might do something, anything, to stop their taking Brule."

The child piped up again from the bedroom: *"Qu'est-ce que cela?"*

"Never mind," Marcy said quickly.

"Then we'll take him away ourselves," said Liss. "Go and get yourself dressed." She went into the bedroom and hauled out a dark dress for herself. "I'll dress the boy."

"Where can we take him?"

"I have friends." Liss's ugly face emerged from the dark folds of a dress she was pulling over her head. She reached for her usual white headwrap, discarded it and found a dark one. Brule was fascinated. "But it's not morning!"

"Non, mon petit. We are going for a—walk. Now hurry, Miss Marcy, dress yourself."

"But, Liss—you know there's yellow fever."

Liss's dark eyes fixed themselves on nothing. Then she sank down on a chair, and for the first time in her life Marcy saw the rugged, ugly face with its deep, drawn lines dissolve into weakness; Liss put both her hands over her face. "God forgive me, I forgot. My friends—they live near the levee. Near the river. No, we can't take him there."

Marcy sat down on Brule's small bed. "We've got to do something, Liss."

Liss's hands dropped. "Listen!"

She had heard it first. Marcy listened and then heard also a kind of thump and distant rattle. Liss sprang up. "It's that Yankee returned. Or the major. I bolted the door to the barnyard. I'll see." She snatched up the forbidding poker again and went out. Marcy followed her and could barely distinguish her figure whirling around the carriage entrance to the stable and out of sight. She stopped at the black cavern of the barn and mews entrance. She heard Liss say softly, "Who is it?"

A man murmured beyond that black cavern, and Liss said, "Yes, sir."

There was the thud and rattle of a bolt being moved, a draft of chillier air, and the smell of the stables swept out of the black void. There was the measured thud of a horse's hooves on the wooden floor of the barn. It was the major.

Liss began: "Sir, *Monsieur le Commandant*—"

"Well, Liss. Thank you for letting me in."

"Monsieur le Commandant—Miss Marcy is waiting. She'll tell you."

"I'll let my horse into his stall. Where is Miss Marcy?"

"Here—"

"What's wrong?"

Liss murmured something; then the major himself came, running out of the blackness; Marcy could barely catch a shining glimpse of an epaulet and brass buttons. "What is it?"

She told him quickly. "Brule—they will take him away tomorrow..." She must have said more in her almost incoherent whispers, for Liss said, whispering too, "My friends, down near the river. We can't take him there! The fever."

He understood. He said promptly in a low voice, "Certainly not. Well, then where can we take the boy, Marcy?"

"I thought—oh, I've been thinking all along, I told you. If I could get to Nine Oaks—"

Liss added, "Along the River Road to the Bayou Reve Road. Away this side Baton Rouge—"

"All right. We'll manage. Get some clothes on, Marcy. You, Liss, dress the boy and gather up some food."

Marcy was almost dizzy with relief. "You'll take us there!"

"What else is there to do? He may not be safe there, of course. But for the time being—"

"Passes," Marcy cried. "I have no pass."

"I can manage that, I think. I'll try. The main problem is another horse. Can you ride, Liss?"

Liss would have agreed to swim the Atlantic. *"Ah, oui, m'sieu. Certainement."*

"Get yourselves ready. I think I know where I can get a horse—" He stopped abruptly as a yellow rectangular patch sprang up over the blackness of the garden. All three of them looked up. Marcy whispered, "It's from Claudine's window."

"Then we must hurry," said the major coolly, and turned back into the dark recess of the stable.

Liss vanished. Marcy crept along the gallery just below Claudine's window. She watched, scarcely breathing. At last, after what seemed to her a long time, Claudine's window turned dark again. Then Marcy sped about, dressing. A riding skirt, hot on that night, still hung in her armoire. No riding boots; they had gone long ago and had not been replaced. A white basque, tight and hot too, but the only one she could find; she left the top buttons undone. She remembered and found an old carpetbag in a corner of the armoire. It was a splendid bag, tapestry with amber handles. She had last carried it on her one journey to Washington. She shoveled a handful of dresses, lingerie, anything her hands could find, into it.

All the time she listened for sounds from the stable and heard nothing.

At the last moment it occurred to her that there were a few gold coins left; and she might need them. She unlocked the drawer of the Empire chest, and clutched at the coins and also, instinctively, at the ruby and turquoise box and the Ortega wedding ring. No way to know or even guess what would be the outcome of that night, but at least she would have a little money and a box and a ring, which at the utmost need could be translated into money.

She slid cautiously down the stairway and again kept to the line of deep shadow below the lower gallery. Claudine had the ears of a cat. Claudine could rouse the house; Claudine would stop them somehow. She had taken less time than it seemed; Liss was still in the kitchen. Brule was blinking sleepily, but dressed and interested in this late-night activity. She hurried to help Liss take out cold, cherished ham and biscuits left over from one of their more lavish meals, and some cheese. They wrapped them up in a red-and-white-checked tablecloth. Then Liss carefully blew out the lamp, and they went out as silently as they could, Liss whispering to Brule that he must not speak. The stable was quiet and black. Marcy felt her way through it and tugged open the door into the mews. There they waited, not speaking, scarcely breathing. At last they heard the even tramp of a horse along the cobblestones of the dark road. A horse? Two horses, surely. Yes, two.

Suddenly there they were, the two horses, the major on one horse and leading the other. No one spoke. Somehow he got Liss into the saddle of a horse, Brule still in her arms. Liss appeared to adjust herself, the boy, and the reins firmly and efficiently. He fastened Liss's bundle and Marcy's carpetbag to the pommel of the second horse. "Lighter weight than the two of us on my horse," he said in a low voice, and then hoisted Marcy up on his horse and slid her before him as he swung up himself into the saddle. She clung to the pommel of the big Yankee-built saddle. Then they started.

The city around them was asleep. Occasionally, some dim night-light burned at a window. The smell of burning pitch was strong at first; it grew less. The major clearly knew his way through the winding, irregular streets.

But the major must have been exceedingly uncomfortable, as indeed Marcy was, huddled as closely to him as she could be. She liked the strength of the arm which encircled her, but she was also painfully cramped and uncomfortable. Gene might have lent them a chaise, easier for the journey; but Gene would not have conspired with them to act illegally. There was the red, smoky flare of lighted pine knots ahead. The major said, "It's all right. A Federal sentry post."

He reined in beside a young man in blue who held the flaming pine knot; he peered at them and said uncertainly, "Why, it's Major Farrell. But—"

"My wife," said the major without hesitancy. "Just arrived from New York. My son and his nurse are behind us."

"Oh." There was uncertainty in the man's voice. He held the pine knot higher. Several dim forms in uniform beyond the red flare stirred and moved toward them. The major said, "It's all quite in order, Corporal. I have my passes, but we are hurried."

One of the other uniformed figures came near. He, too, peered at Marcy and then at the horse behind them. Marcy glanced over the major's shoulder and was thankful to see, in the fitful flame of the pine knot, that Liss was waiting, sternly upright but holding her shawl over Brule's face. Now, if only Brule wouldn't thrust out his face with its lustrous black eyes; if only he didn't inquire in baby French what they were doing. Liss, she thought, caught her glance and moved her head once, nodding as if to say, It's all right.

The sergeant said, "Certainly, Major, if you say so. The couple ahead of you had passes."

Marcy felt the major's body, so closely pressed to her own, tighten. But he said in an uninterested way, "The couple? Messengers? Officers?"

The sergeant looked at the corporal, who removed his small blue forage cap and scratched his head. "I don't know, sir. They had passes. They had a kind of cart."

"A chaise," said the sergeant.

"How long ago?" the major asked, but still as if barely interested.

"About—I'd say twenty minutes. Half an hour. Said they had to be in Baton Rouge."

"Ah," said the major, "it must be the men I expect to meet there."

"One was a lady," said the sergeant.

"A lady?" The major seemed to have little interest in the answer, but the sergeant said distantly, "A small woman, young, I'd say, veiled, in black. Nobody could see her face."

But I can, Marcy thought, suddenly sure; it was small and lovely and had heavy black lashes over bright eyes. Oh, no; she *couldn't* be sure; she had no idea why the thought of Madame Lorne and some ubiquitous escort should leap into her mind.

"Ah," said the major. "Thank you, Sergeant, Corporal."

He spoke to his horse, and they clop-clopped on. But the people in the chaise ahead of them could *not* be Madame Lorne and the escort; how could they have procured passes? Marcy told herself not to yield to fancy. Besides, she thought, there was nothing but the Ortega ring which Madame Lorne could possibly want.

Once fully beyond the light cast by the pine knots, the major reined in the horse. "You are very uncomfortable," he said. "I think I can arrange a sort of pillion. I have a saddle blanket strapped behind."

Marcy heard her own faint giggle. "I've been trying to make myself small."

"I know. But—here, I'll get down and give you a hand."

He slid out of the saddle, and she was oddly regretful for the loss of the strong support of his body and his arm. But he lifted her down, and she straightened cramped legs and arms. The horse whiffled and breathed heavily and stood still at a word from the major. Liss had halted. "He's asleep, thank *le bon Dieu*," she said in a low voice.

The major approved the low voice. "We'll not have another sentry post, not on this road. But there might be guerillas."

"Guerillas?"

He was working with the rolled-up blanket; Marcy could see him only dimly. Never, she thought on a tangent, could there have been so dark and still a night, still except for a chorus of frogs and the whine of mosquitoes. He said, briefly, "Bands of men, some of them former Confederate soldiers, some of them simply renegades out to waylay passengers, steal jewelry, money, anything."

"Oh," She thought of the gold and again of the Ortega ring, and of her mother's ruby and turquoise trinket. He seemed to guess her thought, for he said over his shoulder, "If you have anything of the kind, don't try to hide it in your hair. First place they look."

"No, I—I have one or two things and the rest of the gold you gave me. But they are in my carpetbag."

Liss heard that; her horse moved restively, she clutched the reins and said grimly, "Just let anybody try to get anything from me!"

The major gave a low chuckle. "Admirable woman." He turned to Marcy. "All right. We'll try it this way."

He hoisted her up so she could cling to the saddle and adjust herself upon the rolled-up blanket. After trying it as she would a sidesaddle, to which she was accustomed, she quickly found it even more uncomfortable than before and decided to ride astride. She immediately found a certain amount of ease. Not ladylike, but no one could see her. Her indecorous behavior didn't really matter. What mattered was reaching Nine Oaks.

There was no use in trying to think ahead. She did not know what had happened to the plantation; eventually they would find out. Even if the house itself had been burned, there would be the overseer's house, a small wooden structure quite close to the main house. Or failing that, one of the Negro cabins. Guerillas—she had not known of that particular menace.

The major was in the saddle. "Now," he said, "put your arms around me. Easier for you."

She did so, and at once felt safe, holding the hard-muscled body of the man, still close to her. Close physically, she thought once. He knew her to have spied and lied and yet—and yet he came to her aid when she so desperately needed him. Suddenly she said, "That chaise ahead of us. Are they really—"

"Messengers I expect to meet? No. I was only talking. By the way, do you know—do you have loyal friends in Baton Rouge?"

She thought swiftly—cousins, cousins of Armand's, friends. At last she said dismally, "At one time, perhaps. But now I don't know. There's nobody I could go to, if that's what you mean."

"You may have no need to. It's a long and hard ride. Your house may be in perfect condition. Be sure to tell me when I should turn off the River Road."

Of course, they were on the River Road. She could see little, only the deeper shadows of trees on either side. Occasionally, below the creak of saddle leather, she thought she could hear the slow wash of the river along the bank where it took a yearly toll, nibbling at it, no matter how many willows were planted, or how many levees were built to protect the land. The major reined in his horse and listened. Then she, too, heard a kind of muffled beat somewhere on the road.

"Someone is behind us," the major said. "Too near." He half turned and spoke in a low voice to Liss, who had also checked her horse. "Follow me," he said, and turned his horse into the deeper shadows of the hedges banked up along the road.

EIGHTEEN

The hedges scratched Marcy's face and arms and legs as she clung to John Farrell. As easily as a mountain goat and clearly quite accustomed to taking refuge on orders from its owner, his horse climbed up through the thick bushes, the brambles, the clouds of gnats and mosquitoes. Then it stopped. Liss had followed, but Brule awoke and murmured.

"Stop him. Don't let him speak," the major barely whispered, but Liss's keen ears heard him, and Brule murmured another word or two but was then silent.

Marcy was silent too; there was only the heavy breathing of the horses, the swish of their tails as they tried to fight off night insects. Then Marcy heard the steady trot of a horse coming along the River Road, just below them.

Liss made a movement as her horse uttered a stifled kind of nicker. Marcy guessed that Liss had flung her shawl over his nostrils. "Good," whispered the major and listened again. Even the frogs seemed to cease in their chorus for an instant. The oncoming horse began to gallop.

"Now, I wonder who . . ." the major said softly.

Who? The night rider could be anybody. Yankee soldier,

Yankee cavalryman. Guerilla. Even the word—a new word to Marcy, though obviously well known to the major—gave her a tweak of fear.

The galloping horse went on. The major waited, still patient but listening, until the hoofbeats had completely died away. He waited again then; she could have counted to a hundred. Finally he said, "We'll go on. About how far is it now?"

How far? She couldn't remember the precise outlines of the ancient, twisted, live oaks which hung over the river, defying its muddy and hungry currents and making the turn from the River Road into the Bayou Reve Road. Liss, however, knew. " 'Bout five more miles, *M'sieu le Commandant*. Then turn left."

Liss knows everything, Marcy thought thankfully. But not quite everything, for Liss whispered sharply, "Who that man on a horse?"

The major did not reply for a moment. Then he said, "Whoever it is, he may go straight on toward Baton Rouge."

They were back now on the River Road. Once it had been smooth and easy for the rolling carriage wheels leisurely making their way from the city to the big plantations along the river. Now it was deeply rutted. One jolt would have taken Marcy off the improvised pillion if she had not grasped the major so tight around his waist that he gave a kind of surprised gurgle. Again he chuckled. "All right. You didn't strangle me. Wrong spot for strangling, anyway. The ruts were left by gun carriages."

"Oh." When the Yankees attacked Baton Rouge both by river and land, the city had been obliged to surrender; there were not sufficient means of defense.

"In the daytime this road is no pleasant sight," the major said rather somberly over his shoulder. "All the debris left by the army. It's better at night, in spite of the mosquitoes." He slapped vigorously at one cheek.

She snuggled her face against his shoulder; it protected her in a way from the gnats and mosquitoes, but she also admitted to herself that she liked the feeling of strong support the pressure of his shoulder gave her.

My wife, he had told the sentries calmly. My son. His nurse. they knew him; they must have been well accustomed to his comings and goings; they had accepted his statement without question. Wife, he had said.

The rhythmic clop of the horses, the feeling of warmth and security, the drone of the frogs which never stopped, all induced an overpowering sleepiness; her head resting against his shoulder, Marcy didn't realize that she had drifted off to a kind of drowsy semiconsciousness, through which pieces of questions, like half-seen puzzles, marched dimly.

Claudine might surmise their destination; she would certainly know that Marcy and Liss had the child. On the other hand, she might come to the more likely conclusion that they had merely taken him to one of Marcy's friends. Certainly she would go to Gene. Gene might have provided them with more comfortable transport, but Gene would not have engaged in what he knew was an illegal act. He was Claudine's cousin; they had agreed in affection no more than they had agreed in behavior. Yet they were blood kin, which was always important; somehow, family members clung together.

Once she thought of M. Lemaire, who had so entirely disappeared at the moment Liss approached with her news; it was almost as if he intended to have nothing to do with the action of stealing Brule, which he could have foreseen.

She wondered why the woman who said she had been married to Armand had threatened M. Lemaire. "I know all about you. I denounce you." Was it possible that in the accusation there was anything but anger and a desire to strike at him in revenge for his doubt as to her claims of marriage? If that was so, then Armand must have told Madame Lorne whatever the woman had said she knew. But Armand could have known nothing that could be used against M. Lemaire. There wasn't anything to be denounced, she thought, almost asleep, when a swift, more important and immediate question jerked her awake. The horse stepped into a hole just then and pulled himself up; she put up her head and said almost into the major's ear, "You knew I had—tried to spy on you. You hated me for it."

He did not reply for a moment. The horse jogged on. At last he said, "No, I didn't really hate you. And I had to help you tonight, didn't I? Was there anyone else who could?"

"Nobody."

After another long moment he said remotely, "I was under the impression that this Gene Dupre is your very good friend. He might have provided you with a more comfortable transport."

"He'd have tried to stop me. He says Claudine has the legal right to sell the boy."

"I see," he said, and Marcy caught sight of a dimly outlined, scraggy, enormous shape standing amid the darkness, draped in wispy shrouds of Spanish moss. "We turn here!" she said.

They turned into the Bayou Reve Road, and suddenly Marcy's dreams returned to her. Everything was black; she knew that trees and shrubbery grown wild surrounded them only because she knew they were there. Where was there any danger? Her dreams had been fantasy only; she was becoming superstitious, silly, childish, half believing in a threat which had existed in a nightmare. Yet she didn't like the notion that, just possibly, Madame Lorne and an escort had preceded them along the road. Armand might have told her about Nine Oaks. But there was no way to surmise how Madame Lorne could have learned of their hurried escape from the city tonight, nor was there any sensible reason for her undertaking the trip herself. She wasn't the person, the shadow, so quickly fleeing from the shelter of the heavy shrubbery. But there was her escort, that ubiquitous, never-fully-seen figure, always sliding out of sight. Had he been in the courtyard that starlit night when someone prowling there had crouched over and scuttled out of sight? Had he watched and listened in the garden that night?

Marcy was frightening herself with nightmarish fancy. All the same, neither of the two was to be trusted; she was instinctively sure of that.

They jogged on, the horse finding his careful way over

the corduroy stretches which provided passage across some of the swampy patches.

A wisp of Spanish moss brushed softly across her face, as if warning her of something it knew. The major brushed it away impatiently; she could sense his irritation by the swift movement of his arms. "I hate this stuff. Why do you let it grow all over the countryside?"

"Try to stop it." She heard herself give a faint, uncontrollable laugh; it was as uncontrollable as the Spanish moss. She sobered and added, "It does no harm."

"It's a parasite," the major said shortly.

So his world, his lawyer's world—now a soldier's world— had no use for parasites. "I expect I'm a parasite too."

He did not reply to that. "Do we stay on this road?"

"For about a mile. Then turn right. I'll tell you. We're on Chastain land now."

If it was still Chastain land, she thought; if the Yankees had not confiscated it. Suppose when they arrived they found no house at all, only the burned-out shell. Suppose the slaves had all left. Suppose—no use in trying to see ahead. No matter what had happened to Nine Oaks, it had to provide a refuge for herself and her brother's son.

What would Claudine do when she could not find the boy sheltered by a friend in the city? What would Gene feel obliged to do? Surely it would be too difficult to send anyone after them from a city held by Yankees. There would be only Yankees to pursue them, unless Gene unleashed some of his cohorts among the Defenders. This was unlikely.

Something like a flash of déjà vu struck her; she hadn't experienced this escape herself, but somewhere, somebody had. Ah, she remembered; there was the book written by a Northern woman who had never visited the South. Marcy had read the book and been surprised by the rampant melodrama; a mulatto woman, fleeing with her baby to prevent his sale, leaping over—why, yes, leaping over ice floes, pursued by a slave trader. Her father had laughed at the book, but then had sobered and said gravely that it was a book to stir up fires.

There were certainly no ice floes here. Also, she had for escort a major in the Union army and Liss, who was proving herself unconquerable.

"There seems to be a driveway here," the major said.

She lifted her head. There were dimly white stone fenceposts. "Yes, yes, turn in here."

He turned. The driveway was smoother. Perhaps no Federal troops had visited here. The horse seemed to find his way by instinct, for the trees almost met overhead. More Spanish moss touched her face like a ghostly finger.

Behind them, Liss uttered something, and Brule gave a piping cry of surprise, as if he had just then awakened to find himself in Liss's strong arms, riding through the night. The road turned in on a leisurely, graceful curve, and Marcy leaned forward, striving to see the white outlines of the house. "I can't see a thing," she said.

"Never mind. The horse can find its way."

Then they came out into the cleared circle before the house, and there the house stood, ghostly in the night but dimly visible. It was still there, then. She caught her breath in a deep sigh of relief. It was strange, though, that no Negroes came with flaring torches, either to investigate or welcome them. All around the house it was silent except for the constant croaking of frogs and the whine of insects. John Farrell said, "Funny! Frogs really are antiphonal in their croaks. Is nobody here?"

She prepared to slide down, but he got down from the saddle first and held up his arms for her. She staggered a little, owing to cramped muscles; he held her firmly, but she could see that his face was turned intently toward the house.

She said, "It's not as—elegant as the city house. But it's home and—now I can see the veranda and the door. We go this way, Major." She knew that he was looping up the reins of the horse, with the intent, she supposed vaguely, of tying him to some tree. With thankfulness for reaching Nine Oaks, but also with a terrifying fear that the house had suffered from looting and ravaging, which so often, she knew, accompanied the Union Army, she started quickly for the shadowy white shape ahead of her. She had almost reached the steps to the veranda when there was a swift, strange flash of light, and a thundering crash sent both horses plunging wildly and John Farrell cursing.

He ran to her. "Are you hurt?" He took her hard in his arms.

NINETEEN

It was a shot, that crashing, shocking sound. Birds awoke
and fluttered wildly everywhere. No Negro came running
out from the quarters beyond the house. Liss had got down
from the saddle, and Brule shrilled, "What was that? Tante
Marcy, what was that?"

John Farrell said softly, "They got here ahead of us."
Both horses were still plunging wildly. The major drew her
back from the house into the deep darkness below the trees.
Here he groped for the flying reins of his horse.

Liss had let go of her horse to hold Brule. She came near,
her tall form looming up. "Give me that other gun," she
said sternly.

That other gun? Marcy had felt one of the guns close to
her knees. The major hauled out a second one from somewhere, and without a word handed it to Liss.

"Liss, do you know how to—" Marcy began, and John
Farrell said, "Certainly she does. Aim low, though, Liss,
and don't fire until you see something to fire at."

"Yes, sir," said Liss calmly.

The great water oaks, nine of which had given the place

its name, towered over them like enormous tents curtained in Spanish moss.

They waited, all of them, hearing only the galloping, thudding hooves of Liss's horse. The sounds died slowly away, and the frogs, which seemed to have been shocked into silence, began their iterated refrain again.

John Farrell made up his mind. "You two get away from me, behind that thicket over there. I'll fire a shot and try to find out where they are."

Liss, in full command of herself and of Marcy, drew her farther into the shadow of the laurels, which rustled around them and then quivered into stillness. Presently, at some distance now—proving that the major had gone quietly along under the water oaks—there was a shot, a short pause, another shot. "Both from his gun," Liss whispered.

There was no returning fire from anywhere.

After a long wait, during which there was only the twittering of birds settling back into their trees, the whiffling breath of the major's horse, and a little murmer from Brule, which Liss hushed, quite suddenly a horse whinnied somewhere in the distance, in back of the house.

John Farrell came back, moving cautiously. "Stables back there?" he whispered.

"Yes. Workshops. The Negro quarters are further back."

"Are there usually horses here?"

"Yes. That is, there were. I don't know how it is now. There are no Negroes."

"They all gone," Liss said.

"Are you sure?"

"I know," Liss said. "Somebody would have come out by now."

"You must be right." He seemed to consider it. "Well, then we'll try to make it into the house. I'm sorry you have that light-colored bodice on, Marcy."

At first she thought, oddly for that moment, he's using my name as if he were an old friend, as if he—she cut off that flashing realization to take in the meaning of his words. "Do you mean—was that shot for me?"

"I'm afraid so. That white bodice—"

"But—nobody would try to shoot me!" She didn't believe it; it was not possible. Yet earlier that night, only a few hours ago, someone had stood behind the clump of crepe myrtle and watched her and waited and then gone sliding away into the night. But the danger hadn't been on the Bayou Road; it had waited for her at Nine Oaks.

John Farrell said quickly, "We'll get you into the house. I saw the flash of the gun from the side. Do you have a key?"

"There's always a key—"

"Hidden? All right. Now wait till I tie up my horse." There was a rustle and the sound of the saddle creaking among the shadows. He returned. "Now then. Run."

No shot came from anywhere. In seconds they had reached the steps. She sought among the strong branches of an ancient wisteria which curved over the pillars of the veranda, groped for the nail that had been there since she could remember, and found the great brass key. The major gave a little sound like a smothered laugh as she put it into his hand.

The wooden planks of the veranda creaked under their footsteps. The major found the door. There was the slight rasp of the key in the lock; then the door swung open, whining a little on its hinges. They had not been oiled, Marcy thought. But the door had still been locked. Perhaps the house had not been looted. They entered. The air inside was musty, dampish on her face.

"I think we can light a lamp," the major said. "Whoever shot at us is far away by now. I hope," he added.

"In here. I can find my way." They had entered the wide hall which ran straight through the house with living rooms, dining room and library on either side. She scarcely had to hunt for the great chair which stood beside the fireplace, or the table with its top of semiprecious stones set in mosaic that also stood near the fireplace and held a lamp. The fireplace smelled of long-ago fires and damp. Vestas were kept in a covered box on the table beside the lamp; the box was still there. She struck a vesta, and the reddish flare lighted the major's blue coat, Liss's tightly wrapped tignon, her dark face, the white of her eyes, Brule's excited face, his mop of black hair. Her hand shook annoyingly as she lifted the glass chimney of the lamp, held the vesta to its wick and replaced the chimney.

The major was giving quick glances everywhere. She followed his eyes. Nothing was different. There was no devastation, no destruction. There was only the same old sofa, same worn rugs, same portrait of some distant Chastain over the mantel, same clutter of tables and chairs and knickknacks.

"Does everything look all right?" the major asked.

"The Yankees ain't been here," Liss said.

An odd, sober look came into the major's face. Then he shook his head. "I'll search the house. You and Liss stay here."

He picked up the box of vestas, his gun in his right hand. He went swiftly but quietly out of the room.

She could hear him, striking a vesta, entering the library and then the dining room. Here it seemed he found a candle, for she went to stand in the wide doorway and saw the advancing glow of candlelight. It fell upon his boots as he mounted the curving stairway and disappeared above. She could hear him going through the enormous bedrooms, one at a time, opening armoires whose doors squealed on their unoiled hinges.

Liss calmly put down Marcy's carpetbag and her own bundle, sat on the sofa and took Brule on her lap.

The major came downstairs, heavily this time, with no attempt at concealment. He came into the room and nodded reassuringly at Marcy. "No one seems to have been in the house at all."

Liss rose. "I'll take the boy to bed. Must be bedding where I stored it. Anyway, night like this, he won't need much. I put him with me."

"Yes, please, Liss. Take one of the big bedrooms."

Liss merely scooped Brule up and tramped out of the room. At the door, however, she turned back, the shadow of a grin on her lined face. "Take your gun, Mister Major?"

It was thrust into one of the vast pockets of her apron. John Farrell chuckled. "You keep it, Liss. I'd rather have you at my side than—than plenty of soldiers I know about."

He finished rather grimly and settled himself down on a chair.

"I wonder about that couple in the carriage ahead of us," he said to Marcy after Liss had disappeared down the hall.

A small woman veiled in black, the man at the sentry post had said. Madame Lorne! Marcy was almost as sure of it as if she had seen her. She said, "She may have been in that chaise."

"Who?"

"The woman who said she was married to Armand."

"Married! You didn't tell me that." The major's face tightened.

"I didn't know it. I mean, she didn't tell me until she came to see me. She said she was married to Armand. She says her marriage certificate was in a trunk that has been lost. She wanted the Ortega wedding ring."

"Did you give it to her?" he asked coolly.

"No."

"Why on earth not?"

"It is not mine to give. It goes to the Ortegas."

"Oh." He stretched out long legs and surveyed his boots, which showed signs of their journey, for they were muddied and scraped. He was listening to her, however. He was also listening intently, she knew, for any sound anywhere, inside the house, outside the house.

There was no way to guess why or if in fact Madame Lorne had come to Nine Oaks or what she had wished to accomplish. Yet neither was there a reason to surmise that someone else had felt for Marcy the degree of hatred which Madame Lorne had been at no pains to hide. Still, that was not a reasonable cause for her to try to kill Marcy.

He caught the question in her mind and said briefly, "I think whoever shot at—at us got away. Liss's horse did whinny, probably as whoever had taken an aim at us was getting off toward the Bayou Road and the River Road as fast as he could."

"You said 'shot at us.' It sounded as if you really meant shot at *me*."

He replied evasively, "Only because you were wearing a

light bodice and had moved into an open space where anyone might be able to see you as a—that is—see you.''

''As a target! But that's impossible! There is *no* reason for anybody to try to murder me!''

''We'll see that it doesn't happen.'' His smile was meant to be reassuring. She did not feel reassured. A slow throb beat in her throat. He said, ''You thought at once of this woman who claimed to have been married to Armand.''

''But why? I mean, she may have considered herself married to Armand. She might really have been married to him, I suppose, although I can't believe that. But—I am no threat to her! Why would she want to shoot me?''

The major said quietly (but listening, too; she knew that), ''There could be reasons. Suppose she really was Armand's wife.''

''I can't believe that Armand would insist upon marriage to me while he had a wife. Gene advised me to give her money.''

''You didn't tell me how Dupre happened to know about her. You only said you had met her in his office.''

''Gene learned of her existence through a note, a letter he had found when he went to Armand's room in the hotel. Oh, never mind all that. She came to our house and made a scene. Really, it was dreadful. Especially after M'sieu Lemaire came.''

''What did he have to say?''

''He advised her to find her marriage certificate. She didn't like him.''

''Why?''

''She—oh, she was very angry. she made threats—''

''Threats?'' He eyed his boots very closely.

''Oh, nothing much. Said she knew all about him, she'd denounce him, that kind of thing.''

He turned and examined the sole of one boot closely. ''Denounce him?''

''She was only talking. Angry. Then she—spit at him and flounced away.''

''Dear me!'' He looked slightly amused, either that or the lamp flame flickered.

"I can't imagine why she would come here," Marcy said, but thought again of the Ortega ring.

"The point is, why would she shoot at you?" The major said evenly. "If she claims to have been his wife, how could you stand in her way? I take it Armand had property to leave."

"He did have, once. Nobody knows what anybody has now." She couldn't help the tinge of bitterness in her voice, but it did not appear to affect John Farrell.

He said equably, "War is no happy or peaceful way of life. When it is over, Armand's property may have been returned to him."

"Nobody quite believes that."

He ignored that. "Did Armand have a will?"

"Yes. Gene had it. He let me read it. Everything Armand had went to his wife, me. He drew it up just before we—when Armand expected us to be married."

He was silent so long that she began to discover the various mosquito bites on her ankles and arms and face; the itch was almost intolerable. Her clothes were sticky and hot. She hoped that Liss would find bed linen which was reasonably dry. There was a great linen room, so built with layers of woodshavings and cedar shingles that it was supposed to keep out the all-pervading damp of a house near the river.

Liss appeared in the doorway. "Things in the house just the way I put them away, that August, nearly two years ago. Guess I must have known we'd be away a long time." The major's second gun sagged down her apron pocket. She carried a tray with glasses, a candle and a tall bottle of red wine. "Your pa's wine still in the dining-room cabinet. Now, we'd better eat something. The major ain't had a chance for any supper, is my guess."

"You are right, Liss." Major Farrell rose to help her as she opened the bundle of food she and Marcy had prepared. He sliced the ham with an opened clasp knife. He drew the cork from the bottle. It was an old Madeira; Marcy had a glimpse of the label.

Liss said, "All the people in the quarters have gone, Miss Marcy. Not a light, not a smell of smoke."

"Liss! You didn't go outdoors! Marcy cried.

Liss gave her a scornful glance. "Why, *certainement!* Had to see what happened to that man shooting at us. Nobody there."

The major paused, holding the opened bottle over a glass. "That was dangerous, Liss. Don't do it again. You didn't happen to see a carriage, chaise, anything like that?"

She shot him a dark but understanding glance. "No, sir, Major."

The major brought the glass of wine to Marcy. Liss said something about Brule and went out, taking the candle. The red color of the wine was touched to brilliance in the mellow glow from the lamp. The major's face was very serious.

"Drink that. Whoever shot at us is gone."

Madame Lorne could conceivably have wished to kill her; there had been a shot in the night, and there had been a shrub that changed its shape. "I didn't tell you! Tonight, at home, in the garden, the crepe myrtle moved."

"What are you talking about? What moved?"

"Just before you came back tonight. At home. In the garden. I didn't know that anyone was there. I was sitting on a bench. I think whoever it was must have been there for some time. Then it moved—"

"Drink your wine. That's better. Now, tell me."

There was not much to tell. She finished the wine, which sent a heartening glow over her, and delivered her brief report. "Then you came and said you'd get another horse and . . . that's all."

He was frowning thoughtfully. "Could it have been your sister-in-law?"

"Claudine! No! Nor Tante Julie. Whoever it was slid off toward the stable and the carriage door to the mews. Jason must have left it unlocked."

"Lemaire?"

"No! Why should he?"

He put down his glass. "M'm—why should he! I'll stay here tonight. I'll have to leave tomorrow. Don't let my staying here bother you. I only want to be sure that you— that nobody comes."

"It doesn't bother me," she said crossly. "I'm thankful you are here. I'm thankful you brought me and the little boy here. I'm thankful you forgot what I—what I tried to do!"

He took a generous slice of ham and two cold biscuits. "I didn't forget. It is now too late for anything to be done about it, even if your friend Gene and his associates had believed the message you took to them." He bit into his improvised sandwich and said, "Grant has crossed the river. Yesterday. Successfully."

She stared at him. "But this is April!"

He laughed a little. "Not June. No."

"Then it *was* a trick."

He nodded. "I'm afraid so. I knew someone in the house was far too interested in my affairs. I didn't expect it to be you!"

"You mean you left that scrap of paper in the dispatch case to catch me!"

"I told you. I really didn't think it would be you." He munched calmly on the ham and biscuits.

"You said you never wanted to see me again. You hated me, you said."

"Surely not hated. Never mind what I said. Yes, I was disappointed in you. But after I thought it over, I . . . wasn't. I know you were acting under—not orders perhaps, but some kind of pressure."

"But you helped me tonight. You—"

"Oh, yes. I had to forgive you. You see, you were such a poor spy." He laughed a little, softly.

"Gene was right, then. He said it could be a trap."

He finished his improvised supper and brushed a crumb off his blue tunic. "Actually, I don't think I accomplished much by my stay in New Orleans. I managed to get some supplies Grant needed up the river to him. That's about all."

"You accepted the alibi I gave you."

He nodded soberly. "Certainly. At the time I had to. Nobody, not even the commanding officer in New Orleans, General Banks, was to know the exact time of Grant's crossing. No matter how careful officers may be, far too often there is somebody who forgets himself, makes some allusion which may be caught up by—well, enemy ears.''

"Our ears.''

"You know that. I couldn't let anybody know of the true projected dates. I was then arranging—very cautiously, indeed, very carefully—for the supplies General Grant might require. This demanded a certain diplomacy and very careful negotiation on my part. A full report to General Banks could have threatened General Grant's intentions. Not by way of General Banks, but easily by some indiscreet staff member. So, I still am in debt to you. But you needn't lie any further. I'm being sent to the army in Pennsylvania.''

"You—where? I mean, when?" Dismay, like a cold wave, washed over her.

"I don't know." He looked at her directly. "My exact orders will be at Baton Rouge. My usefulness is over here. Not," he said ruefully, "that I can tell myself I accomplished much. However— Now I'll take a look outside.''

There were heavy yet rather slow and weary footsteps coming along the hall from the kitchen. She cried, "That's not Liss!''

In a second his gun was in his hand, and he had whirled to face the door into the hall.

Marcy had a wild notion that Madame Lorne, pretty, petite, her small face catlike, would come into sight. Or perhaps it would be Madame Lorne's escort, who so far had avoided being seen.

M. Lemaire came into view. He looked very tired, wilted as his frilled shirtfront. He put one hand on the door casing and simply looked at them.

The major shoved his gun into its holster and said, half smiling, "What kept you?"

TWENTY

"But you—but he—you couldn't have expected—" Marcy began.

"I missed the turn onto the Bayou Road," said M. Lemaire with simplicity. He moved toward an armchair which was sternly upholstered in black horsehair, where he subsided and looked at the bottle of wine.

The major emptied his own glass. "If you don't mind using my glass."

"Thank you, thank you." M. Lemaire reached for the glass before the major had finished pouring.

"But—why?" Marcy began stuttering again. "How did you know?"

The major answered. "That horseman following us. I rather expected him but came to the conclusion that I had been mistaken."

M. Lemaire gulped thirstily. "It's the very devil of a night. Black as— May I have another glass?"

The major poured more wine into the glass which M. Lemaire extended.

"You were expecting him!" Marcy cried.

The major grinned. "Do you want to tell her or shall I?" he asked M. Lemaire.

M. Lemaire touched the wine to his lips and said plaintively, "How long have you known, Major?"

"Not long, really. I began to suspect after I had made inquiries about the various people in the house where I was living. You were the only one who couldn't quite be accounted for. I wasn't sure until Miss Marcy proved herself a—rather clumsy little spy."

M. Lemaire gave Marcy a reproachful glance. "But you didn't know?" he cried with an air of being unjustly accused.

"Know what? You are both talking in riddles."

The major waited. M. Lemaire said airily. "That I am a spy."

"You! But how could—why—"

"Easy," said Lemaire. "Just keeping my eyes and ears open. Reporting what I heard."

Marcy stared, unable to believe him. The major seemed almost to fidget; he took his gloves from his belt, turned them over, eyed them closely, put them back again and said, "For both sides. Isn't that right, sir?"

"Both!" Marcy cried. "What do you mean, *both*?"

"He means both sides," M. Lemaire said lightly. "Only thing to do. I was caught in a snare. Not that I minded. Both sides paid me small sums now and then. Besides, I was really of some help to you, Marcy, wasn't I?"

She took a long breath, tried and failed to understand. "But that can't happen! A spy for both sides?"

"It did happen. Probably has happened many times." M. Lemaire had recovered his usual air of friendly, polite insouciance. "Couldn't really help myself."

"*How* did it happen?" Marcy demanded.

"Partly your father's fault." M. Lemaire eyed the cold ham hungrily. "He took me in, you see. Gave me a home—he and your mother. Oh, she really was a cousin," he interpolated. "Very kind to me, both of them and General Beauregard. He and your father were always good friends, and the general knew something of the reason for my coming to New Orleans and—to make it short, he sent word asking me to inform his agents of any news I could discover about Yankee activities. I must say," he added frankly, "there wasn't much to let him know about, except the general situation in New Orleans. News of all that, I sent on. I'm not too sure that my news items, such as they were, ever reached the general's ears. I rather think they were sifted out by whatever officers there are versed in espionage. The man I saw, to whom I passed on such bits of knowledge as I had, is a former ship captain. He contrived to get boats, scows, riverboats of some kind, up and down the river. I'm not sure that I was ever of any great help. Until, of course, you came, Major. I could then watch your goings and comings."

"And did that help anybody?" John Farrell asked.

M. Lemaire sighed. "I am afraid not. But then, you see, I was also interested," he said delicately, "in working for the Union, too."

"Good heavens!" said Marcy.

"Oh, it was very simple." M. Lemaire strolled over, took up a piece of ham and a biscuit and began to gnaw. Marcy said, "*How* did that happen?"

"Oh, I've told you that. I told you the whole thing. Pressure was brought by somebody in the North. They still think, in New York, that I am an escaped murderer. I explained to you that it was a duel. I don't think," he said sagaciously, "that you believed me."

"But you—you told so many stories."

He chewed thoughtfully, then nodded. "I daresay. Had to. Trying to cover myself. Make people think I was a good-natured, lying old fool."

Marcy swallowed hard. "You must have a pass!"

M. Lemaire nodded and chewed. "Of course. On Federal business!"

"You could have helped us anytime! You could have brought all of us here!"

He shook his head. "Oh, no, my dear. How long could I have lasted in—well, in either role if I had trespassed upon my quite legitimate pass? Dear me, no."

"Did Armand know this?"

"He may have guessed and told the Lorne woman. She said she would denounce me."

"I don't know what to make of you," Marcy said hopelessly.

"I'm not really very important. I only—tried to save my own skin. *Sauve qui peut*. The French put these things so well."

"There are other things besides lying that can be said of you!" Marcy said.

M. Lemaire, unashamed, nodded agreeably. "But I am still safe, I think," he said, but rather doubtfully this time, giving the major a flickering glance.

After a moment the major said, "I began to wonder about you when I found someone was searching my room."

"Me," said M. Lemaire with a shade of satisfaction.

"You. Marcy—Miss Marcy seemed to know nothing much about you."

"Oh, I told her some of the facts. Not all, naturally. But I helped her when you found her stealing that message from your dispatch case."

I think I may fly into pieces, Marcy thought. All so easy, so absurdly good-natured. "But you did help me!"

"You did such a good job then of pretending to be drunk that you fooled me for a moment." The major permitted himself another grin. "You weren't drunk at all."

"Merely doing my duty," M. Lemaire said indistinctly, chewing. "That message had to go to the Confederates. But then, of course, I had to let General Grant know that they were expecting him to cross the river in June. That is why I followed you here. You have ways of communicating with him. You must warn him."

"If it troubles you, it needn't," the major said. "He crossed yesterday. I had word tonight."

"Good," said M. Lemaire pleasantly.

Marcy got to her feet. "I can't believe—you two act as if—oh, I can't believe all this!"

The major only looked at her. M. Lemaire said, chewing, "Might as well. It's all true. It's been," he swallowed and said clearly, "rather a strain, really. Kept me going. It wasn't hard to find where you kept your valuables, my dear.

I'm sorry about leaving the Ortega ring in the major's room, Marcy. I hoped he would not suspect me of searching. If he thought it was you—well"—he smiled—"he would feel differently. By the way, who owns that chaise that is standing out in the back, near the blacksmith shop?"

The major's smile vanished. "Chaise! Then they are still there! Did you see anybody?"

M. Lemaire shook his head. "No. Who are you expecting?"

"Not expecting. Already here. You missed your road, and you also missed some shooting."

"Shooting!" M. Lemaire jumped up. "Now, see here—I don't like shooting!"

"Who does?" The major turned to Marcy. "I'll just take a look now."

"Let me go too, sir, Major," Liss said from the doorway. She had his second gun in her hand again. "I want to see what horse it was that my horse snorted at."

"Liss!" M. Lemaire said. "You got here all right! How?"

Liss cast him one dark glance. "Rode. Carried the boy."

"I didn't see that," M. Lemaire said with interest. "I only heard the major talking to my niece"—he still insisted on "niece," Marcy thought absently—"so I slipped out and found myself a horse."

The major said abruptly, "If they are still there . . ."

He went out and Liss went with him. Liss's voice floated back. "I didn't see anybody, Major, sir. But maybe we'd better look again."

The door to the breezeway and kitchen closed. M. Lemaire eyed Marcy solicitously. "You seem a little upset." Upset! Marcy stared at him. A shot in the night. The possibility that somebody was still somewhere in the meshing depth of shadows around the house—and M. Lemaire's utterly fantastic and rather smug confession! "Upset," she cried. "Upset! What a word!"

"Seems *le mot juste*, my dear."

"It is not. That is—" She was diverted to M. Lemaire. "I can't believe you! Double treason. That's what—"

"Not at all. I am a creature caught by circumstance. You

must see that. As a matter of fact, I didn't think I did any harm to either side.''

Probably he hadn't, she thought; in any event, whatever he had done was done, and nothing could be changed.

She left him munching contentedly and went out into the hall to the door to the breezeway and the kitchen, which lay at some distance from the house. She opened it, but she could see and hear nothing. The major and the indomitable Liss must be somewhere outside. No one could be hiding in that darkness. But someone had certainly shot at them on their approach to the house. Suddenly there was a kind of muffled sound somewhere; it became clearer; almost at once it began to assume a kind of rhythm. It was the steady but rapid gallop of a horse. She stepped out into the breezeway and heard more clearly the soft, faraway thuds of a horse at a gallop now, toward the Bayou Road.

So someone *had* been hiding in the darkness, waiting for a second chance? Whoever it was had now gone. The sounds died away swiftly. she could hear again only the drone of frogs off in the swampland beyond the quarters, and the sleepy twittering of some roused bird. The glow of a lantern made a circle of light appearing from behind the smokehouse. She saw within its mellow circle Liss's dark skirt and the major's uniformed legs coming toward her.

The lantern bobbed and swung an eerie light, glancing here and there, touching a cabin, a path overgrown with weeds, the feathery drapery of Spanish moss from a tree.

The major saw her. "They have gone."

"Who were they? I heard a horse."

Liss said, "Somebody heard us and lit out."

The major put his hand around Marcy's arm and took her back inside the house. He put the lantern on a table. "He—or they—took the chaise and their own horse. M'sieu Lemaire's horse is tethered out near the smokehouse. It is very likely that whoever shot at us came here in the chaise the sentry had passed. Two people. They must have waited for another chance out there hidden and then when Liss and I came out together, heard us and got into their chaise and got away as fast as their horse could go. I ought to have gone out at once, searched—well, I didn't. My mistake.''

"What could you have done if you had found them?"

"Something," the major said shortly. "I'll make sure that my horse is still out at the front door."

He swung along the hall. M. Lemaire appeared in the candlelit door of the long living room. "What happened?"

"Oh, I don't know!" Marcy ran along the hall and passed him. The front door was wide open, but she could not see the major. She thought she could hear him pushing through the shrubbery and vines, speaking in low and soothing tones to his horse. Then he came, barely visible in the darkness, leading his horse. He said, "I'll put this fellow in a stable. Find him food and water."

Liss said, "The major knows where to take him. Now then, little Brule . . ." She went upstairs.

M. Lemaire had overheard everything. "Glad they didn't take my horse," he said and yawned.

Marcy sank down on the lower steps of the stairway. She could hear Liss upstairs, talking now to Brule.

M. Lemaire retreated to some easy chair, she had no doubt, in the living room. It seemed a long time before the major returned, and when he did come from the breezeway, his boots thumping, he had found food and water for both M. Lemaire's horse and his own. They were in a nearby stable. He thought they would be safe for the night.

"For the night," she repeated again, all at once desolate. "You do plan to leave in the morning."

He nodded, looked down at her, lifted the lantern and started to blow out the flame, then said, "You'd better take this up with you. Now then, you are so tired you don't know how tired you are. Take this." He thrust the bail of the lantern into her hand, scooped her up and started up the stairs. Halfway, though, he laughed. "You weigh more than you look. Here." He let her down carefully. "Take hold of the bannister."

She did. It wasn't like being held in his arms. She straightened her back and lifted her head, and he chuckled a little. "That's more like it. Not that you don't have reason for feeling a little"—he paused, chose a word, and finally said, with a low laugh—"feeble." Then he put his arms around her waist and—she told herself with a flicker of indignation—pushed her up the stairs.

All the same, she was grateful for the help. Her knees seemed unsteady. Everything seemed unsteady.

They reached the top of the stairs, and the lantern light brought into being the well-known and worn strip of carpeting, the huge barometer fastened on the wall, the tall-backed chair which had always stood there beneath a stiff and unnatural painting of the front of the house with its white, thin pillars and doorway from near which someone had shot at her.

He took the lantern from her hand and put it on the high-backed chair. Then he looked at her, very seriously. The familiar hall seemed to vanish; she could almost feel the warmth of a spring garden and hear distant strains of dance music. He put out his arms, and she swayed toward them; this happened then, she thought. It's the same irresistible wave of belonging. The same when he kissed her. The same long moment, never to be forgotten.

He released her too quickly. The lantern flame made lights in his eyes; she put her hands to her cheeks without knowing what she did. He said, "It's the way it was that night."

He turned abruptly and went down the stairs, the light at first glowing upon his blue tunic and picking out the gold epaulets. The light from the lantern dimmed; she could barely see him turn into the living room, where there was still a candle and M. Lemaire.

Liss came out of her bedroom, picked up the lantern and said, "The boy is asleep, quiet now."

But I'll see the major in the morning, she thought.

I'll see him in the morning. She felt as if she'd had wine, champagne, everything fine and intoxicating, so much that she couldn't possibly sleep. There was too much to live over again and think about. But she did sleep, in such comfort and ease that she didn't waken at all until Liss came to her side with a steaming cup of coffee. "Coffee was in a closed barrel." Liss said and plumped up pillows behind her. "The major, he went away. Early. Said he had to go."

"Oh, no!"

Liss eyed her. "Soldiers is soldiers! Reckon he had to go to Baton Rouge. Then later, he tell me, to Pennslyvania. He tell me to say good-by to you. He peek in here, but you were asleep. Where is Pennsýlvania?"

"Very far away," Marcy said dully. He hadn't even awakened her.

"H'm." Liss walked across to open curtains; sunlight streaked into the room. "M'sieu Lemaire, he gone too. Just left. Not a word to me. Brule is down in the kitchen." She had found some bacon in the smokehouse and some of the nests where the remaining hens had hidden their eggs. "Left some food in tins when we closed up the house," she added. "We'll not starve."

She went out again, and Marcy stared at the worn pink and blue figures in the once brilliant rug. So then, he had gone.

It was the same thing: drawn into his arms, drawn to him in a current she could never have resisted, and now he was gone. Pennsylvania; it was very far away.

She could only accept it. The coffee had grown cold; she drank it anyway, and since there was nothing else to do, tried to face down a sense of utter loneliness, which she knew in her heart might last all the rest of her life.

Five days later Gene Dupre came.

TWENTY-ONE

The five days had passed slowly but in odd segments, like a dream.

Marcy and Liss explored cautiously, Brule trotting beside them: the smokehouse, where ham and sides of bacon still hung, the blacksmith shop and the stables, where a carriage and a barouche still stood, cobweb-draped.

The cabins showed signs of an orderly migration; the slaves had left, probably after due consideration and with some plan. Blankets and cooking utensils were gone; only a few work clothes hung on wooden pegs, and a bottle of liniment, half empty, stood on one shelf. The doors had all been closed, some even fastened with pegs and straps of leather. "Looks as if some of them plan to come back," Liss said.

The first day they did, thankfully, encounter a cow. Liss told Marcy to hold the pistol while she brought a pail and addressed herself adeptly to milking. Is there anything that woman can't do, Marcy wondered with admiration and gratefulness.

"But it hasn't been long since she was milked," Liss said. "Must be somebody hiding out in the woods."

"Somebody?" Liss saw her alarm.

"Not one of our people, Miss Marcy. He'd come right straight to the house, once he knew we were here. But we'll take a look around."

"Suppose he's a—a guerilla, a thug, a criminal."

Liss was not deterred. "Sooner I find out, the better."

Sometime that day Liss quietly disappeared; when she returned, she was satisfied. "I saw him. All in rags and hungry, hardly more than skin and bones. Didn't talk to him. No need. Rags were part of a Yankee uniform. My guess is he's a deserter. Got tired of fighting. Likely he's scared of us."

"Shouldn't we do something about him?"

"Oh, I'll leave him some food somewhere. No need to fret yourself about him, Miss Marcy."

Liss was right.

After that, Liss quietly contrived to leave cornbread, ham, part of whatever they had found to eat, in the breezeway at night. In the morning it was always gone.

It was Liss who remembered the sweet-potato hills, Liss who found onions and garlic and early sweet corn in the little garden plots in back of the slave cabins.

It was a kind of Robinson Crusoe existence, and the unseen man hiding in the woods their Man Friday—if and when he ever gathered up the courage to come forward.

The place was lonely, and at night there were only the familiar sounds of frogs and twitterings of birds. Liss saw to everything, sternly yet with a kind of satisfaction in her bearing; they had rescued Brule, at least for the moment.

They might have been on an island, accompanied only by their invisible Man Friday. There was no evidence of plundering Yankee troops or renegades from either army. The quiet and apparent safety of the place was perhaps due to the isolation of the house, above the River Road yet unapproachable from it. A marauding stray would not know of the Bayou Road and the driveway, which was all but hidden.

The man and woman in the chaise had known. That, too, suggested that Madame Lorne had been on the veranda and retreated when the major had fired shots into the air. Frightened, perhaps, and surprised because they had not known that Marcy and the little boy would be so strongly reinforced. They had slid away into the night, at first stealthily, waiting; then when the major came out, carrying a lantern and armed, they galloped toward the River Road. There was only one way they could have known that she was taking Brule to Nine Oaks.

When she thought of it, it was still more frightening, for it had to mean that the figure in the garden, waiting and watching her, had overheard her plan to take the child to Nine Oaks. Madame Lorne or her shadowy escort? But if they had taken a chaise and preceded them to the plantation, Armand must have told Madame Lorne of the plantation, of the Bayou Road, of the hidden driveway, all about it.

She began to feel that perhaps he had married the woman. The Ortega ring and the ruby and turquoise box were carefully locked away in the room that had been her father's and probably her grandfather's. It was not a very good hiding place; a wall desk with a lid which could be pulled up, disclosing a vacant space below. Anybody who had time and motive for searching could certainly have found it. But what looter would take the time to find the tiny notches where one slid any kind of sharp instrument, a letter opener, for instance, and lifted the lid? Its virtue lay in the fact that a thief would be hurried; a prowling looter would not take time to search for anything so hidden. She rearranged the silver inkwell and the silver candelabra above, shielding the tiny notches. The silver was tarnished.

The house, however, considering the time it had been closed, was in remarkably good condition. They had built well.

Nine Oaks was not a big plantation, not in any way a showplace, but it was solid, enduring, built for generations to come. The teakwood floors, the ebony stairs and bannister, the oak paneling in the dining room, were made to last. The rooms were big and deeply familiar to Marcy; every chair, every footstool, was covered with needlepoint made by women who had preceded her. She could see them, those long-ago women with their busy hands, always white but busy, using the needlepoint as a pleasurable change from work at the endless cutting, measuring, sewing, that had to be done in a working plantation. There were about a thousand acres comprising Nine Oaks. Possibly some of that acreage had been eaten away by the greedy Mississippi.

She loved the grace and beauty of the New Orleans house. But Nine Oaks held for her a different and deeper feeling of home. Her roots were here and were as strongly embedded as the giant, ancient water oaks which gave the house its name. Here she felt as if she breathed her own air, lived her own life more completely than in any other place. Here she seemed to abide in another and happier world.

Yet she listened, too, all the time. The quiet was at first restful and reassuring; as the days went on, however, it became subtly menacing. Suppose whoever had shot at her returned?

Liss felt the threat in the air too. She kept near her the major's pistol; it was never far from her hands, even when she was cooking, feeding Brule, watching him explore the new and, to him, excitingly strange world. He was so like her brother sometimes that Marcy's heart got into her throat; even the turn of his well-shaped head, the quick and well-coordinated movements when he ran or played or chased a butterfly, all were like the other Brule.

But the underlying uneasiness Marcy felt had much to do with Claudine, too. Claudine would guess where they had gone. Claudine would discover some means of getting Brule back into her possession and selling him.

Gene came on a late afternoon. Marcy was on the veranda, Liss beside her, when they heard his horse plodding wearily along the winding drive from the Bayou. Liss had the major's pistol in her hand. When Gene emerged from the shadow of one of the great water oaks, she slid it back into one of her enormous pockets.

Brule, attracted by the sounds, ran to meet Gene, who dismounted, looped his horse's reins over the hitching rail, and stooped to take the little boy up in his arms, laughing at the child's pleasure and then, Marcy thought, suddenly very serious. Gene had many times played with him, admired his beauty, liked him because he was his father's son. He walked toward them, holding the boy's hand. Gene had never looked so little like Claudine, and he had never been so agreeable to her wishes, for he said at once, "I knew you were here. She guessed too. She sent me to bring him back."

"You can't," Marcy said.

Liss said practically, "You better have refreshment, M'sieu Gene. Tiresome ride."

He sank down on the step, tussled a little with the child, who squealed with glee, and then said somberly, "I had to come. If I didn't, Claudine threatened to tell the Yankee general the names of the Defenders. She knew, or guessed, most of them."

"You can't have him," Marcy said again. She sat down beside him on the step, gathering her wide skirt around her. But one little boy against the lives of how many young men? Yes, she could see that Gene felt he must take the boy to Claudine.

"She's a terrible woman," Gene said suddenly. "My cousin—she meant what she threatened, you know."

"I can't give him to her."

There was a long pause.

At last Gene said, "Claudine said M'sieu Lemaire must have come with you."

"Oh, he—" She stopped herself in time. If Gene or any of his associates knew of the double role M. Lemaire had been playing, his life wouldn't be worth a picayune. "No, he isn't here."

Gene merely gave her an absent glance. "He's gone somewhere. You do understand why I have to take the boy back to Claudine."

"Oh, yes. I understand. But . . ." A possible, an impossible, a mad notion struck her. "How much is this man who wants to buy him willing to pay?"

Gene rubbed his hands over his hair wearily. "Not much, really. The market isn't very good just now. I think Claudine said five hundred dollars. He's young, you see. May not survive long."

Marcy rose. "I'll be back." She ran into the house as Liss came out carrying a silver tray, glasses and a bottle of wine.

Her fingers shook as she pried up the lid of the old wall

desk. The Ortega ring meant nothing to her, only an obligation to the Ortega family, which now seemed of no importance whatever. The ruby and turquoise box meant something; her fingers closed around it. Her mother's hand had been slim and white and always loving. Her mother would have said, "Yes, yes, buy him. My grandchild. My son's son."

All the same Marcy lingered for a moment, holding the jeweled little box. She couldn't guess what its purchase price might be; she knew that the Ortega wedding ring had real value. She was only vaguely aware of a kind of stir and movement, a murmur of voices below.

She went slowly down the stairs.

She stopped in the doorway. There were now two horses tethered to the hitching rail. There were two men on the veranda, Gene and the major. Liss said behind her, "Major back. I'll get a glass for him too."

They were oddly alike and as oddly unlike. Gene was very slim, blond, dressed like a fop in a frilled, if wilted, shirt, tight fawn-colored trousers creased from riding, a long black coat which looked and undoubtedly was very hot. The major in his trim blue uniform lounged on the steps too, yet even lounging, there was an alertness about him, something tough and firm. Gene was firm too, in his way.

Another strange thing was that they were speaking in a perfectly friendly way, seriously discussing something and very intent about their conversation.

Both men rose as Marcy came out and the door clicked behind her. Her heart hadn't stopped; instead it was thudding like a drum gone wild.

"Major—" she began, and he said, "I was in Baton Rouge. I had a chance to come here. I see you have been safe."

"Safe?" Gene's gaze flashed to the major. Marcy said, "Oh, yes. Liss is here."

"Nobody else has been here then?" the major said.

She had unconsciously put her hands at her throat, as if to stifle that wildly thudding heart; she felt the pressure of the Ortega ring and lowered it, looked at it and remembered why she had brought it down to Gene. She did contrive to reply unsteadily to the major's question.

"Only Gene today. And someone harmless, hiding in the woods. Gene, I want to buy Brule."

"Buy him?" Gene's slender face was stunned. "But, Marcy—"

"He is my nephew. I have these things," She went to him and put out her hands. "Take them. I don't know the value, but I think it's more than was offered for Brule."

Gene had the ruby and turquoise box and the Ortega ring in his hands, looking at them, turning them over. "Why, I don't know what to say, Marcy."

"Will Claudine accept those as payment for the boy?"

Rather to her discomfiture, the major gave a kind of smothered chuckle. She could guess why; she was, in effect, buying the boy. But not as a slave! Gene turned over the Ortega ring again, his face thoughtful now, a banker's face. "Why, yes. I think the ring is very valuable. But do you really want to part with it?"

"Armand gave it to me. It ought to go back to the Ortegas. But I can't care now about the ring or the Ortegas. Will Claudine accept the ring and the box?"

Gene lifted his head. "How will you care for the boy?"

She hadn't crossed that bridge; she would when the time came. She said confidently, "I'll see to him."

"Claudine will insist that she never set eyes on him again."

"Then she can stay in New Orleans. The boy belongs here. It is his home as much as it is mine. I'll see to everything—education, everything." She didn't know just how, but she knew that she would accomplish it somehow.

Gene shrugged, "Then you'll have to take him north. Although, the way things look now, the North will be coming here."

The major said quietly, as if he felt sorry for Gene, "It isn't over yet."

"It will be." Gene lifted his tired face and eyes to the major. "That message Marcy found in your dispatch case and gave to me—I didn't believe it. But we didn't think Grant could have crossed at all. The message was wrong."

a spark came into his eyes. "Your doing, Major? I thought so. It was a trap, but not the kind of trap I believed. However, it could have made no difference really. We did send a warning that the crossing might be attempted in June, but then we heard that he had already crossed. You knew all that, too, Major."

John Farrell said, "I think you understand."

"Oh, yes," Gene said. "I understand. You had to track down any—any spy." He didn't look at Marcy.

"War," John Farrell said, as if the one word explained everything.

"We'll fight on, but I think it will be over . . ." Gene paused, staring out into the shadows of the live oaks, as if he saw visions he did not wish to see.

The major said soberly, "I believe that when peace comes, it will come to both North and South."

"Yes, yes," Gene said, but as if thinking too far ahead and too wearily. "Well . . ." With a start he looked down at the Ortega ring and the shining little box. "The ring alone will be enough, I should say, Marcy. I think I can speak for Claudine. At least I will speak for her, and she can like it or not. The ring is very valuable. Are you sure, Marcy?"

The great emerald in the ring, the diamonds set around it, flashed with beauty, but none of it was beautiful to Marcy. "Yes."

Gene looked at her for a moment, as if testing her decision; then he slid the ring into his pocket. "The little box won't bring much. However, if you wish—"

"It was my mother's. Brule is her grandson."

Gene put the charming trinket in his pocket and the red and blue stones were gone. "I may be able to induce Claudine to take only the ring. Doesn't it mean anything to you, Marcy?"

"No. I intended to give it back to Armand's cousins. Now it doesn't seem to matter."

Gene lifted her hand and kissed it. "I am sure that Claudine will be satisfied. I'll have to offer her a home." He shrugged. "She's my cousin."

"But home—"

"I meant to tell you at once. Your father has been released."

"*Oh!*" So the major had succeeded.

Gene went on. "He and your Tante Julie were sure too that you were here. They hope to come here and stay here for the duration of the war. That is, if they can procure passes." He looked inquiringly at the major, who said after a moment, "I'll try. I may not be able to. But how did you get a pass?"

A shamed pink went over Gene's face. "I told the Yank—I mean the Federal provost marshal—that the bank holds a mortgage on this place and some others along the river, and that it was my duty to discover what condition they were in, revalue some of them, perhaps. He understood perfectly. The instinct of—"

"Of the Yankees?" the major finished, a slight smile crinkling the corners of his eyes. "Ah well, we are told that we are a nation of shopkeepers. But I think no more than—"

Gene flushed a deeper pink. "No more than the French. I must get back to the city."

The major moved. "I'll ride along with you."

Liss came out with a tray and more glasses.

Gene's thin face flashed into warmth. "That's very kind of you, Major. You want to be sure that no zealous sentry takes a shot at me. But I shall be quite safe, you know."

Again Gene kissed her hand; the major said, "I'll go along, just to be sure. I may be able to stop in again on my way back." Unexpectedly, he, too, took Marcy's hand and kissed it, but rather hard and briefly. Then the two men went down the steps together like two friends, exchanged a word or two near the horses at the hitching rail and got into their saddles. They rode away together. There was an indefinable air of companionship and friendliness between them.

TWENTY-TWO

Marcy stood for a long time, watching as they went out of sight beyond the curtains of the oaks and Spanish moss. She waited until the thuds of the hooves and the slight creaking of saddle leather had died away. Perhaps when peace came, the two armies, the two peoples North and South, could come to an understanding, a kind of brotherly resolution, to change the war-torn land into one of peace, and to mend its scars.

But John Farrell was not in faraway Pennsylvania. He was near. She was lost in her dreaming while Liss stood at her elbow, extending a glass of wine. "Better drink it. Do you good. Them two men—like old friends. You bought the boy. We'll have to take him north, Miss Marcy."

"I don't know." She drank the wine, still in a dream. Liss brooded. At last she said, "We'll do something," called to Brule and took the empty glass from Marcy's hand. "Now then, your supper."

Marcy sat down on the veranda steps, curling her skirts under her for the cushion they provided, thinking, yet not thinking. She would almost certainly see the major again before he went so far away.

She did not hear the thump of the horse's hooves or the creak of the wheels of a chaise until there was a light clatter from the nearest clump of live oaks and laurels. At first she thought it was Claudine, come to claim Brule after all. Too late she realized that she ought to have asked Gene for a paper proving the sale.

She jumped to her feet. The chaise had halted. There was a rustle in the shadows; Madame Lorne emerged, saw Marcy and came for the steps, clutching her skirts. She was wearing all black and the same black-lace mitts. Her little cat face was as intent as if she had seen prey. "I've come for the ring," she said flatly.

Suddenly Marcy wished that Liss hadn't taken Brule back into the house for supper. Probably they were by now in the kitchen; Liss couldn't have heard the woman's arrival.

"I don't have the ring."

"I know you have it. All of Armand's property belongs to me."

"He had no property."

"Oh, yes, he had land. Acres and acres. Rich land. I know. It's all mine. And the ring. I need the ring now. The property can wait until the war is over."

"I gave the ring away."

"You gave—I don't believe you!"

"I did. I don't have it." The woman saw the bottle of wine and came gracefully up onto the veranda. Marcy said, "You were here the night I came!"

Ignoring Marcy, Madame Lorne poured wine into a glass, holding the bottle in one hand and leaving the glass on the steps; to do so, she had to bend her black flounces and her petite face too near Marcy. She lifted the glass but did not sip; she drank thirstily, paused for a breath, said, "A very hot drive," and poured another glassful of the wine.

Over it she glanced sweetly at Marcy. "I tell you, I've come for the Ortega ring. I have to have it. Armand ought to have given it to me. Why—" her black lashes dropped over bright, fixed eyes—"I *was* married to him! His family must recognize me and my claims. The ring is—call it my pass to his family."

"Pass!" Marcy then asked, as if on a tangent, "How did you get here? You must have had a pass."

Again the thick eyelashes fluttered; the pretty mouth curved upward, complacently. "I happen to know a man in the provost marshal's office. Two passes. Simple."

Marcy wondered briefly what would happen to the luck-less man in the provost marshal's office if his dereliction was discovered. Madame Lorne gulped down the contents of her second glass like a greedy kitten lapping milk. There was nothing of the kitten in her brilliant eyes. "Naturally, we—I—knew where to find you. So I came."

"You said 'we.'"

"Ah, yes. My husband—"

"You said you were married to Armand."

"But I was. I understood that my husband had been killed in battle. So I married Armand. But my husband returned."

"He shot Armand." Marcy said as certainly as if she had seen the murder.

Madame Lorne shrugged lightly. "A pity. But it had to be done, of course."

"But why? Did Armand quarrel with him?"

"He didn't *know* of him until—until a few days before poor Armand died."

"Was murdered," Marcy said. And thought, That is the reason Armand suddenly made determined plans for our marriage. That had been surmised; this was proof. For the first time she fully believed in Madame Lorne's claim of marriage, for when Armand discovered that her real hus-band had returned and found her, Armand had felt himself free and had made plans accordingly. Perhaps, too, he was all too ready to disassociate himself from the woman he had married in some weak moment. Yes, knowing some of Armand's weaknesses, Marcy now believed in the marriage which had proved to be no legal marriage at all.

Madame Lorne, watching her, leaped to the conclusion that Marcy at last realized what had happened. "Only Armand knew that his marriage to me was not legal. If we could dispose of him before your wedding, we could profit.''

"But Armand had nothing.''

"But he will have when the war is over. Land, property—and as his wife, it will be mine. My husband saw that chance. Of course, you are still in my way. You wouldn't have been if my husband hadn't missed you when you arrived here.''

"You mean that *he* shot at me. You were the two people in the chaise. You were ahead of us. You waited—and your husband tried to kill me!''

"And didn't succeed,'' Madame Lorne said, not sweet now, but angry. "He said it was because he was sick. Well, yes, he was ill. He died of the fever yesterday. Perhaps it is as well. It would have been a constant problem to prevent the Ortega family from knowing of him. He meant to have his share of the property willed to me. You never saw my husband, but he saw you, many times.''

But I did see him, Marcy thought swiftly. I knew that I was being watched, stealthily, constantly; I knew it. And I saw him, this returned husband, down in the courtyard, having made his way into the garden through the stable door, running through a patch of starlight. It had been atavistic, that sense of surveillance she had felt, and yet it was not quite a thing of the senses only, for she had caught one or two other glimpses of him, a quickly disappearing figure in black slouch hat, black coat—and the night she had sat in the garden, waiting for the major, hopeful that he would take them to Nine Oaks, she had seen some shrubbery change its shape.

"Why did he watch me? Why?''

"We were already making our plans. He intended to—profit from my marriage to Armand. Why not? But you were a problem, you stood in the way of proving my marriage. If necessary, he planned to kill you, of course.'' Madame Lorne said impatiently, "The ring! Give it to me.''

"I haven't—I can't . . .'' The shadow had not been a shadow, but a watchful threat of murder! How could she evade now? Should she induce the woman to wait while she pretended to go upstairs to get the ring? Surely Liss would come and make short work of Madame Lorne.

She did not reckon on the wily, agile mind behind the lovely face. "I believe you really did give the ring away! It will take longer without the ring, but I can still trace down the marriage certificate or the record of it once this war is over. I'll find that! When Armand decided to marry you at once and even showed me the will—the fool—and I saw how it was worded, I knew and my husband knew what must be done. First Armand, then you."

Madame Lorne's right hand came from her shielding flounces; it held a small but dangerous-looking gun, which she pointed at Marcy.

Marcy backed away. *"What are you doing?"*

A flash of exasperation shot into Madame Lorne's eyes. "How can I make the Ortega family believe that I was Armand's wife if you are here to make your own claims. They'd never believe that Armand would plan to marry you when he was already married to me. After the war, there'll be property. That will of Armand's; he didn't mean it that way, but I come first, 'His wife'—then 'or' your name, but 'his wife' is first. Your name is there, but you were never his wife! So . . ." She steadied the gun, which looked very large in her small hand. Her eyelashes fluttered almost coquettishly, but there was nothing of the coquette in her fixed bright gaze.

Scream for Liss? She couldn't possibly get there in time to help her. Talk, but Madame Lorne, in spite of the heat and weariness or because of the wine, had talked and clearly felt it a waste of time.

She must have made a move, for Madame Lorne said, "Stand still! I don't want to kill you, but it's the best way, and then I'll be safe. Armand's wife, in his will. Stand still!"

But something behind Madame Lorne was moving. Don't look, Marcy's senses screamed at her. In a second a tall, blue-clad figure leaped up on the veranda behind Madame Lorne and clasped her and the pistol in his arms.

She fought. She fought hard and viciously, and then another figure came into being too. A strange figure, bearded, his hair long and his blue uniform ragged, his feet bare. "Just give me that gun, Major," the newcomer said. "Here is some rope."

Marcy dropped down on the top step of the veranda. She seemed dimly to understand the presence of the unkempt figure, who was very effectively tying up the struggling, wiry little woman. The major helped. Once the woman was tied but still biting and trying to scratch, the major took out a handkerchief, pushed it very deeply into her mouth and said, "Thank you, Corporal. Now take her—"

"I know. Yes, sir. Come along, now—"

So that, Marcy thought, is our man of the woods; that is our recipient of eggs and sweet corn, living in the woods. The major sighed. "Corporal Calhoun," he said. "Deserter. He's been hiding out in your woods for some time, he told me, and became devoted to you and Liss for your kindness to him. He saw the woman come back toward the house. Your friend Dupre told me to look out for this woman, Madame Lorne. The first sentry we came to said a young woman had passed him. I came back and met the corporal. He told me she was here, and that she had been here the night we came, and some man had shot at you—"

"Yes," Sometime she'd tell him the whole ugly story of Madame Lorne.

She didn't need to.

"Gene Dupre told me of Armand's will." He was still breathing quickly. "He said it had been on his mind since he had seen the Lorne woman, because the phrasing was so ambiguous. Armand wrote it himself without legal advice and brought it to Gene only to keep safe for him. If this Madame Lorne really had married Armand and could prove it in any way, then she might succeed in inheriting anything Armand had to leave, ever, but then you would stand in her way. You had the ring, and the Ortega family knew of your formal betrothal and Armand's plan for an immediate wedding. So, she had an imperative need to get rid of you. I suppose she wanted the Ortega ring to help prove her claim. Don't look like that, Marcy. It's all over. I'll see that she is put away safely, somewhere. The general in New Orleans will see to that. I am sure the corporal will take her there gladly. I can arrange for leniency in the case of his deserting. Marcy, lean against me. Stop shaking.''

She leaned against him.

There was a curious, still moment or two. A bird somewhere twittered softly. The frogs had not yet set about their evening chorus. The evening shadows were long and blue. A rosy light lingered over the tops of the trees. At last the major said, ''I've got to get back to Baton Rouge.''

The war. Pennsylvania. She said as if from a great distance, ''Grant will besiege Vicksburg.''

''Oh, yes. It may take some time.'' He spoke wearily. ''It's all a waste. Grant will win. But lives—''

''You have to go?''

''Yes. Is Liss still here with you?''

''She's back in the kitchen with the boy.''

There was another long pause. Then the major laughed quietly. ''So, you own the boy, legally. I nearly forgot. Gene Dupre remembered and gave something to me for you. It's a bill of sale. All proper, he says.''

She took the piece of paper, hastily scrawled on, but since it came from Gene, she was sure that it was perfectly legal. The major said, ''Of course, when the war is over the slaves will be free.''

''He's not a slave.''

''I know. Well, I must go. You should be safe here until your father can come.''

The shadows had lengthened across the lawn; the gray wisps of Spanish moss felt a breath of evening air and gently moved. She heard herself saying words she had not intended to say. ''Will you come back to me?''

But she *had* intended to say just that. She knew it when he took her hands, looked searchingly into her eyes and finally said, as gravely as if he were taking a vow in church, ''I'll come back to you. Believe me, I'll come back. My dear love.''

Liss had come out and stood behind them. ''Well, I do declare,'' she said.

Marcy jerked her head up and twisted around in his arms to see Liss—ugly, cross Liss—smiling. ''Yes, sir, Major, sir. You must come back." She slid into French. "*Que le bon Dieu vous benisse.*"

She stood beside Marcy when the major rode away, looking back with a kind of salute with his lifted hand as his horse and his tall figure faded into the gray-blue shadows of the night and the Bayou Road.

And more Great Mysteries by MIGNON G. EBERHART